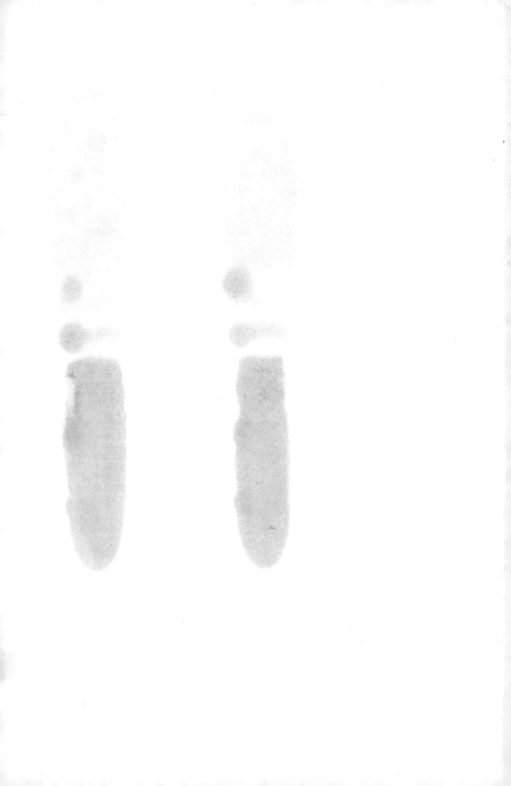

A View by the Sea

Modern Asian Literature Series

A View by the Sea

Yasuoka Shōtarō 1920

Translated by Kären Wigen Lewis

Columbia University Press
New York
1984

The Japan Foundation, through a special grant, has assisted the Press in publishing this volume.

The translation of the novella *A View By the Sea* was awarded the Japan–United States Friendship Commission translation prize in 1981.

Library of Congress Cataloging in Publication Data

Yasuoka Shōtarō, 1920–
   A view by the sea.

   (Modern Asian literature series)
   A novella plus five short stories translated from Japanese.
   1. Yasuoka, Shōtarō, 1920–   —Translations, English.   I. Title.
PL865.A7A24   1984   895.6'35   83-21081
ISBN 0-231-05872-1

Columbia University Press
New York   Guildford, Surrey
Copyright © 1984 Columbia University Press
Printed in the United States of America

Clothbound editions of Columbia University Press books are Smyth-sewn and printed on permanent and durable acid-free paper.

Contents

Foreword, by Van C. Gessel   vii

Acknowledgments   xiii

Yasuoka Shōtarō:
A Biographical Introduction   xv

Bad Company   1

Thick the New Leaves   29

The Moth   61

Gloomy Pleasures   77

Rain   91

A View by the Sea   103

Modern Asian Literature Series

Foreword: "Views" of Home
in the Fiction of Yasuoka Shōtarō

A few mocking smiles were exchanged within Japanese literary circles in 1977, when novelist Yasuoka Shōtarō's name appeared as the co-translator of Alex Haley's *Roots*. The assumption was that Yasuoka, who had not published any significant fiction in over six years, was making ends meet by riding the crest of Haley's popular wave. Because Yasuoka is a writer who has always depended heavily on his personal experience for the threads to weave his fictional webs, many concluded that he was caught in another of those personal slumps that are the creative bane of the Japanese autobiographical novelists.

Now that Yasuoka has published a major interpretive history of his own ancestors (*Ryūritan* [Tales of Wanderings, 1981]), however, it is evident that his interest in Haley's quest for origins was anything but pecuniary. Indeed, the student of Yasuoka's fiction is struck by the persistence of a single theme that courses like a subterranean river just beneath the surface of all his literary works: the search for a lost home. The first story he ever wrote, "Kubi kiri banashi" (A Tale of Decapitation, 1941), has been—appropriately enough—lost. But it was a story about home and family in a sense—a historical tale dealing with one of Yasuoka's own progenitors, Kasuke, a rural samurai in the mid-1800's who broke away from his family and its traditions, fled his domainal home, and finally was executed for participating in a political assassination long after his co-conspirators had been hailed as heroes for the act. The same Kasuke appears over and over in Yasuoka's fiction in a variety of guises, but he resurfaces as the central figure in *Tales of Wanderings*, bringing the corpus of Yasuoka's work full circle in yet another historical search for the meaning of "home."

In essence, all of the characters that appear in the stories translated here are manifestations of some part of Kasuke—that is, they share a sense of failure, of uprootedness; they hunt in vain for a comfortable spot to roost. Unable to locate any tranquil nesting-places, they stumble clumsily about, never able to abandon their hopeless quest. They seem to have persistent itches they can never scratch; like the protagonist in "The Moth," they behave as though an insect buzzing around inside their heads will not grant them a moment's true peace.

It would be no exaggeration to suggest that the underlying motif in each of these works—whether explicit or not—is the yearning for a home, tempered by a realization of the struggles that abound therein. Yasuoka, a member of the Japanese war generation wrenched from home and school by the call to battle, concentrates in his stories on homeless individuals who feel antipathy toward their origins (specifically, toward their enfeebled fathers and overbearing mothers), yet yearn to go someplace where they can get away from the demands of society and enjoy all the comforts of home without having to shoulder any of its implied responsibilities. Like the protagonist in Yasuoka's 1971 novel *Tsuki wa higashi ni* (The Moon Is to the East), who is flying in an airplane between a destination he wants to avoid and a starting-place to which he never wants to return, they long for time to freeze over, for an eternal limbo.

This sense of homelessness and the inability to act that

accompanies it assumes many forms in Yasuoka's fiction. Take, for instance, the strong sense of failure that is second-nature to the hero of "Gloomy Pleasures." He has persuaded himself that he cannot succeed as a worker in society, yet he feels guilty accepting the veteran's unemployment compensation for which he qualifies. Unpleasantness awaits him on all fronts, and the only "pleasures" in his life derive from the anticipation of the next "gloomy" experience that lurks ahead. Clearly he is looking for some kind of repose, but he has no idea where to find it.

Similarly, the heroes of "Bad Company" and "Thick the New Leaves" carry a burden of loss about with them. They long to do something "evil" of their own volition in order to break away from the control of their mothers. But there is a countermanding fear that mother will discover what they are up to— that terror keeps them from doing anything truly delinquent. Unable to be a part of the family, they are likewise prevented from totally severing the ties with home. In "Bad Company," the protagonist's confused feelings about home are, ironically, framed by statements regarding the deepening Japanese involvement in the war effort. Yasuoka's generation, knowing neither leftist protest nor right-wing fanaticism, harbored that same sense of ambivalence toward the war which robbed them of their youth.

Even in "Rain," the desperately ludicrous hero (a frantic parody of Raskolnikovian decisiveness) attempts his robberies because he has nowhere to go—no home to assuage his fears of isolation. And his impotent dreams of thievery are shattered when he hears a potential victim mutter the words he surely hears ringing through his own head: "I can't go back again."

Nowhere in modern Japanese literature is there a more moving account of the loss of home and the collapse of the nurturing, protecting family than in Yasuoka's 1959 masterpiece, *Umibe no Kōkei** (*A View by the Sea*). Shintarō's nine-day

---

Kaihen no Kōkei is an alternate reading of the title—KWL.

vigil beside his dying mother affords him the opportunity to examine just what his family has meant to him. By intertwining and overlapping several layers of past experience with scenes at the asylum where she lies dying, Yasuoka is able to bring time to a veritable halt, just as Shintarō has solidified in his mind distorted images of his own father and mother. Once she has expired, the "view" that opens before Shintarō's eyes is of a desolation that lies deep within his own heart, of a loss that he can comprehend only sketchily.

One of the fine subtleties of this short novel is the manner in which the negative emotional reactions that Shintarō has toward his parents are very delicately contradicted by the scraps of fact that the narrator slips in between the lines. The sensitive reader will have limitless compassion for the awkward frustration of the father Shinkichi, while recognizing that Shintarō himself is bereft of love for or understanding of that tormented man. And the causes for his mother's insanity are infinitely clearer to us, for Yasuoka gives us glimpses of the family that Shintarō has never cared to try to understand.

This work is based once again on largely autobiographical materials, but Yasuoka here brings a new element of insight into the Japanese "I-novel" by creating a critical distance between himself and Shintarō, thereby seeing through his hypocrisy and egotism. *A View by the Sea* is one of the crowning achievements of postwar Japanese literature, a tightly constructed narrative told in a controlled but casual style, and loaded with images of sight, sound, and smell. Yasuoka here creates a world devoid of intellectual or philosophical concerns—his characters bemoan their lost roots in the sensual realm of the emotions. Yet overseeing it all, Yasuoka towers above the selfish baseness of his lost characters and details their lives with cool, detached clarity. Along with others of his generation, Yasuoka has opened up new vistas for the modern Japanese novel by affording his readers a critical vantage point from which to observe the actions of his characters.

Yasuoka Shōtarō was one of the first postwar authors to describe the collapse of the traditional Japanese family unit; he remains today one of the few to continue a search for something to fill the void. Because his concerns are so human and so immediate, these stories come through in translation with the same overwhelmingly moving power they possess in the original Japanese. And because he has so tenaciously probed after his own roots, there seems every chance that this self-styled "failure," now one of Japan's most respected writers, will be able to go home once again, successfully.

Van C. Gessel
University of California, Berkeley

Acknowledgments

The generosity of many individuals has made this collection possible. Peter Grilli and the Japan Society offered the initial impetus and support for publication. John D. Moore and William Bernhardt at Columbia University Press gave freely of their expertise at the publishing end, while the Japan Foundation provided a grant to see the volume through. Miwako Tomizuka helped establish translation accuracy; Dr. Van C. Gessel provided valuable assistance with the final copy and with biographical information; and Jim Hynes gets special thanks for helping make *A View by the Sea* readable. Deepest gratitude to Dr. Kathryn Sparling, who many years ago inspired the project, who guided the bulk of the work, and who has always given unstintingly of her friendship and talents. None of this would have been possible without the contributions of all these people and more. The translator of course takes full responsibility for any inaccuracies that remain.

Kären Wigen Lewis

Yasuoka Shōtarō
A Biographical Introduction

Yasuoka's fiction has been from the first a close reworking of the author's life as seen from the inside. With his breakthrough into literary fame in 1953, at the age of 33, it also became overnight a decisive influence on his life from the outside. For both reasons, a brief biographical sketch seems in order for setting in context the stories that have been chosen for inclusion in this anthology.

Yasuoka's boyhood was an unsettled and uneasy one. Born in 1920, the sole son of a veterinary officer in the Japanese military, he had to move frequently as the family followed his father from one post to another. In addition to the difficulty of changing schools six times in twelve years, the young Yasuoka (if his later stories are any indication) also had to face embarrassment in front of his classmates over his father's line of work. In the process he understandably came to despise school. By the time he was a teenager, Yasuoka was regularly truant.

Graduation from Tokyo City Secondary School was thus a relief—for a time. Japan's escalating militarism having already drawn his father overseas, Yasuoka found himself newly freed from both the authorities under which he had chafed throughout his early years. But the same militarism that resulted in a suspension of the ordinary rules of life at home also posed a threat to the freedoms it inadvertently created. Before long, Yasuoka would either have to get into a university or face the draft.

For three years after graduation, as he tried the former route, Yasuoka lived the aimless life of the *rōnin*—a Japanese appellation both for samurai without a lord and for students without a university. For three years he nominally enrolled in (though did not exactly faithfully attend) a special preparatory school for the annual entrance examinations. Fully three times he failed those examinations. During this *rōnin* interval, Yasuoka and friends purportedly dissipated much of their time in coffee shops on the Ginza, reading novels by their heroes Kafū and Tanizaki, and imitating what they knew of their ways of life.

Finally Yasuoka was accepted into the literature department at Keiō University. If anything, his boldness in flouting authority increased while there. He chose to further his so-called "research into the habits of the Tokyoites" by taking a room in the Odawara, one of the city's famous night spots, and had to appear before the Information Bureau in a censorship case involving a literary magazine he and some friends were publishing. His first fiction to be printed—subversive inasmuch as it exposed the hypocrisy of the interwar years, and clearly sided with the underdog—appeared in this magazine.

By 1944 Japan was pulling out all stops in its effort to win the war, and even university students were called into active duty. March of that year saw Yasuoka drafted and sent to Manchuria. But within the year he was sent home with a lung infection and discharged from the army while in Kanazawa Military Hospital. In October 1945, not two months after Japan's surrender, he went back to Kugenuma in a body cast to recuperate under the care of his mother.

For a few intimate, sheltered months, mother and son managed to suspend recognition of Japan's defeat. The finality of it came home in full force only when Yasuoka's father returned from the Pacific the following May. Now Yasuoka was plunged into a dismal reality indeed, with abysmal poverty, family squabbles, and the lingering illness piled one on the other. In the midst of it all he managed somehow to graduate, working mostly from his bed. In 1949 he was once again put into the hospital, where he proceeded to write three remarkable stories: "Jingle Bells," "Gloomy Pleasures" (included here), and "Glass Slippers," for which he won an Akutagawa prize nomination in 1951. Thus encouraged, he followed in 1952 with "Homework" and "Prized Possessions." At last, in 1953, the new story "Bad Company," along with the earlier "Gloomy Pleasures," won him the 29th semi-annual Akutagawa Prize for Literature.

The event marked the turning point in Yasuoka's life. Literary recognition not only brought him into a circle of new colleagues including such respected writers as Kojima Nobuo and Endō Shūsaku, but also enabled him finally to rid himself of his Pott's disease, to marry, and to move out on his own.

In 1957, however, Yasuoka's mother died, and in 1958 a friend and literary critic committed suicide. These experiences moved the author to write two major fiction pieces: the novel *The Angel Who Stuck Out His Tongue,* and the mid-length masterpiece, *A View by the Sea.* The latter created a sensation in the literary world. It won for Yasuoka both the Mombusho (Ministry of Education) and Noma Literary Prizes, and was widely hailed as the first fruit of his maturity as a writer.

For the next decade, Yasuoka put out mostly short stories and essays, beginning with a collection of impressions from a 1958 visit to the U.S. undertaken at the behest of the Rockefeller Foundation (*Sentimental Journeys in the United States,* 1962). He showed himself as much at home in the essay as in fiction, with a keen, idiosyncratic judgment particularly manifest in "Shiga Naoya: An Interpretation" (1968) and "A Novelist on the Novel" (1970), as well as in a range of pieces dealing with movies, music, painting, and even social criticism. The year 1967 saw the publication of his next major fiction work (*After the*

Curtain), awarded the Mainichi Prize for Literature but considered secondary to the earlier *A View by the Sea*. A 1973 short story collection *(Run, Tomahawk)* was awarded the Yomiuri Literary Prize, but again failed to stir the critics as had his earlier work.

For a number of years, Yasuoka kept a relatively low profile, serving on the Akutagawa Prize selection committee, translating *Roots* into Japanese, and laboring on a two-volume work, *Ryūritan*, which has been called a Japanese version of *Roots*. In 1981, Yasuoka's name made a spectacular comeback with the publication of this latest work. The book was awarded Japan's highest literary distinction, the Grand Prize for Literature.

As a result, Yasuoka has reached a new stature in Japanese literature, and as of this writing his reputation is undoubtedly at its all-time high in his homeland. It is only fitting to commemorate the event by making some of his finest stories available to an international audience.

Bad Company
(Warui nakama)

The China Incident was just beginning to be one more commonplace episode in our lives when my friends and I began to see our faces clearing at last of acne, that plague of the middle-school years. It was the first summer break after we had advanced to college-preparatory school. I had turned down an invitation from a classmate, Shingō Kurata, to visit his home in Hokkaido and, having no plans of my own, had decided to kill time by signing up for a summer session French class in Kanda.

One day I walked into the classroom to find someone else's belongings spread out at the front-row seat I always took. The desk hadn't been specifically assigned to me, but I moved the books to the next empty seat anyway and sat down, then went back out to the hallway for a cigarette. But when the teacher came and I went back into the classroom, a short kid in a blue shirt was sitting in my chair. He looked like a sissy, with his skinny neck and wearing an oversized shirt of a color that belonged on a woman's apron, but his weakling looks only made his brazenness all the more striking. I walked up to the desk and deliberately snatched my textbooks out from under him but he didn't bat an eye. He just sat there with his wan face turned to the front, irritating me more than ever with the profile of his big, unsightly nose. I had no choice but to take another seat—not the empty one next to him, though, but one as far away as possible. Presently the teacher began to call roll. Each student was supposed to answer with the French "*présent.*" When our teacher, a thin blonde named Mademoiselle LeFolucca, looked up at the class over her spectacles and read off, "M. Fujii," the boy in the blue shirt shot up and practically shouted in a long, high-pitched voice,

"*Je—vous—réponds!*"

Then with a ladylike flourish he sat back down. . . . This queer response shattered the harmony that normally reigned in the classroom. The backs of the small boy's ears turned bright red as he curled his back and hid his face like a baby bird on its perch. "Idiots!" I muttered to myself. Komahiko Fujii told me later that he had been trying to come on to Mlle. LeFolucca that day. I was stunned. Mlle. LeFolucca was an ugly, mean-tempered woman.

      One day on the train home from school I happened to end up in the same car with Fujii. To my horror, as soon as he picked me out he came over with a big grin on his face and sat down next to me. My nostrils were immediately assaulted by a strange, abhorrent stench. He greeted me like an old friend, but with big, exaggerated gestures; as he warmed up he started flapping his arms around like wings, exposing in the process a pair of cuffs blacker at the wrist than any I have ever seen, and letting off even more of that horrible smell. Wondering how long it would be before I were rid of him, I asked,

      "Where do you live?"

      "Shimokitazawa."

      My luck—the last stop before mine. The whole way there he talked in a steady stream, telling me how his family was from Shinuiju in Korea; how he was staying for now in his brother's apartment by himself, while his brother—who was a medical student—was home for vacation; how this was his first time in Tokyo (his high school was in Kyoto); and so on, and so on. At the least response from me he would scoot forward and excitedly rub his thighs together, sending up a new wave of that rotten onion smell every time. . . . By now I had quite forgotten my irritation at his having taken my chair in class the other day: all I wanted to do was to get away from that smell. Just as we came within one stop of Shimokitazawa, he changed the subject and asked,

      "What do you know about Kurt Weill?"

      I was somehow flattered. In those days there wasn't anything that could have made me feel as proud as being asked a question like that. I jumped right into telling him all about the man who had composed *Three Penny Opera*. Despite the fact that he was now on the listening end for a change, Fujii's mannerisms were as exaggerated as before. He nodded his head up and down emphatically with every word, and leaned so close to me he practically rammed his ear into my mouth. But this time I was not dying to make my escape the whole time from this embarrassing situation. Furthermore, I wanted to show off my *pour vous*'s, rare items in those parts, and the programs and stars' photos I'd been collecting since junior high. So when Fujii started to get off at his station I invited him to come home with me. His answer was not what I expected.

". . . . I'd be embarrassed, going to your house." His cheeks and eyelids turned red, and he laughed weakly. Then he said, "Why don't you come to my place instead? It's that one, there," and he pointed to an apartment visible from the window. I didn't know what to make of his attitude, but I agreed to visit him later that afternoon.

I didn't take this promise to Fujii very seriously. When I got home, a cousin from Denenchōfu had come to visit. Now that she had gotten herself engaged she hardly ever dropped in anymore, unlike before. She also seemed to me to have started looking more like a lady. To taunt her I did mocking imitations of her fiancé's Tōhoku accent, as well as of his table manners, his way of greeting people, and other quirks of his. Though I didn't quite understand why, the more this seemed to fluster her, the more I enjoyed my little game. . . .

The next day, as soon as I walked into the classroom, Fujii bounded to my side and demanded, "Where were you yesterday?"

I said nothing. "I bought apples and bananas and sat there waiting for you," he said, staring straight into my face. . . . The whole scene was somehow comical. But when I tried to laugh, no laughter came. There was nothing in his eyes that I could identify, something I hadn't noticed until now. Mouthing a wordless reply, I realized that for the first time in my life I had let down a friend on account of a girl. "My old lady got sick and I couldn't come," I said.

That afternoon—perhaps out of guilt for having lied to

him—I went straight from school to Fujii's apartment. Oddly enough, from that day on I was never again put off by his overpowering smell.

From our first get-together Komahiko and I quickly became close friends. With my father away, Komahiko seemed to feel less uncomfortable at my house than he had expected. I for my part was intrigued by Fujii's independent life in his one-room apartment, where inkwell, school cap and books lay side by side on a shelf with the frying pan and coffee pot. . . . When I went to the apartment early in the morning, Komahiko would thrust one naked arm out from between the rumpled sheets and beg a cigarette. When I handed him the cigarette and matches, he'd open his puffy eyelids to a slit, look at me, and smile. . . . At such times I found myself unconsciously acting out love scenes from books and movies. Komahiko was slight of build, and except for his nose being too big, his face had a kind of clear-eyed beauty. . . . Not to imply that I thought of him as a weakling. He had a measure of brazenness that I just didn't have; I noticed it when he talked to his landlord or his neighbors. Furthermore, he could sit down unperturbed in a tiny, filthy restaurant and calmly—even with seeming enjoyment—proceed to eat a piece of fish that was covered with flies. . . . But none of this had particularly impressed me yet.

There came a day, though, when I had to be surprised. The two of us were walking down the street together when somehow we got to talking about how hungry we were. In the fanciful mood that camaraderie seems to conjure up, we started talking about *kuinige*—skipping out of a restaurant without paying the bill.

"What do you say we do it?"

Komahiko was already pushing open the door of a restaurant on a side street when he put this to me; at the moment, I had no intention of actually going through with it. For me, eating away from home itself counted as an adventure, *kuinige* or no. Furthermore, in this kind of formal, European-style restaurant my head was soon swimming over questions like whether to tuck my napkin in at my chin or to lay it across my lap. . . . The dining room was fairly crowded. The waiters hurried back and forth but always gracefully, flitting about like white butterflies. The two of us chose a table overshadowed by a large, hairy hemp plant, ordered two dishes, and had our meal. When we had finished, Fujii smiled and said, "Ready?" I absent-mindedly answered, "Sure." Then Fujii took hold of one fiber of the hemp plant and struck a match.

Suddenly there was a burst of light in front of me. In a flash the trunk of the hemp plant was a pillar of flame. Pandemonium broke loose. All the patrons were on their feet at once, and instantly the place was transformed into a classic fire scene. . . . Dazed, I leapt up from my chair when above the din of breaking crockery I heard Fujii's voice at my ear and, snapping out of it, I dashed after him full speed toward the exit.

The whole thing had turned out so unexpectedly that I thought surely I must be dreaming. But what really amazed me happened after we lost sight of each other running down crowded back streets and got separated. . . . As soon as I was by myself, I was seized with fear; this on top of the excitement and the running had my chest pounding alarmingly. I wandered restlessly in circles, not knowing where to go or what to do, greatly agitated, setting out to find Komahiko one minute and wanting to tear off running again the next. The sunlight glared harshly off the concrete sidewalk, and though my back and chest were pouring sweat, my body was chilled. Hounded by fear and remorse, I had almost completely given in to my guilty conscience when at last I saw, up ahead, the familiar oversized blue shirt: it was Komahiko, the sun behind him as he strolled down the broad avenue toward me. . . . Immediately my heart did a complete turn-around: now I was flushed with triumph.

"Hey!" I could have hugged him.

"Hey!" he called back.

Full of my own excitement I started telling him all about the packed streets I had run through when I noticed a large mysterious package in one of his hands. "What's that?" I demanded. He mumbled nonchalantly, "Oh, miso, dried sardines, . . ." I was shattered. Here he was telling me that within minutes of doing something that dangerous he had calmly stepped into a grocery store to do his dinner shopping. My sense of high drama was dashed. What had been a terrific adventure for me had been purely a practical affair for him.

I had always been intimidated by restaurant workers before, thinking of them as nasty "etiquette police;" after this episode, I saw them instead as people who had become malicious by scurrying around to serve other people for too long.

One day toward the end of summer vacation, I went to Fujii's apartment to find wire, wire cutters, nails and whatnot strewn about the place and Fujii himself facing the window hard at work. . . . As he fiddled with a hand-held shaving mirror, Fujii explained that he was setting up a periscope for seeing into the bathroom of the house kitty-corner to his flat. I was overcome with this fantastic idea, and let out a loud exclamation. Fujii reproved me. Then he asked, "Didn't you have a mirror at your place that was a little bigger than this?"

"I think so," I said, perking up again, and dashed out of the room. But when I got back with the larger mirror, the wire and the wire cutters were gone, the whole mess cleaned up, and Fujii himself was acting deliberately nonchalant. . . . At a loss for anything else to do, I set about constructing a reflection device of my own.

"Forget it. It's too dark to see anything now."

Something cold in his tone made me bristle. Fine then, I'll do it myself, I thought, and without a word I continued with my work. But sure enough, as the sun began to set, the light in my mirror all but went out; the bath, lit only by a single electric bulb, was also half dark; and before long all I could tell was whether someone was in there or not. When I refused to give up even then and kept fiddling with the mirror, Fujii said tauntingly from where he lay,

"Do you really want to see it that much?"

"What about yourself?" I retorted.

"Why, me . . ." Fujii began, and then broke off with a snicker. I persisted. He said, ". . . . Well, you know, until two or three days ago I could see straight into the bath of the house across the street. Shame they had to go and close the window."

I was furious.

"Why didn't you say something sooner!"

At this Fujii, still slumped across the bed, crossed the legs that had been thrown open toward me, let out a simpering laugh, and said, "I . . . I couldn't, especially not someone like you."

In a flash of intuition I knew then that Fujii had had a woman. . . . In that split second my image of Komahiko was turned on its head—a hidden something inside him, a secret domain so vast that the eye could not take it all in, suddenly stood bared before me. Feeling as embarrassed as if I had mistakenly strayed into someone else's house, I completely clammed up.

. . . The truth was that I thought constantly about women. Whenever I daydreamed about the future, whenever I imagined myself in the kind of role I wanted to fill someday, inevitably there was a woman beside the hypothetical "me"; besides that, I entertained various sexual fantasies of women. But in spite of all this I had never once thought of approaching a woman in real life. To me, women were too distant to be anything more than objects of fantasy. My several female cousins were somehow of a class apart from the rest of womankind, and all my other relationships with women were on the order of passing on a bus or train: I could see them but I was cut off from them. . . . So now, though Fujii lay right near me, I felt a sharp difference separating us. He was a man from an unknown world.

I went back home that evening and thought about nothing else all night. In my exposure to Komahiko during the short
space of this summer vacation, I had felt an attraction stronger
than anything I had ever experienced before. If I was still unable to go into the dingy restaurants he frequented, it was not
out of any great scruples of mine over nutrition or hygiene, but
because the dark, damp gloom of the place scared the wits out
of me. Likewise with prostitutes: more than a question of disease or morality, it was something harder to overcome that made
me avoid even the thought of going to them. Nevertheless, now
I was coming to believe that I would have to learn to love precisely these things that I had always avoided. . . . Just as a man
begins to perceive the woman he loves as mysterious, I began
to think of Komahiko as a boy with awesome powers. The
smallest detail of his way of life seemed to take on a whole new
splendor. By the logic of a child who imagines a miniature or-
chestra inside a phonograph, I began to see a woman inside
my friend. . . .

From the next day on I tried on various pretexts to get
him talking on the subject of women, but Fujii remained elu-
sive, and I only grew more perplexed. Unfortunately, at this
point I had no power to pressure him with. It was not until the
day before he was to go back to Kyoto, as we walked the streets
together that night, that I finally got him to talk about it. It was
the first time I had consciously played on his vanity.

"Listen, it's an incredible bore," Komahiko reprimanded
me. "You're bound to be disappointed, so I'd drop it if I were
you." It turned out, however, that since coming to Tokyo Komahiko had gone to amuse himself several times without my
knowledge.

Autumn came.

When Shingo Kurata, back from his family home in
Hokkaido, first saw me at the start of the new term, he was
taken by surprise. He seemed not to know how to respond to
my subjects of conversation, my vocabulary, even a lot of my

gestures and mannerisms. To me, on the other hand, this old friend and classmate seemed like a dumb horse. . . . It bored me to death now to sit around with Kurata, listening to records and nodding stupidly to the beat, or hearing him brag about his tennis playing. He talked eagerly, gesturing emphatically with his long neck, but I turned a deaf ear to almost everything he said.

Suddenly, at one of my mumbled replies, Kurata turned his long, sun-burnt face straight toward me. The conversation broke off as his voice trailed away to a mumble. I too was silent. From the opening of his short sleeves came a scent like the sweet smell of dried hay. . . . This must be the smell of virginity, I thought, and that odor I noticed when I first met Fujii, that must have been the smell of experience. . . . Which smell did I have now, I wondered. The day after I had said goodbye to Fujii, I had found my way, going by the topography of a famous novelist who had written about the place, to a brothel across the river.

The shock I had received at Komahiko's hand was now to be passed on to Kurata. . . . Only half aware of what I was doing, I began to retrace the course Fujii had marked out over the summer. *Kuinige,* stealing, voyeurism . . . The only thing was, my actions were marred by something that smacked of revenge, something that wouldn't be satisfied until I had forcibly shaken Kurata up. With *kuinige,* for instance, the way I handled it was not to let him in on it ahead of time but to spring it on him out of the blue and force him to make a run for it. The only time I was a hundred percent successful was when I stole a spoon from a restaurant on the main strip of the Ginza. That time Kurata's admiration was spontaneous.

. . . The pattern on this particular restaurant's teaspoons was an unusual combination of straight lines and circles, and it struck my fancy. As we got up to leave I pocketed mine. But as we were on our way out, the waiter ran up behind us and said, "Excuse me, sir, I believe you have our teaspoon? . . ."

I turned slowly around. "You mean I'm not allowed to take this?" I asked, taking the spoon out to show him. . . . The waiter was flustered. Blushing, he waved me away, saying, "No, go ahead," and he actually went away beaming as if he had brought his customer some forgotten belonging. Kurata, who I thought was standing next to me, must have fled at some point, for the next thing I knew he was about twenty-five feet away and staring at me wide-eyed. When we were outside the restaurant, he let out a sigh like a man confessing, and applauded my calm, saying, "You are really something else." It was the first time I had impressed Kurata without contriving the effect. Just how impressed he was became clear as early as the next day, when he pulled the same stunt himself at a cafeteria near the school. His performance there was so good that the waitress ended up giving him a cutlet knife almost as big as a butcher's knife. This unwieldy token of her admiration was too large to fit in his pocket, and he couldn't very well ditch it along the side of the road, either. In any case, there was no mistaking that Kurata too felt an inexplicable fascination for adventures of this sort. Now the most important of these by far was undisputably my trip to the quarter across the river. But when this subject came up my desire to advertise what I had done and my desire to lead him on yet a while through a net of enigma got all tangled up together, so that in the end, every time I looked at Kurata it was me who fell into a quandary. . . . True, perhaps I had been disappointed on returning from the other side of the river, as Komahiko had predicted. But "disappointment" in Komahiko's sense was precisely what I had set out to find. The indefinable dissatisfaction I felt had nothing to do with that. If anything, though, I had in fact had more than enough of this kind of disappointment: for two or three days afterwards, I couldn't look at a female without being overcome by the absurdity of it, so much so that I nearly found myself in trouble. . . . But this wasn't what I had had in mind. What I'd been hoping for was some kind of a sign. Nothing visible to strangers, but something I could recognize as a sign—that's what I had thought I would come away with. But if I had, it must have been stuck to the middle of my back, or hanging behind my ear. Though I followed in Fujii's footsteps, I was totally on my own.

"You really want to see this that bad?" ——Sitting in the front row at the Asakusa Revue, I was planning to turn to Kurata and say this to him. But somehow when I went to open my mouth it seemed like I was the one who wanted to see the show. . . . What would Fujii have done in a situation like this? Wanting to come across just as he had that time, I rehearsed his glance and other mannerisms in my head. But nothing I tried would make me sound like that. This only made me more and more irritated, until I finally blurted out,

"This is boring. Let's go."

My saying this for no apparent reason when the show had barely begun, especially after I had insisted so adamantly on bringing him here, made Kurata angry, but he didn't want to be the one to say he wanted to stay, either, so he had no choice but to follow me out. . . . In the end, it was doing what I could to humor Kurata out of sulking over the bind I had put him in in the first place that finally put me in a good mood myself.

In short, the whole time I was with Kurata I thought only of Fujii. The more progress Kurata made from being a horse to being normal, the more I became like Komahiko, or so I thought. So I took care not to treat Kurata like any dumb horse. . . . Once in a while, though, I would be tormented by the nightmarish possibility of Kurata and Komahiko somehow meeting up, though I was sure Komahiko was in Kyoto. If that happened, what would become of the false image of myself that I had been at such pains to plant in Kurata's mind?

This nightmare came true. Roused from sleep one morning by the maid, I went downstairs to find Kurata and Fujii standing together at the front door. They had just happened to come on the same train. Fujii carried no baggage except for the raincoat he had thrown over his shirt.

"I was getting fed up with Kyoto, thought I'd come up here for a while," he said.

This coincidence turned out to be not the disaster I had imagined, but a totally unexpected joy. The atmosphere was festive, and soon the three of us were feeling like old chums. The really peculiar thing was that Kurata, who was generally withdrawn and rarely spoke a word to someone he had just met, acted with Fujii as if he had known him for years. For he had already become familiar with another Fujii, the one inside me.

The conversation between the three of us was animated to an alarming degree. Now that the real Fujii had appeared, I had no doubt faded to a pale shadow in Kurata's eyes. This meant that at the same time that I was struggling for Fujii's approval, I also had to work to shore up the image Kurata had of the Komahiko in me. And what with Kurata and I outdoing each other to ingratiate ourselves with Fujii, he had to talk twice as much as usual in order not to lose either friend. . . . With all of us trying to impress each other this way, the boasts grew by the minute. Finally, hoping to dump Kurata, I proposed that we go to the other side of the river.

As a scheme to upset Kurata, this completely backfired. Contrary to my expectations that he would blush and have to mull it over first, instead he immediately joined in. . . . Thinking back on it, I can see now that this was the last thing I should have done. Kurata was like a man at a fire: he had that freak strength to perform incredible feats without feeling any pain. I had thrown away my most valuable trump card. And the worst of it was, I didn't have a bit of fun once I got there. What happened was, the three of us split up when we reached the place to seek our respective adventures, but almost as soon as I started walking I was picked up by a policeman on a juvenile delinquent beat. This after I had been trying to come off as an old hand in front of Kurata.

Finally released from the police box three hours later, I ran across the street and was heading for a dark corner to hide in when somebody called out,

"Hey. Over here."

It was Kurata and Fujii. My initial joy at coming back into the fold was short-lived. It came out that these two had stood in the shadow of a yakitori stand at the side of the road and watched for over an hour as I bowed to the crowd of policemen surrounding me, or raised my arms against threatened blows and pleaded for mercy. . . . They told me all this with an air of the utmost concern.

Fujii left again for Kyoto. But I could not go back to treating Kurata like a horse. . . . Fujii had stayed only two nights in Tokyo, but those two nights had been like two years of ordinary time, if not more. Like a guide on some whirlwind tour, he had led us from one place to another, seeking out his favorite spots—specialty seafood restaurants, coffee houses, theaters; we would hop in a cab to go some ridiculously short distance, and then traipse along on foot for hours and hours around a particular district that he liked. We didn't need any alcohol to intoxicate ourselves. Three abreast we strode through the back streets of the Ginza, Fujii in the middle, firing off our automatic lighters like pistols. . . . The third day ended with the fanfare of a carnival. But Komahiko's image only grew larger as he receded. In Kurata's eyes I was now but a shadow of Fujii—even the incident with the spoon now appeared as a mere imitation of Fujii's exploits. At first this was unbearable. But as the days passed each of us came to feel a certain pleasure in bringing out the Komahiko inside the other. We walked the streets we had walked with Komahiko, we went into the coffee shops we had visited with Komahiko, we made a leapfrog game out of taking turns playing the part of Komahiko. . . . We imitated even completely trivial things like the way Fujii held a coffee cup to his mouth. He never picked up a cup by the handle, but would always take hold of the cup itself, lift it slowly to his mouth, press it to his thickish lips, and then, extending his tongue slightly as if to lick the rim of the cup, let the coffee dribble slowly down his throat. It made him look greedy, as if he were trying to suck the last bit of flavor from every drop. Another thing was we both started unconsciously stooping our shoulders. Fujii, who was short, always walked erect, his chest thrown out and his head back, but in our efforts to imitate him, the two of us preoccupied ourselves with just the opposite, rounding our backs. Both Kurata and I had always been finicky eaters, but now we outdid each other by eating anything Fujii had pronounced good. My mother could not figure out why all of a sudden with the arrival of fall her son should develop an appetite for tomatoes. . . . In all things Kurata and I served as each other's inspectors. Neither would allow the other to copy Komahiko directly. If Fujii had worn a pair of socks embossed with a fish design, for example, that specific design was out of bounds. A bird or butterfly pattern was the loyal as well as the tasteful choice in a case like this.

The letters between Tokyo and Kyoto flew thick and fast. . . . These letters were everything to us. With all the stunts we pulled, the thrill of the thing itself was nothing to the pleasure of writing about it afterward. Fujii always compared and rated the letters from the two of us in Tokyo. His letters from Kyoto were invariably addressed in both of our names, and mailed to each of our houses by turns. When we showed them to each other, each of us would secretly judge the thickness of the letter sent to the other's place.

In this way our mental image of Komahiko grew more idealized every day. Even in our striving to outdo each other Kurata and I were united. And at every turn we'd think, "If only Koma were here." Even if a bus crammed with passengers were to break down in the middle of the road and be unable to move, we'd look at each other and think, "If only Fujii were here. . . ."

In Kyoto Fujii was killing himself with this correspondence. Almost every other day he had a letter to write. At least if his correspondent had been a woman the work of letter writing would not have been so grueling. All you have to do to evoke a woman's emotion is to write down the same old things you've been doing every day of your life. With another man, though,it doesn't quite work that way. . . . The letters coming in from these two buddies one after another raised Fujii to a dizzying height before he knew what was happening. Looking about him, he could hardly find any explanation for it. In this precarious, intoxicated state, like walking on clouds, the one thing that was clear was the importance of stringing along for as long as possible the fellows who were making him so drunk. . . . But before long Fujii tripped up in a misleading suggestion he himself had thrown out. To whit, like Kurata and I, he too started believing that the real source of his life's beauty was his intimacy with women. The result of this was that Fujii started making a veritable religion of frequenting the licensed quarters. And all to stir up inspiration for his letters to us. . . .

One day I arrived at Kurata's house in Harajuku to find him clearing his father's golf trophies off the ornamental shelf at the front of the entry hall.

"What's going on?" I demanded, but he seemed highly agitated and wouldn't answer, and kept hurling the cups one after another into a closet on top of his little brother's toys. "What's going on?" I demanded again, but looking into Kurata's disturbed face, suddenly I felt I would burst out laughing.

So it's getting to him, too, I thought. Kurata's family was a lot like mine. My father had gone off to northern China with the military; his father was an executive in a munitions company, and went around the country to inspect regional plants. As a result, both of us were largely free to do as we pleased from one day to the next. But recently I had started to find my house somehow constraining, confining. It wasn't that anything in particular had changed at home, so much as that the pact between the three of us was starting to bind me even at home. For instance, when I came in late at night I mustn't hesitate or be scared. That was definitely a disgrace. It was also against the rules to wash your hands after going to the bathroom. There were a host of new injunctions like this binding us. Since the goal in all things was to achieve "beauty" (beauty equalling Fujii's way of life), this outcome was inevitable. . . . I had no choice but to be a complete slob at home. I happily let my clothes and my room get as dirty as I pleased. It was as if I were trying to drown out the household mores I had found so oppressive in a heap of junk and garbage. . . . But Kurata had another kind of pain to bear. While all I had to do was sit back and watch as dust and cobwebs covered the photographs of starlets I had pasted up on the wall, Kurata's room was decorated with things like skiing equipment, a tennis racket, the tail of a broken glider, and even a sterling silver model of a naval bomber that he had secretly taken from the guest room mantel piece in his father's absence; these things had once been his pride and joy. Recently, however, like Jean Valjean's troubling tattoo, they had become a daily torment for him. Now, to make his humiliation complete, in order to escape his friend's judging eyes he had come secretly to return the bomber to its original spot. . . . The accumulated rage that this torment had built up inside him had finally exploded until he had lashed out even at the trophies in the entryway.

Once you start doing battle against a parent's hobbies like this, there's no stopping. Every inch of the house is their territory. . . . For me, it started with my father's sword that had been placed on display in the decorative alcove; then the hanging scroll and the flower vase began to irritate me; and after that I got so I couldn't tolerate things I had never even noticed before—down to the pattern on the sliding paper doors and the cracks in the pillars. Especially the food: it got to be downright ridiculous. Everything on the table irritated me. Even when I had my mother fix up a separate dish of something that I had liked when I ate it with Fujii, it seemed to lose all its taste as soon as I took a bite of it at home.

Needless to say, both Kurata and I began to spend less and less time at home. We passed the better part of every day in a den-like coffee shop. As our allowances tended to be on the low side for regular eating out, we came up with halfway measures like spreading butter on roasted potatoes we could buy on the street, and this was the sort of thing we lived on.

In those days all of Japanese society was behaving every bit as eccentrically as we were. Everyone in the country was suffering from a whole array of fictional observances which had their basis in the moral code of a "new" era. For instance, once when a line of people waiting to see a performance by some famous movie star had wound all the way around a certain movie theater, someone decided the crowd was being unnecessarily frivolous and turned the fire department's hoses on their heads. Periodically a signal corps of soldiers could be seen riding around in the streets—more for display than for lack of any other place to practice. Suffering inconceivably under the heavy copper cording wrapped around their chests, all they managed to do was obstruct traffic. . . . Apparently under some kind of orders from somewhere, the school would hastily assemble the students on the playground for a lecture from the principal. The principal, wearing wheat-colored gloves and standing like a bronze statue, would say something like, "The way to discipline a monkey and train it to dance is to take it when it is still young and make it walk on a red-hot sheet of iron. When it feels the heat, the monkey begins to prance about. This is the meaning of discipline. Now the same goes for you boys. . . ." A number of us students would be fighting hard to keep from laughing out loud. . . . The idea of us being little monkeys! The deeper symbolic meaning of this story was truly beyond us. Nobody—the principal included—had any idea of what the sheet of iron stood for. . . . Afterward, many of the students who had heard this speech were wounded or killed in combat. Among those who suffered burn injuries was none other than the principal himself.

Already it was getting to where a person could be publicly reprimanded for anything at all. Surprisingly, it happened more often in demure places like the coffee shops that sold nothing but pastries, places frequented only by the quietest students, than to those wandering through the licensed quarters. Dim-witted students who had been spotted in front of a pool hall during school hours would be hauled off to the police to get paddled and come back blubbering. . . . We were completely in the dark about when this sort of thing would happen and what form it would take. The one thing we could be sure of was that when the day to day tedium was starting to kill us, when we began to get the feeling that we'd misplaced something but were completely helpless to remember what it was—then these things would suddenly spring at us. For when we fell into a mood like that (which we called "stagnation"), we were itching to pull something off ourselves.

We hit stagnation pretty often. Naturally the thrill of a dare wore off after the first time around; as the repetitions mounted, stagnation was sure to follow. The arbitrary punishments already mentioned helped us out at first. That topsy-turvy state of affairs had grown more remarkable with every passing day, until even the military police were drawn in to help round up juvenile delinquents. For us, the effect of all this was exactly the same as sitting in a chair and "traveling" by watching a panorama go by. . . . But as these disciplinary actions, too, became commonplace, we gradually lost our nerve. Both Kurata and I skipped most of our classes, but we had no desire to do anything else, either, and we fell into spending whole days sitting in that grimy downtown coffee shop, staring at each other and feeling as if we were starting to rust away. Seeing Kurata huddled like an old man over the damp-smelling charcoal brazier, I would automatically think of Komahiko. I'm sure I conjured the same thoughts in Kurata. . . . We would start in animatedly on the subject of our program for a new round of adventures, knowing all the while that it was mostly a lie. But that too would as suddenly break off. . . . For the figure of a soldier with a bayonet—on the prowl for some runaway comrade—had passed across the darkened window like the silhouette of evil.

The letters coming from Kyoto became more and more frenzied. Unaware that the pair of us in Tokyo were stooping to gross exaggeration in our competition to impress him, Fujii—determined not to be outdone himself—was pushing himself to the limit. . . . His letters were full of wildly idiosyncratic theorizing, replete with dogmatic pronouncements, morbid images developed to an extreme, and nearly indecipherable leaps of logic, all written in an eccentric style. Then one day in the dead of winter came a letter bearing the following enigmatic poem.

> Desolate as when I came—
> Taking leave of Kyoto at springtime.

This was accompanied by the news that he had been expelled from school, was seriously ill, and was thinking of going back to his home in Korea.

The letter had come to Kurata's first. Kurata arrived at my house in Setagaya panting like a post horse, his breath a white vapor in the cold.

One look at the letter left me so dazed I could barely think. I was too afraid to read the whole thing through. Kurata was undoubtedly in the same state. Hastily we left the house. Trance-like, we walked for some time, then would stop in the middle of nowhere, occasionally making loud, meaningless attempts at conversation. . . . I didn't know what to do with myself. All our escapades of the past half year had seemed to take place in a dream. In fact, a real human life had been at stake in all these "dreams" of mine. . . . And all the while, Kurata and I had been having a ball.

Is it because this is all too frightening that I actually feel cheerful? I speculated. The truth, though, was that another part of me refused to acknowledge that I was rejoicing at my friend's misfortunes. . . . I was, at least, aware that there was something despicable in my reaction. Accordingly, though I thought I was saying the opposite of what I "really" felt, I ironically spoke the truth when I cried out,

"This is a day to celebrate. Let's go out and have a feast."

Kurata replied with apparent relief,

"You're right. Today Fujii sets out on his greatest adventure of all."

Together we picked the fanciest restaurant we could find. I decided that at a formal place we were likely to be so preoccupied with wielding our forks and knives properly—cutting a piece of meat without sending it flying off the plate, or carefully winding slippery spaghetti noodles onto a fork—that we wouldn't have a moment to think about anything else. As we soon found out, however, self-inflicted suffering while dining did nothing in the least to alleviate our inner pain.

"Let's at least send a telegram to congratulate him," I said, coming out of my private misery to make another jaunty suggestion.

"Good idea," Kurata answered.

But when we left the restaurant we went to the usual dingy little coffee shop and sat there until closing time without any plans to do another thing. Until we split up that evening, not another word about the telegram passed between us.

That night I was upset—not over the business with Fujii but over the inscrutability of Kurata. . . . It was perfectly clear that if we carried on much longer the way we had been, we too would fall prey before long to a fate like Fujii's. I dreaded being saddled with a fate like that. Not that I would have known how to answer if asked to explain my dread. I could only have said that I was terrified of the uncertain, insecure future I imagined. . . . In a case like this, regardless of whether I had any intention of deserting him in the end or not, I at least wanted to bring it up for discussion. Although the only possible motivation for doing so was in actuality a desire to turn traitor.

Kurata was by nature the more withdrawn of the two of us. From the next day on, while paying lipservice to Fujii's character and outlook on life, I began dropping hints here and there about the misery that awaited Komahiko in the life he was likely to lead from here out. . . . If I could somehow maneuver Kurata into saying he was going to desert him, my plan was to follow in his footsteps.

The scheme worked. More than there being any particular force behind my warnings, the truth was that something in Kurata was waiting to hear them. . . . In the growing frenzy as final exams approached, deals were being made all over the classroom for the swapping of notebooks.

"I hear more guys flunk the first-year exams than any of the rest." "Yeah, and they say if you fail the first time around you're stuck for good, too." . . . In our present state of mind this kind of talk, even from a crowd we normally jeered at, was enough to get to us. "Shall we go to Mr. F's grave and pay our respects?" I asked cynically. Every year on the birthday of F————, the school's founder, the whole student body paid a visit to his grave; tradition had it that anyone who didn't go along would fail his exams. The two of us had been absent that day, as usual.

"Yeah, let's go," Kurata said, brightening. . . . The day was clear, and it felt good to walk through the cemetery. Hoping to boost the results still further, I worked to put him in a genuine class-outing mood. Before I knew it I was feeling like a regular doctor treating a sick patient. Out of the pleasure of taking the initiative for once, and looking forward to seeing Kurata again, I actually left for school the next day in time to make the first period class.

Kurata wasn't there. Second period came around and he still didn't show up. At that point my suspicions started working on me. It suddenly hit me that Kurata was somewhere with Fujii. Sitting in my iron-legged chair listening to a boring lecture, I wished that I had slipped out before class had started. But as each lecture ended, I had a feeling Kurata would show up for the next one, so I passed up my chance and stayed in the room. Kurata didn't come to a single class even in the afternoon. . . . I had never felt this impatient waiting for Kurata before. But then again, was it really to wait for Kurata that I was here? If I really wanted to see him, surely it would have been faster to go to his house, or to the cafe where we always hung out. Was I remaining in the classroom truly out of solicitousness for my patient, Kurata?

When I got home there was a note from Fujii.

"——Came up to see you before I go back to Korea. Staying at a flophouse in Asakusa. . . ."

So I was right, I thought, with a touch of self-satisfaction at having guessed right, and not particularly surprised. A map in Fujii's distinctive handwriting accompanied the letter. I took a cold and cursory look at it. (. . . It's too bad about him. But if I sit here and feel sorry for him, I'll end up going right down the hole after him.) By this time I had put Kurata quite out of my mind. . . . Having sat waiting around all day myself, I felt as if it were me who had been betrayed by my friends. And since I felt I had fulfilled my obligation to the friendship in that one act, I felt clean and clear, as if my demon had been exorcised.

I dare say this change of heart, this resolve to shape up and fly straight, was merely a matter of convenience. The proof of this came the next morning when I had already begun to backslide. In other words, my real desire—to take the easy way out—showed its true colors. Arriving in the middle of rush hour at the station where I had to change trains, I sat on a bench and let one train that would have taken me to school go by. As I smoked a cigarette there, I got a frighteningly vivid image of the cold iron chairs and concerete floors of the classroom, and let the next train, too, pass me by. . . . My attendance record was bad in the extreme. It was possible that missing today's class would mean I would fail for sure. These hours were far too precious to squander. But for that very reason, idling this time away proved to be an unmatched pleasure. . . . When I had watched the last train that would have taken me to class on time pull out of the station, still full of commuters, I stood up and muttered to myself, "What's the difference, it's just one more day."

I myself did not see my traitorous heart for what it was. Like a habitual liar who believes his own lies even as he tells them, I too failed to see just what I was doing. Or more precisely, I made no effort to see it. . . . Having given up on the idea of going to school, I went instead to our usual cafe. The place was completely deserted this early in the morning, and smelled like a rotting kitchen drainboard. There was a dazed, vacant feeling to the place, like that of a man who hasn't had enough sleep. I tried to burrow my way into that state by sitting in the furthest corner chair and staring at the soiled curtain or the stains in the wallpaper, merely marking time. . . . What was I doing there? Maybe a certain dog-like element in me, with the loyalty to follow after its master even when left behind, was keeping up the way of life I had been living until a short week ago. But the rational part of me didn't notice that at all.

When it got close to noon, I started thinking about lunch, and though I wasn't hungry, I was just wondering what to have when suddenly I heard familiar voices advancing across the fields toward the shop. . . . It was Fujii and Kurata. I shot up as if I'd been yanked out of my chair, and as soon as I came to my senses, dashed out the back door and up a different street. The first thing I felt was an unspeakable terror. Discomfort and humiliation brought on by ruminating on my own cowardice followed soon after. . . . While my mind wavered between retreat and return, my feet took me farther and farther away.

What had terrified me so? Like an overcoat lining exposed by the wind, the intentions I had been hiding from myself had appeared in a flash as soon as I heard their voices. If I turned back now, there might still be a chance. But fast on the heels of this thought was another one, that they were probably talking right this moment about my betrayal and about those intentions I had just seen exposed; now it was this fear that made it impossible for me to go back.

Walking blindly from street to street wherever my feet led, stepping in the broken tiles and the puddles of wash water that were strewn across my path, I tried to forget the two voices that still rang in my ears. . . . They were not easily erased. Then I knew why: that was the last time I would ever hear those two speak. . . .

When I had come far enough to think I really couldn't go back, I stopped and looked over my shoulder. . . . If I hadn't heard those voices, if they hadn't approached the cafe talking so loudly, I would still have been sitting in that chair. And if that had happened, the three of us would undoubtedly have become buddies again as before. . . . I was sure of it—for something in the recesses of my heart was waiting for just that to happen.

In fact, the final act of my betrayal was yet to come. This was not to take place until evening, after I had gone home. As long as I stayed in the city, there was still some connection between us.

That night a woman in a black kimono jacket showed up at our house. It was Mrs. Kurata, Kurata's mother. . . . My mother answered the door, then called me.

Mrs. Kurata had been worried sick about her son, who had left the house two days ago and had not been seen since, when today she had opened a dresser drawer to discover that the family's savings passbook was missing. Besides that, two Boston bags, her husband's duck-hunting cap, a tie pin with a precious stone in it, and even a large sum of cash were all gone. . . . Searching through the diary and memos on her son's bookshelf and through the mound of letters, she had gotten the gist of this appalling situation.

"I wonder where he went," I sighed, not without envy. Mrs. Kurata, however, interpreted this as the most obvious sort of playing dumb. . . . She had suspected me from the start.

"Come on, I want the whole truth now. . . . Where has my Shingō gone off to?"

I could only answer that I didn't know. At this, Mrs. Kurata suddenly broke into a strong Kyushu accent and lashed out at me, saying the original fault was mine. A bead of spittle gathered at the corner of her clay-colored mouth. . . . The woman's words only increased my determination. I looked over at my mother. She looked back at me. After the wasted, embittered face of Mrs. Kurata, I could hardly miss the flush of triumph in my mother's round face, the beaming pride of one whose son has been compared with another and won.

Seeing this, I knew it was safe to excuse myself.

"Well, I guess I'll go out and look for him then," I said, and after locking up my bookcase, just to be on the safe side, I left the house.

Night had fallen. Naturally, I had no intention of tracking my friends down, despite my promise to Mrs. Kurata. When out of habit my feet began to turn toward the coffee shop, I changed direction and walked down streets I didn't know. I didn't know where to go or what to do with myself. A warm wind blew from a starless sky . . . On an impulse I stopped a cab and gave the name of one of the red-light districts across the river. Maybe I would run into them there. So I said to myself. But of course that was not what I was hoping for.

When the cab took off, I was lured by the car's speed into a sentimental intoxication. Looking at the lights reflected in the window as they went past, what I saw were the flickers in the depths of my heart of my feelings from the time when I had loved my friends. . . . But as the car picked up speed, the sheer joy of moving obliterated everything else. Each time we crossed one of the numerous bridges, the midsection of the bridge girders would float into view in the light of the headlights, as soon to be buried again under the body of the car and disappear. . . .

At some point I rose half out of my chair, put both hands

on the driver's seatback, and slipped into a fantasy that I was moving on my own power.

. . . That winter, a new set of countries came into the war against Japan.

Thick the New Leaves
(Aoba shigereru)

So, this year he'd failed again. It was an odd feeling.

Juntarō had lain in bed awake that morning and listened to the maid come up the stairs. Her footsteps were lighter than usual, almost as if she were keeping time: a suspenseful foot-fall.

The tip of this maid's nose was repulsive—always red and spotted with big pores, as if only that part of her face had been steamed. But if you could stand this she wasn't totally bad looking. There was the little dimpled chin, the slim and grace-ful neck above her sloping shoulders, and then those narrow eyes that would sometimes flash up at him so crossly. . . . Juntarō lay with his eyes shut waiting for the sliding door at his head to open, quite as if he expected that at any minute this figure would roll right into his bed.

——Hmm, I wonder if she'd ever take it into her head to get in bed with me—oh but what am I thinking . . .

Still, it isn't necessarily out of the question. Isn't that the real reason she's coming up to the second floor this early in the morning when I'm the only one around?——Talking back and forth to himself this way, Juntarō began to get anxious that at any second on her way up the stairs the maid might just drop the idea and turn around in her tracks. But the footfalls stopped at the head of the stairs. The screen parted quietly. Juntarō pre-tended to be fast asleep, keeping his eyes shut and doing his best to look natural. He was convinced that this was the most conveniently vulnerable position . . .

Finally he couldn't bear it any longer and opened his eyes. There, half-peeking from the shadow behind the screen, was the maid, smiling. The red nose as usual, he was thinking, when she spoke up.

"A letter for you, sir."

It was a postcard, stamped Special Delivery. The return address was marked "Z_____ University Preparatory Course Administrative Offices."

Once more Juntarō felt himself jolted out of his dreams.

At the same time he conjured up a mental picture of the yel-lowish, pointy-roofed school building.

Examinee Number #12989   Abe Juntarō
Results of Selective Examination for admission ap-plication to this University's Preparatory Course hereby deemed
UNSUCCESSFUL

Having so determined we hereby so inform you.

For a long time he stared vacantly at the purple-stamped word UNSUCCESSFUL. He thought he must still be asleep, dreaming up this improbability. But the tapping steps of the maid going back down the stairs made him realize for the first time that his eyes were really open.

The morning sunlight was streaming in through the fixed windowglass at the foot of the stairs. . . . Outside spring was already full-blown. And this year he had failed again.

From the habit of these last few years, "spring" and "failure" had become inseparable in Juntarō's mind. He went downstairs to go to the bathroom. Light, filtering through the twigs of the garden shrubs, filled the sunny porch and made little dancing specks on the paper screen, just like the dimple on a girl's laughing face. And instantly Juntarō understood the meaning of the maid's smile he had glimpsed peeking out from the shadow behind the sliding door. ——She had read that postcard. And she purposely brought it to my bedside just to see my face when I got it.

While he was urinating, Juntarō imagined the maid's cold, whitish eyes. Then he suddenly remembered something. He looked down at his crotch and muttered, "wouldn't you know, today it's not up."

It was true. This one morning the symptom that had been bothering him every morning until now had not appeared—the symptom that he'd always had to camouflage from the time he got out of bed until he reached the bathroom, shifting his pajamas or just slightly lifting a hem. Was it from the shock of the failure notice?——But for having just taken a shock I sure don't feel at all sad, or pained, or anything like that. But maybe that's because the same thing happened last year, and the year before, and the year before that? Could be.—— There's nothing a person can't get himself used to, no matter how absurd or how painful it is. The question was, though, how to break it to his mother. It was the same every year: she would undoubtedly weep, and shout, and eventually scratch and pinch him just like some schoolgirl in a fight. Of course, whatever happened she couldn't seriously hurt him, hers being merely a woman's strength, and it wasn't anything he couldn't avoid, but still, the thought that someone might happen to see it made him unbearably embarrassed. Things were especially bad since that maid had gone and looked at the notice before him.

His mother, being disposed to luxurious morning sleep, had not gotten up yet. Juntarō tiptoed to her bedroom, silently inserted the postcard between the sliding doors, and decided to go out for a walk.

But escapist strolling did nothing to relieve him. Once he left the house that purple seal UNSUCCESSFUL glittered everywhere he looked, despite the fact that he'd tried to dismiss it as nothing. Even when he lowered his head and stared at the ground the UNSUCCESSFUL stamp would print itself fast on his forehead and his brain, until he wondered if it would follow him the rest of his life. Reluctantly Juntarō went back home.

By the time he got back his mother was up, sitting in front of her breakfast tray.

Why did the hugely fat body, seemingly wider than it was tall, seem somehow less so this morning? Do people's bodies look smaller when you're nervous? The thought occurred briefly to Juntarō as he made his way through the entryway and past the glass door, glancing quickly into the sitting room.

"Well, d'you see it, the postcard?"

"Why yes, I did. Since you're lazy I'd figured things would turn out this way."

With this uncommonly straightforward answer his mother finished her meal at leisure, then went into the living room and loudly started practicing classical recitation.

Maybe this time she had finally learned to give up. For a long time Juntarō's mother hadn't been able to forget the Ichikō student in *Tales of Kugenuma*, the novel by Naitō Chiyo or whoever that she'd read when she was young. Terribly upset by her marriage to Juntarō's father, a soldier, she had kept alive a burning desire that at least the son Juntarō should go to a first rank school—or, if that didn't work, anywhere, just to send him off to high school in a white-banded cap. . . . This blind desire of hers was, by virtue of its very blindness, fiercely persistent.

But, predictably, his relief had come too soon. As the saying goes, disaster strikes when you least expect it; in any case, that afternoon who should show up but the tailor. . . . This old Chinese tailor, his sweaty yellow face beaming, had come bearing the uniform ordered after the recent Preliminary Examination Results announcement for Z_____ University.

Now some people might call Juntarō's mother hasty. Nevertheless, it was the one trait they had in common.

Juntarō had taken his first entrance exam at a high school in a hot-springs region of Shikoku. Since it was really a trial run he stopped over with some relatives in Osaka on the way back to see the Takarazuka Revue. The next year, being somewhat serious, he went a little farther south to one with a reputation for being really easy to get into. This time though, because he and his friend H_____ (a boy who had come with him) wandered into a "coffee shop" that turned out to be a rather special sort of café, he failed again. To their surprise the waitress sitting next to them at the table had nothing on under her long-sleeved white apron. Bent on salvaging their pride somehow, the two of them ended up polishing off a whole load of

"Apple Champagne" wine. So . . . when he changed course and aimed for a snowed-in school in Tōhoku the next year, he remembered his lesson from the year before and didn't take a single step outside the place he was staying until after the exam; but, as usual, he failed. Personally he'd expected to show pretty well in all the subjects this time, but . . . . Juntarō had only applied to public schools until this year. Now he couldn't afford to stick to that line any longer. Juntarō had become eligible for the draft. Thanks to that, he figured, he could aim for any school that would take him, and he shouldn't have to study that hard. So thinking he had applied to the Preparatory Course at Z_____ University.

The public school results still hadn't come out on the day Z_____ University's preliminary exam scores were announced. So Juntarō's mother, sensing that she couldn't be wrong to forecast this lesser course, had rushed off to her tailor and ordered, from his steadily shrinking wool supply, a Z_____ University uniform.

"My, how ah, very warm it's gotten . . ."

The tailor faltered as he spoke to Juntarō's mother, planted on the entry platform and staring without a word. Not knowing why in the world he deserved to be glared at so fiercely, the tailor wrinkled up his yellow face with a laugh and said, "Just a little something in congratulations to your son." He pushed forward a little package, wrapped and set in a clothing box.

Still Juntarō's mother didn't say a word—the air around her completely froze up. The Chinese tailor was at a loss. His glance flitted restlessly here and there until he discovered, propped inside an umbrella stand in a corner of the entryway, a dust-covered sabre. Fear flushed his whole face. He barely had time to pocket his payment before he cleared out.

"Juntarō!"

Almost before the tailor had cleared the gate, Juntarō's mother raised a hysterical cry.

"You sit yourself right there. Straighten up!"

It had started again. This was the fourth of these annual events now since the year before last.

"And just what are you of a mind to do now, young man? Your father's at the front, your mother's not going to live on forever, and I'd like to know how you expect to feed yourself if something should happen. What, are you going to end up a soldier?"

But having spoken this far she stopped short. Careless Mother had suddenly realized that the year had actually come when her son finally would become a soldier, not just in her threats and nagging but in real life. This time her voice trembled as she came back to ask,

"Really, what are you going to do?"

. . . Her son was going to be a soldier. For one who, so people said, didn't show the years, this had two implications that were hard to face. Could she really be the mother of a son old enough to be taken off to the army? On top of that, though, however abusive she may be to Juntarō, was the feeling deep inside that compared to her husband Junkichi her only son was clearly a better human being. And she could not fathom the possibility that this same Juntarō, as a private, would be like a slave to her husband, a colonel.

"At least behave yourself, will you. This is no joking matter."

She had to say it to relieve her own anxiety and anger and frustration. But when she saw her son just staring down, head bowed no matter what was said to him, she couldn't stand it all over again.

"Oh, oh, how I despise this. If your face doesn't look more like your father's every year. . . . It may be hard for you to imagine, but in his own way even your father could study when he put himself to it. You though, you only take after him in his bad points."

Her son cowed his head all the more. For whenever he didn't he could feel some kind of invisible, phosphorescent stuff emanating from the inside of his mother's fat, pale, bloated body, stabbing at and stinging his skin.

In any case he at least had to get himself enrolled in a draft exempt school. A number were known among the students for their willingness to oblige in this regard, but word was that with the pressure of the times it had gotten terribly hard to push through the procedures of getting in.

Juntarō decided to try out a college of math and physical sciences on the bank of the outer moat.

The cherry trees along the moat were in full bloom. Boats were afloat here and there; the mud-colored water sparkled brightly. The school sat deserted, facing the railroad track on the opposite bank, and the gloom was just the sort to make you think of some secret society or decaying political party. Going downstairs to the basement reception office, Juntarō saw a crowd of students in black coats and worn, stiff-collared jackets—at a glance he could pick out the ones who had failed their entrance exams—going by turns up to a little window that they practically put their heads right through while they consulted about something or other. He was about to approach the window in behind a line of four or five people when someone tapped his shoulder from the side.

"Hey."

He turned. It was Yamada. This boy, with his long face, huge conspicuous nose, and thick glasses, had been with Juntarō in the preparatory school all last year, but until now they'd never so much as said hello.

"What, you too?" Juntarō answered, betraying more earnestness than he intended.

Fixing a cold eye on Juntarō for a second from behind his thick lenses, Yamada said, "You know, once a person's lost his chance in life he might as well hang it up."

He laughed a weird laugh—all in his throat, without any voice.

Juntarō remembered how in the classroom this boy would always sit in the last row and stretch out his neck at attention, peering all around the room.

——What a jerk, he thought, but his words came out opposite his feelings.

"But last year must've been just your second try at the first-rank school, right?" he let out, too kindly.

"Hardly. A third-rank place out in the sticks. Same with him."

So saying, Yamada gestured with his big nose to one corner of the room. Looking over, Juntarō saw Takagi, squatting on the concrete floor alone with a newspaper spread out in front of him.

Juntarō had also seen this boy in the same classroom, but they'd never talked. He always had his head down so far his long, square chin would be almost swallowed up in the front of his clothes, and his expression was pure gloom.

"Takagi, huh. So he flunked too?"

Juntarō said it just to play along. But Yamada answered,

"Listen, if it has to do with getting in here, go ask Takagi. I already got through. He's been out four years now, and at this place for two."

"So that's it. I thought he seemed awfully relaxed."

"Look smart-alec, who's laughing? The truth is he's a genius. In middle school he was top of the class, right from start to finish, and supposedly he's known for being the smartest in the school's history. So it looks like everybody back home thinks he's already going to the Imperial U." Yamada clamped his jaws shut and nodded his head, as if to agree with himself. Come to think of it, Juntarō remembered Takagi with an application for Z——— University spread in front of him back at the beginning of the year when everybody had sent for college applications, and now after Yamada's story this made sense.

It was just as he'd been told—Juntarō was able to go through a clerk Takagi knew and dispense with the formalities.

As soon as the picture he'd brought along was pasted on the
form and got the official stamp, voilà: he had a student ID.
Sticking this in his pocket made him feel somehow calmed. After
all, a school was a school, wasn't it?

"What do you say the three of us go eat someplace?"
Juntarō fell right in with Yamada's suggestion, and together they
quit the basement office.

The sky was blue and clear. The sunlight was dense and
stuffy. Different smells rose up from each one's clothes while
they walked.

Takagi's clothes stood out most. His overcoat was
strangely discolored to a shade not exactly navy, or purple, or
brown either. The hem was too short and hiked up in the back,
so that the front part hung down by that much extra. Furthermore, the seat of his pants was totally worn out, and the dif-
ferent-colored material that had been stuck on from above
flapped open and shut like a bellows everytime he took a step.
Yamada's clothes looked somehow like a missionary's. Maybe
it was because his black stand-up collar, otherwise the same as
everybody else's, wrapped itself around his long neck particularly stiffly, and because his body was like a rectangular box.
. . . To Juntarō, though, whatever they looked like, the clothes
of his two friends seemed more bearable than his own. He was
wearing that new outfit. He'd taken off the buttons with the
Z_____ University seal and changed them for ones from his
middle school; and for a hat he was wearing one with the badge
from the preparatory school on it. The uniform was just something concocted from material on hand, something only the tailor who had made it could have found handsome. Compared
to the blue knit he'd been wearing, it was light to the point of
being silly, so that although it fit him closely it certainly didn't
feel good. Flapping limp and clinging around his ankles, it made
him feel sloppy. That smell peculiar to new cloth hit him every
time he moved—a constant reminder of his mother's rashness.
Yes, her, the one who wanted now to play sister, now friend,

now lover.——Suddenly it felt to Juntarō as if he were looking at the world from under water, as if his body had been swallowed whole into a dark, sticky mass.

How can I be such a different person here with my friends from the me I know at home? Juntarō thought to himself. And with this thought it was as if he threw off a heavy, oppressive overcoat he'd been wearing on a too-warm day.

The three followed a road along the dirt bank of the moat. Three or four girls about their age were coming from the other direction. They were students in the home economics department of the girls' junior college that faced the technical college from across the moat.

"Hey, you know what they say about us around here?" Yamada said, looking back at the other two.

"No, what?"

"It goes, 'If the home-ec department is the moat's flower garden, the tech school is its dump.' "

"If that's a flower garden, those are pretty sorry flowers."

The girls passed by while Takagi was talking. They had on green *hakama* and carrot-orange stockings, like the Takarazuka Revue girls, and they let off a mixed odor of cold perfumes and warm body smells.

"What've they got to dress up for, bunch of hicks," Yamada said, turning around again.

"I had a fiancée once, you know; she's at a Catholic girls' college now. . . . But last night I wrote a letter and broke it off. I'd feel sorry for her having to wait till I got through school."

"I know what you mean," Juntarō chimed in, but he was actually thinking that Yamada was in some ways more childish than himself. In class Yamada acted so superior, his nose in the air, putting people off with his looks; yet here he was today chattering on about personal things the other two hadn't even asked to hear. How his father had a Ph.D. in engineering, for instance, and was a director at S_____ manufacturing plant, while his brother-in-law was a lieutenant engineer for a shipyard; in short, his father had groomed the whole family to be engineers. "So no matter how long it takes I have to get into an engineering school or they'll never forgive me. But I'm getting sick of listening to them, and next year I'm going to try literature for a change. I do like machines though. At least they're straight—they don't tell you lies."

Next to Yamada, Takagi seemed positively serious. As they walked along he kept his head to the ground and would only let out an occasional evasive "oh," or "I see," to Yamada's chatter—yet without coming across as cold, either. Yamada seemed to look up to him too, because when he heard one of these indirect responses he'd stop talking and stand still for a second. Takagi, laughing a self-conscious little chuckle, would disown even his evasive answer. Then Yamada would relax and start up again enthusiastically about his fiancée's school or his father's work—all absolutely irrelevant to his listeners. So it went.

Before long the three of them wound up at Kanda. At every used book store or tailor's shop, little clusters of students in their new white-banded school caps would stick out like a sore thumb. But this time, unlike last year and before, Juntarō didn't really feel jealous or inferior. In fact he couldn't help thinking they were ridiculous, wearing those junior-high uniforms and changing only the hat, then hanging those silly towels from their hips like some kind of magic charm.

Little cafés lined a back street, the whole place crowded with students from private schools. Jazz records blared at top volume. The prettiest girls from each store stood in the doorway to attract customers.

Lips painted heart-shaped, wistful expression, skirt pulled tight over her hips—it was a standardized type. Every shop had one, looking this direction from the semi-darkness behind the glass doors. In front of one, Takagi suddenly stopped and said, "Why don't we go in here?"

Yamada and Juntarō looked at each other. This was the first time Takagi had shown a will to do anything. Further, the whole style and feel of the place didn't seem to fit his personality. But then Juntarō noticed that Takagi's eyes, glittering conspicuously, were riveted on the girl at the door. He spoke up.

"I'm game. Let's go in."

Yamada seemed to be at a loss, but since Juntarō was going along he made an unhappy face and followed them in.

The inside of the café was dark and smoke-filled. Yamada ordered a drink, Port Twist or something—watered-down wine with sugar. Juntarō decided on the same thing.

"How about you, Takagi?" Yamada had the presence to ask, for the benefit of the waitress standing beside their table. Takagi answered, his long face turned down and blushing.

"I don't know, Chinese noodles I guess . . ."

Yamada was visibly flustered and cut Takagi off midsentence.

"Listen, smart alec. They don't sell Chinese noodles here. If you're hungry get a sandwich or something."

The girl laughed, upsetting Yamada even more.

"What're we doing in here? Let's go."

"Hold on, we're alright. Wait'll we've had our drinks."

But even as he calmed Yamada down, Juntarō realized that, come to think of it, he too no longer understood why Takagi had spoken up for coming into the place. Could he have known Yamada would feel uncomfortable and done it to tease him? Or was there no special reason except that he'd never been in one of these cafés before and had suddenly wanted to try it out?

As for the girl at the door, she continued to watch the street as intently as ever. . . . Since the sun was shining on the street out there you could sit in the dark interior and see clearly even the eye movements of the passersby. When somebody met the gaze of the girl at the entrance she would instantly throw the door open, and as soon as the new customer came up to it the waitresses inside would all call out a loud chorus of "Good afternoon!"

Juntarō took in the scene without really looking at it. Customers came in at a rate of about one every ten minutes. Some would enter in rhythm with the jazz; others swaggered in coolly like actors, their shoulders back: the various poses for crossing the threshold showed everyone's consciousness of being watched, and they all gave away some sign of nervousness. But once they sank into a chair in the café, it was as if no one were watching anymore, and all fell to absent-minded sipping on their Port Twist straws. They couldn't even strike up a conversation with the girl at the doorway, much less fondle her or hold her hand.

As he looked on, Juntarō suddenly remembered the maid's face, her white flashing eyes and pointed chin not without their charm if you could overlook the red nose. But when he also remembered that she had brought that UNSUCCESS- FUL postcard right up to his pillow, there was no way around seeing that he'd fallen into the same trap as the virtually im- prisoned customers around him.

When Juntarō looked around now, having thought this— at Yamada, sitting with his questionable drink half unfinished, his long neck upright and his eyeballs riveted in space as if to ward off the people surrounding him; or at Takagi, face down, refusing to lift his head—they all started looking to Juntarō like misfortune itself.

Back at school, the new term had begun.

Last year Juntarō had won an award for going one year straight without missing or being late a single day. This was of course no proof of his dedication. If anything, it proved the ex- tent of his laziness. The fact was Juntarō hardly knew what it meant to play. Maybe it was that he didn't have any brothers or sisters, and had lived alone with his mother since he was small; in any case, Juntarō had never learned baseball rules and couldn't even play Japanese chess. Since he hadn't wanted to play house or shoot marbles with girls, either, in the end he had done nothing. An occasional teatime outing with his mother had been his sole thrill in life. So although he hadn't particularly been morally educated, he had no inclination toward delinquency. . . . But this way of life was steadily growing intolerable.

Luckily, since his mother wasn't the doting type, Juntarō wasn't followed all day long and nagged at for such trifles as how he held his chopsticks. Even so, just to look at her was suffocating. Instead of saying "go do your studies," she would whine at him. "Oh, you were such a bright, adorable little boy till you went off to school."

Once this got started it would go on and on, from how he breast-fed well as a little baby to how he graduated from kindergarten with flying colors, never breaking, never ending. If it wasn't his childhood, it was his future wife. Since he kept failing, though, she had more or less dropped that one lately. But there was another thing, though it wasn't something he liked to talk about: Juntarō's mother wore her clothes badly. A shirt-front or the hem of a robe would be left carelessly open for any length of time. Especially in the summer. Maybe this shouldn't seem so bad once a person got used to it; but it just wasn't the same as taking a bath together when you were little.

At any rate, such things made going to school with his friends infinitely preferable to staying at home. The school didn't ask them to prepare or review for class, and the school had a no-flunking policy. There were no rules or punishments, and no military training. Better yet, there was no appointed model student, and no class president, so naturally no one was polishing apples trying to be teacher's pet.

And this year going to school had gotten to be more fun. Because Yamada and Takagi were there. The saying may have it that out of sight is out of mind, but for this trio it was just the opposite. While they may not have been a perfect match for each other, these three got to where if they weren't constantly doing something together they missed each other unbearably.

Once Juntarō got to know them, both Yamada and Takagi turned out to be pretty decent fellows. Lately both of them were fanatical about literature. "Fanatical" may be a funny expression, but in Yamada's case at least there was no other way to put it.

"All apologies to your father, Jun, but the fact is Japan is going to lose this war. When that happens, being in industry won't be worth a thing. Culture—the arts—that's where it's going to be."

So saying, he went off and bought tickets to shows and concerts like a madman, taking off almost every day for some auditorium or exhibit hall. But then that wouldn't do either.

"Japan doesn't have an international cultural university yet. You know, where students from all over the world could get together and teach each other about their own country's culture and religion. . . . Since Kimi Yūsuke is a friend of my parents, I think next time I see this Mr. Kimi I'll get him to set one up. If we do get it, you guys will have priority for entrance, so you'll have to work hard and be the first graduates."

He insisted on these preposterous things with the utmost seriousness.

Takagi, by comparison, was closer to the real thing—your true "young man of letters." For a while he crammed his notebooks full of stories and poems and the like; then, making statements like "I just don't have confidence in Japanese anymore," he started writing poetry in some phonetic system he'd come up with himself. But what really surprised the other two about Takagi was that he knew women. In a conversation about his life in the country he had casually touched on the subject. From then on, Takagi was to Yamada and Juntarō a separate species of humanity, on a level of existence one step above their own.

But on second thought this was odd. It wasn't as if Takagi were the only friend of Juntarō's who had had experience with women. When he was an elementary student, a shop boy in a laundry where he used to go had talked to him about those things, and he'd not only been totally disinterested but had actually felt sick to his stomach. When he had grown up a little, a classmate in junior high had had the same experience, but Juntarō had even felt sorry for that boy—certainly never jealous. Why was it that only Takagi began to seem to him as a person concealing something great, something vaguely threatening? Was it that he had reached the period now where he was supposed to be wanting "it" more? Maybe so. But then, it wasn't as if he'd had no interest in it at all when he was younger, so this explanation wasn't completely satisfying either.

And here was another strange thing: why had Takagi become so flustered in the café at Kanda? Until now Juntarō had always assumed that the reason for his own inordinate shyness and self-consciousness in front of people was his virginity. It seemed something to that effect was written in a book about these things, and he had more or less believed it. So what did it mean that Takagi had turned so red and lowered his eyes? Didn't "that" have anything to do with shyness?

Before long, the cherry blossoms fell. Every year at about this time Juntarō's mother quit grumbling about his failure: for her, it was cause for short-term unhappiness only. Naturally, Juntarō could breathe more easily then, too. Accordingly, since he had started failing the entrance exams, the cherry blossoms were depressing for him; the new leaves just coming out were beautiful.

In fact, ever since Juntarō had started taking these tests he had been increasingly sensitive to the changing of the seasons. The year before last, last year, and now this year, too, he had to suffer the same agonies from the same workbooks and the same textbooks, always with the same threat of disappointment lurking in the road ahead. The workbooks only frayed around the edges, the underlining in the textbooks got heavier—nothing else changed. He thought about exams as follows: There are some people who can do everything smoothly the first

time, and there are some who can't do anything until they fail
once; the failure types fail even at the easiest things, it's like a
warm-up for them; but entrance exams never allow you to fail
that way. Therefore, even if I try for three years, I'm just turning around and around in the same orbit without any hope of
landing.

But this year already something different was happening.

Juntarō's cousin Kyōko came to visit.

Kyōko was trying lately to get herself engaged to the man
who had been Juntarō's tutor, and his mother was playing
matchmaker. She had helped Kyōko once before with marriage
arrangements—that time, so rumor had it, the man had been a
real Gary Cooper look-alike. Curiously enough, ever since then
whenever Juntarō saw a picture of Gary Cooper he was overcome with anger that he couldn't explain as jealousy. For some
reason, that match had broken off. But this time it looked as if
things were moving successfully. His mother's only emotional
outlet these days was to recount every detail of the affair to him.
"What do you think, Juntarō? I do believe Mr. Yoshino is taking to that girl." She chuckled. "You know what he said to me?
'She has very nice eyes, doesn't she.' " His mother put this to
Juntarō with pauses that carried biting overtones.

"I'm sure it'll go just fine."

Juntarō answered with his face averted, head down,
wanting to keep the agitation inside him from being noticed.
Again, his mother spoke in a tone that could have been either
comforting or sarcastic.

"Well, I wonder. It sounds like the people in Kyōko's
family were thinking that you two would have made a perfect
pair . . ."

This was his mother's coy way of reminding Juntarō how
long he had been failing exams. By now, if he had gone straight
through, he would have just over two years until graduation.
In Juntarō's case though, simply getting into school, assuming

he ever managed to do so, would have taken more than three.

Kyōko arrived with Juntarō's aunt in full Japanese dress. As she had come straight from the hairdresser, it looked as if she were wearing a wig. Kyōko had only been out of the girls' school for a little over one year, but already she had the stereotypical look of a person who belonged in the adult world. She looked just like a mannequin of the kind on display in bridal-shop windows. She bowed for so long a person might have thought the tatami mat had swallowed up her forehead.

"My dear aunt, it has been such a long time. Is my uncle at the front active and in good health? And once again, to Jun—"

Here the words that had been rolling out like a recording came to an abrupt halt.

Once she's come this far, Juntarō thought, she might as well add, "our deepest condolences." But Kyōko didn't say another word. His aunt hastened to say something but Juntarō's mother took over and blundered through a greeting of sorts.

"Yes, well, we are letting him take his time."

Now what was he supposed to do with himself at a time like this? Be ashamed, was that it? But even if it were, Juntarō couldn't begin to figure out how to feel ashamed on demand. His face wouldn't turn red when he tried to make it blush, and it was silly to scratch his head. . . . The only thing to do was to run away from this disgusting scene, and fast. But for some reason this was the one thing he was unable to do. Something deep inside him refused to give in to them. ——But who says running away from here means giving in? And what is it in them I don't want to give in to? Juntarō had no idea.——He ended up simply sitting fast where he was, listening to the chatter about Kyōko's wedding date and whatnot, and trying very hard to look nonchalant.

It was two or three days later. Takagi took Juntarō along with Yamada for a stroll across the river.

By this time, even Juntarō was sick of sitting in front of

the same desk, opening the same workbooks, having the same lineup of teachers write Ptolemy's theorem or the usage rules for the definite article on the same blackboard for the third year in a row at this cram school, and even when he did walk out of the house carrying his bookbag, he rarely went to school. He'd meet up with the rest of his trio instead to wander around between their respective houses or boarding rooms and the coffee shops.

That day, too, the three of them quit school halfway through and walked aimlessly from Ginza to the Kachidoki bridge to take in the view (namely, the newly built Spring Bridge, looking like it might spring off at any minute). After they had watched the river scenery from the bridge for a while, Takagi said,

"Do you want to go to Tama-no-I from here?"

Takagi no longer looked embarrassed the way he had in the Kanda coffee shop. Quite the opposite: he knew the layout of Tokyo by heart, and he would go first, guiding them with no sign of flinching through places Yamada and Juntarō had never been. . . . Still, Juntarō was shocked to hear the name, "Tama-no-I."

Juntarō had heard that Shinjuku was another district around here where women could be had for a price. Many sleepless nights he had been curious to go see it. Though he did not know the details, he pictured the district as being lit entirely with bright red lights, with murky black shapes moving about inside it—it would be a place that would respond easily to a person's desires. But he had never felt like actually going there. Come to think of it, there was one time, on his way back from the test at a certain school in the south, when he was looking for a movie theater in downtown Osaka and had mistakenly wandered into one of those districts. The main street, like the entertainment district of Asakusa, was lined with theaters and movie houses and trinket shops and restaurants, crowded with people walking along with their families; but literally one step behind it he found himself on a wide street with nothing except black-walled houses along it. It was totally deserted. It all meant nothing to him, and Juntarō was about to go back to the main street, when—

"Boy! Come here!"

——a middle-aged woman with her hair up in an old-fashioned knot called out to stop him. In that split-second, Juntarō caught on that this was "that kind of place." This street without a soul on it in the middle of the day; this row of houses deathly still behind their black walls: it couldn't have been farther from what he'd imagined that kind of place to be like. The difference left him terrified. He immediately bolted. . . . But this time it ought to be different. If he were careful to avoid disease and policemen, there shouldn't be anything to worry about. Still, the "let's go" came as a shock.

Gulls reeled above the river, as vast as an ocean, and the breeze off the surface blew in Juntarō's face as he looked to Yamada.

"What do you say?"

"Let's do it," Yamada answered enthusiastically, almost as if to get back at them for that time in the Kanda cafe.

"By 'go' I don't mean 'go in.' We're just strolling through for a look," Takagi said, checking their enthusiasm by his tone like the elder that he was.

There certainly are some strange places in the world. From the moment they set foot in the place, Juntarō could hardly believe that he wasn't watching a movie. It was different from anything he had ever imagined, and so bizarre he could not believe it was real even while he walked right through it.

One step in from the main bus route, along a street so narrow that a single person could barely pass through, was a row of houses with only little one-foot-square windows open to the street; framed inside each window, as if at the bottom of a well, one could see a woman's face.

It would have been a ridiculous layout for an ordinary section of town; then again, the place was too much like something out of a fairy tale to be a site for carousing with alcohol and women.

The three went flying along the incredibly complicated twists and turns of the street, Juntarō and Yamada flushed red the while. Wherever they looked were nothing but women's faces. Many times as they passed it would seem as if someone had called out, but when they turned to look they couldn't tell which face it had been. All Juntarō could see was colors—red, pink, green—moving about inside the little windows. . . .

Juntarō completely lost track of how long they had been walking. Following Takagi out of what looked like someone's back door, he suddenly found himself back out on the bright, sunny main street once again.

"Well, was it interesting?" Takagi asked, stroking his square chin.

"Yeah, it was interesting."

"It was interesting alright."

But actually they hadn't retained a single impression of what they had just seen. Juntarō felt his face still cramped in a smile. He could not rid himself of this half scared, unconscious grin. Of course, anyone would balk at first on finding out that so many women—there must have been a hundred at least—could be had for sheer money.

"Want to walk some more? It goes on over there," Takagi said, pointing to the other side of the street. But both answered, and honestly, "Oh no, that's enough. We're tired." To tell the truth, it took a lot out of them even to speak. Riding the train back to Asakusa, though, Yamada gradually recovered his spirits and enthusiastically pushed for going back to the place one more time. Then, suddenly dropping that tone, he said in a voice full of emotion,

"But you know, just to think all the women in those windows are merchandise . . ."

"So true," Juntarō agreed emphatically. He was painting the scene over in his mind—with Kyōko on display in the windows.

Back home, Juntarō's mother was waiting up for him, stern-faced, with his cold dinner tray before her. Today's excursion wasn't quite the same as cutting class to go see a movie. Had she managed to smell where he'd been already?

But Juntarō's line of thought was mistaken. His mother wasn't the type to pry into every little thing she didn't approve. She gave weight only to what she could see with her own two eyes. What had happened in fact was that today, having gone to Kyōko's house on some engagement business, she had learned that Kyōko's younger brother Takeo had gotten into high school this year.

"Well, what do you think now?"

"Think of what?"

"He's five years behind you, you realize."

"So what, of course he is. He's young for his class, too."

A rice bowl shattered with a crash. Here we go again, thought Juntarō, at the same time tensing to make a getaway. Long experience told him this would be the start of thirty minutes worth of wild, uncontrolled raging. Times like this, it was no use fighting back. In an hour she would have calmed down, and by the next day she'd have completely forgotten about it. . . . But today for once he was off the mark. After the one broken dish, there wasn't a sound. Looking up, Juntarō saw that though her face was white as a sheet, she was somehow keeping her calm. As he cautiously watched, she leaned over to the chest, spreading her fat thighs, and pulled out something in a brown envelope.

"Very well, Juntarō. At this rate I assume you're planning to give up on getting into school and let yourself be drafted. If it's to come to that, I suggest you at least volunteer. Here————."

So saying she handed him the envelope: entrance requirements for the naval school of accounting.

Juntarō was shocked. ——Something must have happened for her to think of making me into one of those soldiers she hates so much. And how on earth did she come up with the idea of making it the navy, and at that to have hunted down an obscure field like accounting. She must have heard about this at Kyōko's house.

"Well, don't just sit there, it's high time you got your picture taken. And be sure to change your underwear before you leave."

Wondering why he should have to change his underwear for a picture, Juntaro took a closer look at the regulations. There it was: "Attach two (2) 5″×7″ photographs, full body, unclothed." Still, getting out of the house seemed safer than staying there, so Juntarō dutifully changed his underwear and hurried off to the studio.

The next day, Juntarō gave Yamada and Takagi a full report on the previous night's events. Naturally, both of them looked surprised. Yamada especially wrinkled his brow with concern (making his big nose look even bigger) and said,

"But you surely don't want to apply to that school, do you?"

"Actually, I do. I know I'll fail anyhow, so why fight it?"

"But what if you pass?"

"If I pass, then I'll go there, of course. I think it'd be sort of fun, being a navy accountant—get to ride on ships and boss around all the little privates on KP."

"Are you serious? How naïve can you be. I'm telling you, Japan is going to lose this war. Maybe it's just China we're up against now, but before long England and America are sure to be in it, and who knows, the Germans might come over too. And you carry on as if it doesn't worry you at all!"

"So, if we lose, we lose. Then it'll all be the same anyway."

"Anybody who can say something like that doesn't have brains enough to be called stupid!"

But no matter what Yamada said, Juntarō kept his calm. Above all, he was sure there was absolutely no need to worry about his passing, so it seemed ridiculous to get upset about anything beyond that; besides, even this might be worth it if it would get his mother off his back.

But when the application pictures came back from the studio, Juntarō was more than a little depressed. These two pictures—one from the front and one from the side of his naked self, here blown up to double the usual size for application photos—no matter how he looked at them, these pictures reminded him more of some creature stripped of its skin (like a full-length shot of a criminal, or of some rare primitive captured alive) than of an applicant to the navy. His eyes glistening vacantly, his body standing there without the least resistance—really, the only assertive thing about him was his navel, strangely and conspicuously facing forward; and then, where his bowlegged thighs came together, the painfully contorted thing strangled in the fresh underwear was also immediately visible from the outside.

The test was given June first, at the site of the school in the Odawara district of Tsukiji.

Juntarō had no idea of what sort of place the naval accounting school would be, or where it was, but to his surprise it turned out to be at the foot of the Kachidoki bridge, where he and Takagi and Yamada had had their conversation the other day about strolling over to Tama-no-I. But that was not to be his last surprise. Standing in the entrance to the testing room was Yamada himself.

"What're you doing here?"

Yamada burst out laughing. "I felt awful sending you by yourself, so I decided to take it, too."

There was no sign that anything devious was going on, but still, Juntarō felt tricked.

"That's downright low, to go around calling a person stupid like that and then . . ."

"No, listen. I went home and had this talk with my dad. I was worried about you. But the old man turned around and got all excited about the idea, and he said I had to take the thing too."

"How come you never said anything?"

"I just wanted to give you a little surprise."

Juntarō didn't care much about things like that anyway. He was just glad one of his buddies was here.

The applicants starting to assemble were somewhat different from those you might see at an ordinary school. A surprising proportion wore glasses, although according to Yamada's theory, this was because the standards for the physical exam here were looser than at other navy schools. ——So he'd even been looking up this kind of information without Juntarō knowing about it.

A number of people he recognized from the cram school were coming in—all of them on their second and third rounds by now. As with the physical standards, the age limit here was broader than that for the marines and the rest. Asking around about their reasons for taking the test, Juntarō found quite a few that sounded word for word like his own.

But one in the group, hearing that Juntarō had been taking tests for three years already, came up to him just to say, "So, this is your last chance, is it. Make it a good one."

These were the types who would set all their hopes on getting into a navy school. But they didn't impress a person as being too intelligent. In fact, for a moment the thought that he might actually pass this test raced through Juntarō's mind. . . . And what if I do—what then? . . . But he imagined he could bear it, riding on ships and lording it over the privates.

A bugle sounded. Some sailors rounded up the students and turned them over to an officer. The officer looked them over and then—laughing or angry, they couldn't tell which—bared his teeth and boomed out,

"The test begins!"

Within an hour Juntarō had walked out the gates of the naval school of accounting. He stood leaning on the railing of the Kachidoki Bridge with the river breeze blowing in his face.

The test had begun with a physical. First they had measured his height, weight, chest size, and grip strength, and then there was a short-arm test and rectal examination. Juntarō went in behind the screens where an army doctor, sitting with his thighs arrogantly spread apart, was belting out in a voice that echoed through the whole gymnasium,

"Since when do you think you're going to be an officer in the Imperial Navy with a thing like that?"

How ridiculous, Juntarō thought. What right does he have to insult somebody who's just here to take a test and isn't even in his division yet?

Juntarō was next. He stood in front of the doctor, a captain who reminded him immediately of a man who used to come over to visit his father, Junkichi. That man was probably doing something along the same lines right now in some other gymnasium. ——While he was thinking this, Juntaro pulled on the cord to his trunks, and promptly had a knot in his hands.

"Cut it off! If it's that long cut the damn cord off!"

But Juntarō only slowed down the more. He purposely took his time undoing the knot just to aggravate the doctor.

After leaving there, though, he went to the chin-up station, and somehow he simply could not get in the mood to lift his own weight. He hung lifeless from the horizontal bar.

"What's the matter with you!" the officer in charge yelled, and as if that were his signal, Juntarō let go of the bar. The rule was, if you failed one item of the physical, that was it for the exam. Wonderfully efficient.

Now that he was past the gates, though, standing here in the wind, Juntarō was suddenly knotted up with anger. Why had he come to this stupid place just to be stuck with the dirty label UNSUCCESSFUL? Hadn't he let himself be tested enough by now?! As he had been leaving the exam room, Yamada had called out, "Wait up! I'm almost through!" But Juntarō hadn't felt like waiting around for anybody in a place like this. Somehow, he had had to act on his own for once.

Juntarō looked up. A white ship was pulling out to sea.

I wish I could go somewhere, too, he thought. Oh, but

where! Joining the army and getting sent to the front is the only way to get out of Japan right now. ——A picture of a deserted street floated up before his mind . . . A solitary soldier is walking head up through the thick fog of a port town. He has no parents, no brothers, no wife, no girlfriend. Just now he has thrown away his citizenship, his military service . . . he had carried the thought this far when something dry suddenly rustled inside him. Oh, you're just thinking of a Jean Gabin movie. What's really got hold of you is your own mother. Why can't you be more independent? If you hate taking exams, why don't you out and say so? If you hate school, don't go. Most people in the world do actually work and get married and live happily to a ripe old age without ever going to school, don't they? Things might not always go smoothly, but you could take responsibility for yourself. So hard times might be waiting for you down the road. But you have to realize that taking that road is still better than letting things go on the way your mother wants them to.

——Then what should I do to break away from my mother? he asked himself. The answer came right back.

——Go to that place.

Juntarō spent the rest of the day in Asakusa, and at dusk he called a cab and went straight to the place.

"This is it, mister," the driver announced, and Juntarō got out at a three-way intersection next to a pickle shop and a kitchenware store. ——Oh no, this can't be it. The driver must have tricked me, he thought, already in despair. But he pumped up his courage, took a look around the corner from the pickle shop, and suddenly there it was. Voices were calling out to customers, but it didn't seem that any were calling him.

"Hey, you, the student! Better take off your cap. If a cop comes by you'll get picked up." Juntarō quickly pulled off his hat and turned around; the face in the window was laughing and inviting him in. It was as in a dream; the face looked like Kyōko and the red-nosed maid at the same time. When he came near, the woman said, "Hurry!" and opened a narrow door next to the window. Juntarō dashed inside, exhilarated.

The interior of the house was not much like what one could see from the outside. It felt more like a soda shop he had walked into. The woman parted a hanging cloth screen with a little bell on it and started up the steps. He figured he should follow her. Upstairs, in a room with sooty-looking folded mats and a low table, he drank the tea that was brought out, and then the woman thrust out her hand and said, "Please make your decision."

This was a different face from either Kyōko's or the maid's. There was something pinched about her shoulders; she seemed totally alien to him. Having no idea how much he should pay, Juntarō handed her the single ten-yen bill he had stuffed into his inside pocket.

The woman immediately became meek. "Thank you most kindly," she said, bowing her head, and she set the money on a tray and took it downstairs.

Juntarō was left with a gnawing, uneasy feeling. Not only had his money been stolen, but now he had been trapped in this room. . . . But presently the woman was back. "Gracious! Are you still over there? This way," she said, in the same gentle tone, and she opened the faded, paper-paneled sliding door. There was a thin mat covered with reasonably clean sheets.

"Just a minute." She untied her sash. Juntarō stared wide-eyed. This was where the miracle would begin. But the woman stayed on her feet, stuck her hand up under her kimono and fussed about for a while.

"I get cold so easy, you know," she said, and pulled out a piece of black wool cloth from under her hem. So that was it. He had thought she looked too thick from the waist down. While Juntarō was wondering if a cat might not jump out from between her legs next, the woman lay down on the bedding with her inner gown still fastened, spread her thighs, and said, "Well. Show me you're a man."

But Juntarō just stood where he was, shocked, and didn't

lift a finger. Was that what he had been dreaming after all these years, this black thing stretched out under the white stomach? It was ugly, even grotesque, but he did not turn his eyes away.

"Why aren't you taking off your pants? Hurry up, your underwear too . . ."

The woman's words reminded Juntarō of the doctor at the naval accounting school. He couldn't believe that could have been this morning. It seemed like ten years ago—no, longer.

"What's the matter with you? Have you been drinking or something?" Expressing her displeasure overtly now, the woman moved to pull her skirts back together.

"Wait a minute." Juntarō tried hastily to stop her, but he didn't know what to say next. Suddenly the woman brightened.

"Oh, I get it. You're the straight type, right? . . . Me too. I hate all that heavy-mushy stuff."

Juntarō felt complimented and nodded his head once as if to agree; but he was still not satisfied.

"Not exactly," he said, holding down the quiver in his voice. "But you don't mind if I look some more, do you?"

"Go right ahead. As long as you don't touch," the woman answered, laughingly, as if she knew everything.

She seemed like a warm person, and Juntarō wanted somehow to take her into his confidence. But before long a bell rang downstairs.

"Noisy buzzer, huh. Time's up, you know. Promise you'll come again? It's not nice to break promises."

Juntarō nodded, satisfied, and went downstairs. The woman laid out his shoes neatly, then turned her back on him and sat down in front of a mirror stand. The mirror was positioned just at the angle from which her face could be seen through the window.

"I'll be back," Juntarō said, waving to the woman in the mirror. The words that slipped past her lips just then caught him off guard.

"Do forgive me for my poor hospitality . . ."

Juntarō didn't know where or how long he had been walking. Following his own feet, he came out at the riverbank. The name "Shirahige Bridge" loomed up before him.

Well, Juntarō mumbled, is that it? Is that enough, am I independent from my mother now? The woman's "sorry for my poor hospitality" made him nervous. ——Did I do something rude? Or, was she rude to me?

Juntarō walked on along the bank, turning this over in his mind, walked on beneath a row of cherry trees dense with damp, heavy leaves.

And kept walking.

The Moth
(Ga)

*I*t really was incredible. Why something like that ever happened is a problem I could think about forever and still not figure out. I suppose the whole incident can be written off to chance. But somehow I get the feeling there's more to it than that. It may be irrational, but I get a feeling this could only have happened to me—a thing like this could only have happened to a fool like me.

I am constantly hounded by restlessness and irritability. . . . The sensation is impossible to convey in words, but you might say it was a cross between the itchy feeling you get right before a toothache, and the ticklish feeling of having the most delicate feather drawn across the underside of your foot—only this is all over my body. It's probably because I have trouble with my spine. My vertebrae, deformed in an illness, seem somehow to irritate my spinal column. . . . But this sort of talk is beside the point. The most detailed scientific explanation would mean nothing to me. The queer sensation that is neither a pain nor an itch nor a tickle would persist as before, and what's worse, an explanation like that only makes me imagine my decaying spine all the more vividly, crumbling away to expose the nerve bundle inside, like a stalk of flayed celery, now bathed in pale yellow discharge (though this vision is about as fanciful as a little kid's picture of a man from Mars). . . . In any case, I have little faith in doctors. These past six or seven years, my spine has gotten alternately better and worse with absolutely no relation to what a host of doctors have said about it. But I don't intend to criticize the medical profession on that score. No matter how skillful their diagnoses or how effective their medicines, I still wouldn't be able to work up any affection for them.

When I was first examined in the orthopedics division of K_____ University Hospital, the head doctor simply listened to my own description of my symptoms and then pronounced, "What you have is spinal tuberculosis."

This was more or less what I had expected, so I wasn't particularly shocked; I just stood there. Apparently that was not an acceptable reaction.

"Do you take some exception to this? . . . Alright then,"
he said, and ordered me to take off my clothes. He then called
in seven or eight medical students, said "Ready?" and proceeded to tap on my spine with a hammer, occasionally paus-
ing for what was to me a meaningless exchange of questions
and answers with the students—"You there, will this bone tend
to move up or down?"—"That one will move down. No, up.
That one will move up. But in rare cases it will move down."
In short, he made it clear that I was nothing more nor less than
a model tuberculosis case, and even said to me, "I had you di-
agnosed the minute you walked into this room." . . . This head
doctor's extraordinary rudeness may be the exception. But the
only difference is that he was up front about it. Every doctor in
the world is like that on the inside. The greater part of their job
satisfaction, aside from the money, lies in this sort of thing. Who
hasn't gone to a doctor with some personal concern only to be
told "there's nothing to worry about" and to come away humiliated? It seems to me that in an instance like this the patient
has been ridiculed for his caution. In fact, he ends up as ashamed
as a soldier who failed to pull off some outstanding feat in front
of his commanding officer. . . . Ultimately, the reason I don't
like doctors is that I get the feeling they can see right inside
me. For better or worse, I consider my body my own, and I
guess I just feel uncomfortable having a stranger know everything about it. When I complain of my ills it's to let someone
know that there is "pain" inside me——I'm not asking them to
cure it. There is such a thing as making a companion of your
suffering. A headache can make me feel as if I'm dreaming. I
get a certain thrill out of suppressing the urge to defecate. I even
rather enjoy the smell of a fart. . . .

I don't go out of the house much. Not for health reasons; it's just that I'm an "indoor" type. Being inside all the
time, though, I do get so I want to go out once in a while. Certain sights in the district called the K_____ Ginza, with its rows
of department stores and bakeries and barbershops, give me

pleasure: a window display for a store that sells European wines and cooking utensils; the fair-skinned girls with red-painted fingernails handling fresh produce in front of a department store. . . . If in spite of this I don't actually want to go there, it's because they don't seem to look kindly on people who just stroll aimlessly around. Suppose I'm walking down a street where all the pedestrians are going one way when I suddenly get bored and turn around. Immediately all the other passersby and all the shopkeepers turn to stare at me. Though they don't say a word, they are all criticizing me. ——Just what are you up to, loitering around here like that. Then either I have to pretend I just remembered something, and say out loud, "Damn, I knew there was something else," or else I have to act as if I'd turned into a ghost, slowly, quietly gliding away. But there's something even worse than the ordeal of turning around, and that's "bowing." Every time I've ever thought of this bowing business, I've wished I were a dog instead. If only I were allowed to turn tail and run away like that whenever I wanted to! . . . There's the eternity it takes for someone who looks familiar but then unfamiliar to approach and finally pass you. The awkwardness of tilting your upper torso forward without slowing your pace, saying two or three barely audible words to the other person, and walking past. And then the sickening feeling you get when the spirit that haunts such greetings stirs the faintest breezes of suspicion and manages to ensnare both of your faces head-on in each other's line of vision, as if in some invisible spiderweb. . . . Of all the people I know, though, the ones who make me most uncomfortable of all are Dr. Imokawa and his family, who live in the house diagonally across from ours, and above all the doctor, Shunkichi, himself.

Bowing with Dr. Imokawa is in a class by itself, completely unlike bowing with anybody else. A greeting between the two of us is not the usual affair of faint, haunted stirrings; we are drawn toward each other with inexorable force, as if by a pair of cogwheels, to salute with one hand and let out a loud "Yah" upon passing, or sometimes to drop our heads to our chests with a thud. To an outsider it must look vigorous and direct and manly. In fact, it is the opposite of all those things. . . . I never do look him in the face. But even without looking I can tell he's got an eerie grin on his pale face. For the simple reason that I'm always grinning the same way myself.

My bedroom commands a view of the entire back side of the Imokawa house. With its large garden pond stocked with edible frogs, and surrounded as it is by huge pine trees, the house has always looked like a mushroom to me. . . . When Shunkichi comes out through the shadows to the wellside with his nurse (a role filled by his mother) and pharmacist (his wife), all wearing their white smocks, I sometimes try to imagine what they might be conferring about. At such times, with the three of them silhouetted in their white coats against the dark, mushroom-like house, I'll suddenly think of them as a stubborn little trio of elves, living a queer life of some kind. . . . Shunkichi Imokawa only moved to this town on the K_____ coast about two years ago, but his name was a household word throughout the vicinity as soon as he arrived. The reason for this was a needlessly large sign at his gate, reading "Imokawa Clinic." Further, rumor had it that between his gate and his front door he had set up no less than six doorbells in a whole range of sizes. The fact that this talk reached even my house leads me to conclude that the doctor's publicity campaign was rather successful. Judging from the way he advertised himself, I formed an image of the doctor—without any particular basis—as a short, round-faced, cheery sort of fellow. Apparently this kind of illusion was general: on discovering that the tall, lanky, pale man who passed regularly through the gate was not a patient but the doctor himself, almost everyone was taken aback. To have any kind of preconceived image shattered like that always leaves a person severely disappointed. Furthermore, as a final mark against Shunkichi, he looked to be only thirty-two or thirty-three years old, a good ten years under his true age. . . . Whatever the reasons, one thing was clear: the Imokawa Clinic was not exactly popular. Only once, when out for a walk, had I seen the doctor hurrying off somewhere with his mother accompanying him carrying a medicine kit. (Having his mother for an assistant only exaggerated Shunkichi's seeming youth.)

The elder Mrs. Imokawa occasionally called on my family. Each time she came she would exchange a few words with my mother, and then come over to the veranda where I'd be lounging in a reclining chair to say meaningfully,

"Why sonny" (I was thirty-three years old at the time, and still addressed this way), "you're looking so pale, is anything wrong?"

or,

"Look at you, you've been losing weight again," and then fix her eyes on my face with the mournful look of a dog passing a butcher shop. After repeating herself several times without any response from me, she would abruptly change her expression, spit out a hostile "Take care then," and stomp away as if she were pounding nails into the ground with every step.

Meanwhile, about this time another bizarre rumor about Dr. Imokawa began to make the rounds. The latest was that, whereas he had advertised himself as a former navy doctor competent to handle anything from internal medicine to surgery and pediatrics, every patient who had approached him these past three or four months had been turned away, and he was accepting neither house calls nor office visits. . . . This rumor reached me through my mother in the form of anecdotes, tales of the personal experiences of Mr. A_____, Mrs. B_____, and Mrs. C_____. Mrs. C_____'s story, for instance, ran as follows: one night her four-year-old son's throat became blocked and he started having trouble breathing; she ran straight to Dr. Imokawa, who told her it was tonsilitis and proceeded to rattle off a list of adenoid symptoms and their treatments; despite her repeated pleas that he make a housecall he made no move to come with her, but leaving the frantic and increasingly angry Mrs. C_____ standing at the entrance, merely flung in her face the words, "You'll have to excuse me, I'm feeling sleepy tonight," and disappeared without more ado into the house. The others' stories were similar; in every case the reason given for refusing a house call seemed to be purposely feeble: he'd say he was drowsy, or weary, or—in extreme cases—that it was just too much bother. . . . I didn't know the extent to which Dr. Imokawa really persisted in turning clients away like this, but I was fairly sure that he had no means of earning a livelihood other than working in his clinic, and furthermore, that with him adopting an attitude like that, it was unlikely his wife or his mother would be able to find outside employment. In this light, such behavior on his part could only be seen as suicidal; it was too extreme to be dismissed as an eccentricity.

As time went by, the grin with which Dr. Imokawa would greet me when we passed in the street began to seem positively sinister.

That night it was hot and humid, so I had the window wide open as I read.

There are a lot of insects in this part of the country. A whole lot. Late at night when the lights in the neighborhood are out, hordes of them—especially drone beetles, long-horn beetles, and moths—fly into my room; they stick wherever they land, on the walls or on the ceiling, creating a paisley effect. . . . They bother me, and I would have tried to kill them but there's no end to them, so I let them be.

Suddenly—just when I had pulled the lamp over because the print was starting to get so indistinct I couldn't read it—I heard a fluttering sound by my ear, and some kind of bug flew up into my right ear canal. I put my finger to my ear, hoping to force it out, but only succeeded in blocking the bug's way out, and it quickly flew deeper in. . . . Even then I couldn't believe that a bug would ever fly inside a person's ear and simply not come back out. So I decided to ignore it, leave off fiddling with my ear, and turn back to my book. But as soon as I resumed reading the bug started flapping its wings, as if to tell me, "I'm still here, you know." I felt as if I were in a dream.

Stepping up my efforts to get the thing out, I rolled my eyeballs around in their sockets, as if that would do any good. (It wasn't me doing the thinking but my eyeball, saying—hey, there's somebody in here behind me. And my hand, thinking—of course you can't catch bugs, they can fly away; houseflies, butterflies, dragonflies, you name it, if it can fly you haven't got much chance to catch it.)

So there I was, alone, in the middle of the night, pacing around my room with my arms outstretched to empty space like a blind wandering minstrel, muttering "shhh, shhh. . . ."

"Hey—hey—what's going on?" By the time I heard my father calling me, I was stomping up and down the hallway.

"I've got a bug in my ear."

"What kind of bug?"

"A moth. I think it's a moth. . . . Think you could take a look at it for me?"

"Which side?" Father got up, put on his bifocals, and took hold of my earlobe. Instantly my nerves were shattered. Without thinking, I let out a loud yelp. From the moment I heard that holler resounding in my own ear, I lost my reason completely.

"I can't see anything."

Almost before the words were out of my father's mouth, I jumped to my feet, pounded my head with my fists, and roared as loudly as I could. Now my mother, too, awoke from a sound sleep. Confronted on waking with this scene, she was completely bewildered. . . . Seeing my parents gape open-mouthed at their son's mad antics, I grew even more crazed over my own wretchedness. In fact, every time the bug fluttered its wings, my body was jerked upward as if I were being hoisted from inside the ear by something powerful like a crane, and I tottered precariously on my left leg.

I raved on like this until morning. Gradually the movements of the bug inside my ear slowed down, and the slower it became, the more my own exhaustion increased, until finally I fell into a stupefied sleep.

How long I slept, I don't know. I opened my eyes thinking of the bug in the dim recesses of my consciousness. I sat
up, took my groggy head in both hands, and gave it a good
shake, thinking even as I did so that it was really too much to
believe that the bug could still be inside there. And in fact, even
when I shook my head like a moracca I could hear none of the
fluttering of the night before. . . . Having more or less re-
gained my calm, I went out and sat down in the cane chair on
the veranda and casually lit a cigarette, when instantly the dream
was shattered. The second the smoke reached the back of my
throat, the pattering started up. I flung the cigarette away and
started leaping about just as I had the night before. My parents
had just sat down to lunch. The dust danced all through the
house. . . . Finally my father hollered angrily, "Hey! Keep it
down out there!"

"Try telling this bug to keep it down."

"You could go to a doctor."

"I could do whatever I please."

Even as I said this, however, I registered a shock. . . .
It might be fair to say that I am a man who is fussy about appearances. Maybe I'm one of those men who has no patience
for bad form. . . . Suppose I go to an ear, nose, and throat
specialist. I'm ushered into a chilly room and made to sit down
in a chair with straps on it that looks like a medieval torture
rack. After a long time the doctor enters, wearing a white tur-
ban with a little round mirror affixed to it, and I have to give
him a complete rundown of my symptoms. . . . The mere
thought is unbearably humiliating.

In any case, I decided to try and calm myself down a little more. After all, I just had one little insect that had moved
in on me, right? I could go to the beach. I could sit on the sandy
shore simply looking out over the ocean, which practically em-
bodied freedom itself, and see if it didn't help my own anxious
heart to unwind.

I left the house. But instead of heading for the beach, my
feet led me toward the K_____ Ginza. Quite suddenly I stepped

into a pharmacy, and heard myself say, as if I were possessed, "Five ear picks, please."

As I looked at the bundle of bamboo picks I had been given, it occurred to me for the first time that my mind might no longer be functioning altogether normally. I decided my head needed cooling down, so I went to a seafood shop where there was also a counter for serving food and proceeded to eat two ice-creams. . . . What I did next was a terrible mistake. All there was left of my mind at this point was a capacity for mischief. This devil now came up with some kind of twisted reasoning to order me off to a barber. The barber I picked was one of those vain ones who take snapshots of haircuts they've styled, label them "Composition Number So-and-so," and put them up on the wall; through his speech and the way he carried himself in general, he tried to give the impression that he was more than just some fellow who cut other people's hair. Accordingly, I figured I'd slyly butter him up and have him, rather than an ear, nose, and throat man, secretly dispose of my bug. I walked in with an innocent expression on my face and said,

"How would you like to do an ear cleaning job?" As it happened, there were no other customers in the shop.

"Just your ears, sir?"

"That's right. . . . But I'll have to ask you to be gentle. For a certain reason I can't trust it to anybody who's indelicate with these things."

My scheme worked beautifully. The barber said he would be delighted to take me on, and with a scornful laugh at my bamboo ear picks, proceeded to take out a whole array of tweezers and other instruments. But when he took a needle with an alcohol-soaked cotton wad on the end of it and put it into my ear canal, the moth went into an incredible flurry of activity. No mere fluttering of its wings but a flinging of the creature's whole body against my eardrum, this set up a thundering and booming that penetrated to the deepest recesses of my brain. In a rush of alarm I pushed the barber's hand away, hollered out like a veritable madman,

"Thank you! That's fine!" and—almost before the words were out of my mouth—dashed headlong out the door.

"If it's that bad you should have gone to a doctor in the first place!" the barber shouted angrily after me. . . . Barely knowing which way was up by this time, I made for home, hopping through town on my left foot with one hand clamped over my ear. . . . I was just about to turn into the path that led to my house when a figure with a tattered parasol and a shopping basket suddenly came into view. It was the elder Mrs. Imokawa. I automatically came to a halt and straightened up.

"My, my, hot out, isn't it." The old woman spoke first, bowing her head. Then, "is something wrong today?" she said, staring at my face with that look of hers.

That night my mental state went into yet another phase. I finally began to accept that there indeed was a bug in my ear. . . . Though I still raged and stomped around the house every time the bug acted up, now it was with a certain sense of resignation—perhaps an inner peace from coming to see hollering and throwing fits as my vocation, and from feeling that at least as long as I was doing that, I knew who I was.

Furthermore, I was beginning to develop a sort of rapport with the bug inside my ear. . . . It seemed as if we had kept up some kind of running exchange since this morning, when I had lit the cigarette and sent him into a flurry of wing-beating. But even after I began to think of it that way, I got irked at this impudent insect for daring to try and push me around, holing up like that in a spot beyond my reach, and I flailed away at my own sideburns until I nearly scratched right through my cheek at the earlobe. . . .

As night fell, a flock of insects began to gather again around the lamp in my room. I looked at them now with new eyes. Especially the moths, alighting on their front legs in patches of darkness, in the shadow of the desk or the bookshelf, to rest their heavy wings: I found myself actually sighing as I watched them. They may be completely intractable rascals, but they're my friends. . . . That was the sort of strange, mixed sentiment I was feeling. I was sure the bug in my ear, too, was getting used to its new home, and had been able to calm down there. In place of the earlier exasperating fits of activity, its wing and leg movements had now taken on the character of an occasional playful scratch.

Whenever the bug moved its front legs inside my ear, I felt a sticky, gummy sensation, partly painful and partly ticklish. It made me imagine the moth was feeding himself on my brain matter (which had probably turned chalk white by now, what with the moth beating its wings against it all this time and showering it with scales.) . . . The feeling this gave me was absolutely indescribable. And then to think that this same insect was watching my every move, from the time I woke up in the morning to the time I went to bed at night—no, even while I was asleep—positively thrilled me.

(Come on, there must be something more vile, something more disgusting I could show this guy.)

Goaded by the bug, who was now crawling back and forth across my eardrum, I suddenly thought of Shunkichi Imokawa. . . . By now Dr. Imokawa's pleasure in purposely maddening his patients made sense to me as an emotion of my own. He, like me, was preoccupied with appearances. "We'll make a name for ourselves for sure," he had undoubtedly boasted to his wife (who though she had a flat nose was something of a beauty), and he had probably made similar claims to his mother; but when he had opened the clinic's doors, no one had come. This humiliated him in front of his family as well as his neighbors, and the subsequent suspicions about his capability had mortified and tormented him further, until after chafing under this day and night he finally came to find a singular pleasure in this sort of rudeness. . . .

I resolved to go ring all six of the buzzers at the Imokawa clinic and have Shunkichi attend to my bug. . . . I would hound him doggedly for as long as it took. I wouldn't care if I got thrown into that frog-stocked pond in the process. I wouldn't even care if, in his humiliation and rage, Shunkichi killed the bug altogether.

As it turned out, the whole thing came to a completely anticlimactic end.

The gate with the huge signboard on it was warped; no amount of pushing could force it more than halfway open. I finally squeezed through the opening and entered, to find that the majority of the buzzers were either missing part of their mechanism or otherwise broken. So I tapped on the glass sliding door at the entrance and called out in a loud voice.

Who should come to the door but Shunkichi himself. I had wanted to act nonchalant when I told him why I had come, but, perhaps as a result of having shouted out at the entryway, I was already worked up, and ended up sounding like a damn soldier reporting for duty.

"Well, this is a surprise," the doctor said, though he didn't look surprised in the least. Then, saying "This way, please," he ushered me to his examining room. At that point I should have turned right around and gone home. I went on in. The room was predictably cold and had that peculiar examining-room smell.

"Now, when did the bug get in your ear?"

"The night before last, about 11:00."

"What? And you let it go all this time? You certainly don't seem to be in any hurry."

"Actually, I would have come earlier but I was embarrassed to bother you for such a little thing."

"Ha ha ha. Don't worry yourself about that."

Don't worry myself about that. In other words, I was the patient here, he was the doctor.

"Now then, which side? Here, lean this way. . . . Ah, good. Still kicking in there. We're alright then," he said, then in almost the same motion hollered out to his wife, "Sachiko!" and picked up a cardboard tube and a flashlight. . . . What followed was really too ridiculous. Shunkichi held the cardboard tube to my ear, aimed the flashlight into it from the end, and with less effort than it takes to blow your nose he flushed out a small moth, about a quarter of an inch long. It would have been better if the moth had at least flown straight to the window and out into the sky. . . . But as soon as it emerged, the insect—possibly stunned by the sudden light—fell to the floor. I was sitting there without any reaction at all yet, feeling a chill as if I might catch cold from the grey walls around me, and heard Shunkichi say,

"This sort of thing happens all the time in the country-side. They say that the peasants who tend the vineyards in France will make up a story about somebody killing a bug in his ear by pouring wine in on top of it to cover up when they've been helping themselves to the master's wine. . . ."

Listening without interest to this stream of talk, I happened to look down at my foot and see the moth; its grey wings sagged heavily, but it was still managing to move its legs in an occasional, feeble kick.

Gloomy Pleasures
(Inkina tanoshimi)

Once a month I make a trip to an office in Yokohama, capital of my home prefecture of Kanagawa, to receive a certain sum of money. Now I imagine that even in the case of an honest wage, the split second when a person's money is actually being put into his hand must always bring with it some kind of humiliation. Since my claim to this money is so tenuous as to be practically nonexistent, that queer, uncomfortable feeling is much more pronounced. The story is, I fell ill due to a back injury incurred in the army seven years ago and I am ostensibly not strong enough to work yet; hence I collect these payments. ——When I put it this way, the reader may find the whole setup perfectly reasonable. But for me, the claimant, it's another story altogether. The truth is, I don't know what to think. I ask myself whether I could possibly earn this kind of money every month if I were well. This is no frivolous question. True, it only comes to 2000 yen a month, but considering that I was drafted straight out of school and managed to fumble my way through sixteen months in the army without even being promoted to private first class, sometimes I seriously wonder whether I have some basic defect, whether maybe I just don't have what it takes to hold down a job. . . . If this is true, my collecting a pension on account of my illness is essentially a sham. At least, that's how I always feel on the day I go to get it.

When that day arrives I am invariably a nervous wreck. Partly, no doubt, because of having slept badly the night before, I can hardly taste my breakfast. Anxiousness may be intrinsic to the state of anticipation, but in my case, beyond the general uneasiness over whether or not they'll actually give me the money this time (for if the supporting documents are the least bit out of order they refuse it), there is another, more specific anxiety, though admittedly a totally foolish one: I'm afraid that on that very day, as soon as I reach the office, my illness will disappear, and that it will be obvious to the most casual observer that I am the very picture of health. What would become of me then?

"So, how are we feeling today?" The clerk who handles

my case will be particularly jovial as he asks me this or something like it. But without a moment's warning his mood will change, and suddenly he'll be eyeing me suspiciously, like an inspector who's just taken a coat off the rack and discovered a sizeable burn mark on it. Then, even though his suspicions are completely groundless, he'll have me panicking, trying to explain the miraculous cure that must suddenly have come about inside me—my cheeks turning redder and more healthy-looking by the minute. . . . In one scenario after another, this nightmarish fear keeps turning up. I try to block it out, but it's no use. For something in my body, against my will, holds out a hope that its illness will miraculously go away. . . . Eventually this anxiety gives rise to a sense of guilt. When in the course of my monthly trip I have happened across a sight such as that of a young man in handcuffs being led off like a monkey by the police, I find myself moved less by curiosity or compassion than by the feeling that a dark, ominous shadow has fallen across my path.

From the K———— coastline it's an hour's trip by train and streetcar to Sakuragichō, by which time I'm already starting to feel tired. To the right as one leaves the station, a mountain called Yake-yama hovers high over the grey rooftops like an island suspended in midair: the prefectural offices perch on its summit. I cross the tracks, reach the foot of the hill, and begin my slow climb. . . . The cement retaining wall at my side stretches as far as I can see; my breaths shorten, the foul air suffocates. This suffering is a comfort to me. Since I want to avoid being invigorated by the walk, I keep my face turned toward the ground as much as possible. A car zooms up from behind and passes me, its back side glinting in the sun like a beetle as it kicks up a spray of muddy water. I take this opportunity to purposely let myself be splattered. . . . By the time I reach the crest of the hill, the combination of exhaustion and fright makes it woefully tempting to stop and rest, but I fight that impulse and, guarding the pain in my chest as closely as I would my wallet, I walk on through the gate and into the government building.

Inside the Division of Reparations for Victims of Disaster, I am by now so consumed with the wish to look like the very personification of disease that I genuinely feel half dead; but there is one girl who particularly intimidates me. . . . As I make my way up the creaking stairway I always pray she won't be there, but every time I open the door, there she is. . . . A big red mouth and a pair of close black eyes under thick eyebrows dominate her broad face; she wears too much makeup for her age, but I'd say she's about eighteen. Even if everyone else is gone she's sure to be there. They always make me wait at least forty to fifty minutes to get my modest sum—on a bad day, sometimes two hours—and for that whole time I am subjected to this girl's savage looks. (In the dim light of the room her eyes positively glow. . . .)

K_____ , the head of the division, is probably close to forty. A short man with a broad forehead, he always wears a dirty black suit and a pair of black-rimmed glasses held together with masking tape. This K_____ is the one who looks over my papers, but he has all kinds of other duties here as well. . . . He'll take the documents from my hands, furrow his brow and examine them mistrustfully, then suddenly leap up and dash off to turn on a light. But not content to stop with one, he'll swoop around like some gigantic bat from one table to another until he has flicked every switch in the room. Returning at last to the documents, he'll find his place, shake his head a couple of times, abruptly show the page to a colleague at the next desk as if to ask, Don't you think there's something fishy about this?, and then confer with him in a voice too low for me to catch. Finally he will nod his head, take up his pencil, and begin to fill out the application, but at the second or third word he will drop his pencil again, jog over to a wall clock, and reach up to wind it. . . . He moves in fits and starts, with the jerking motion of a set of cogs that don't quite mesh. This restlessness reflects back on me, compounding the anxiety I already feel, until with every break in his movements my own heart skips a beat and a chill runs through my entire body. I slide one hand inside my shirt to press on my chest through the plaster cast, shooting fearful glances around the room only to see that girl glaring at me with rock-hard eyes. . . . That stare of hers reduces me to the lowest kind of money-grubbing impostor.

I decide to steer my thoughts toward the pornographic. . . . The girl is wearing a white sweater with a low neckline and a blue jacket with crimson lining. Tight, olive green skirt, fat thighs, a nickle-plated necklace across a buxom chest. . . . I try to imagine the private places on her body. But it's no use. . . . Rubbing one sweaty thumb against the base of a forefinger inside my pants pocket, I strain after an image, but can't even picture a single undergarment. There she sits with her chin in her hands, red-painted lips pushed into a pout, those unblinking eyes scattering all my efforts to the winds. And gradually making my feelings of inferiority a reality.

. . . At last K⎯⎯ 's disdainful voice breaks in.

"Here's for this month. . . . Come again next month on the Xth," he says, and he hands me the money. The moment I feel that damp sensation in my palms my tension peaks. . . . As I turn and start to walk toward the exit, I can feel a thousand pinpricks the length of my back, from my bottom up to the back of my head, and my mind is reeling with the old stories like that of the famous kettle thief caught by Ooka Echizen* and all the others who bungled grand schemes with one last-minute slip. The wood-floored hallway to the exit seems to stretch to infinity.

Am I really as desperate as all that for money? I'll admit money is one thing a person can never have too much of. And it's also true that my mother spends what I bring home on things

---

*A judge of the early Edo period, immortalized in a collection of contemporary suspense stories.

like rice and dried fish, and maybe a little candy. Necessities, in other words. That's why I keep going to the prefectural office and putting myself through this terrible ordeal . . . or is it? The fact is, that's a lie. The claimant doesn't have to appear in person at all, as long as he sends his signature seal. So why do I do it? There are a number of reasons I could cite. That my mother tends to get confused with paper money or to lose it, for one. Or that my father gets tongue-tied and can't talk in front of strangers. . . . But when you come right down to it, I don't understand my behavior myself. I go because I enjoy it. And I purposely dredge up my most disgusting emotions and come back absolutely gorged on humiliation. For that reason, for all I say I hate it or I dread it, the truth is I can hardly wait for that day to come. It's my own gloomy pleasure.

When I picture Yokohama to myself from back at the K_____ coast, I see it as a distinct "district," cut off from the rest of my life: a place full of possibilities and temptations. The reason is that for that one day I get to walk the streets there with money in my pocket—even if it is only mine to carry home.

Once I clear the gate of the Prefectural Center, I run all the way to the bottom of Mount Yake. The feeling is partly one of wanting to get away from a threatening place, and partly that of a little boy who, though normally forbidden to run, has just been granted a rare exception. Racing madly like this, I begin to feel as if there were actually something to look forward to at the other end. . . . I reach the bottom of the hill, cross the tracks, and suddenly I'm in town. An unbroken string of shops lines either side of the street, while temporary stalls are massed together right in the middle of the already narrow roadway like a clutch of insect eggs, and from the shops and stalls all manner of merchandise—food, clothing, housewares, even small animals—spills out onto the pavement itself. . . . Gaily painted restaurants and coffee shops throw their doors wide open to the street; in a sewing store, colorful fabrics cascade across an entire wall. Next door is a pickle vendor with barrels piled every which way and looking ready to come tumbling down any mo-

ment. But none of these are of any use to me. I can't buy anything, and I can't eat anything, so I choose something else. For
instance, I sometimes stand in front of the brightly polished
display window of a certain food store. . . . Plump, glossy
sausages dangle on a string; a ham shank rests in a bed of celery and lettuce leaves with a frost-covered pipe for a pillow. I
stare and stare until the thick glass all but melts. At last the
greasy flesh seems to come to life before my eyes; the ham, sliced
open to reveal a vivid cross section of white bone and pink meat,
and the sausages, stuffed full to bursting, look like the trunk
and chest of a freshly slaughtered animal. Suddenly they start
to move. They rise up imposingly before me, or mount a steed
and thunder past, just grazing my face. At this point I feel an
indescribable pleasure . . . at the way my poor stomach shrinks
in revulsion . . . and at the way passersby gape at me as I stand
there with my nose practically pressed to the glass.

After that I take the long way around to walk down another, broader avenue. This is an area of nothing but souvenir
shops and restaurants catering to foreigners, so I spend my time
there watching them shop and eat. . . . To stand behind an
American soldier as he fumbles with his camera until I am
shooed away with a swift kick in the seat is middling good.
Better yet is to come upon a whole family being escorted out of
a restaurant by their Japanese waiter. The wife emerges first,
strewing compliments right and left—her way of padding out
the tip. Next comes the meek-looking husband, and lastly the
children. . . . This lucky family group fascinates me. Surely they
must belong to a different race than ours. Next to them the
waiter positively looks like a monkey. And I'm a whole notch
below him. . . . Meanwhile, this is where my fun begins. The
adults, busy conferring about where to go next or something,
turn their backs to the children and walk on ahead. I grab this
chance to make scary faces and glare at the children. They immediately turn white. . . . I can imagine why. To have a stranger
whose shoulders are disfigured by a bulky cast glower at you

with a face that was half pig and half demon would be too much for anyone. The little one's eyes immediately cloud over between their blonde lashes. (Ah, the pleasure of it.) Hardly able to believe this nightmarish horror, the terrified child would turn around again to see whether his eyes deceive him, but his oblivious parents push him into the back seat of a sky-blue Studebaker and drive off.

By now my back is worn as a washboard from this unaccustomed exercise, and I'm in a near stupor of self-loathing. I buy a cup of watery coffee for ten yen from a stand near the Bridge of Tears, where the bums congregate, and then head for home.

One day I seemed to be blessed with uncanny luck. It was near the end of November, one of the last clear fall days, and there was a bracing chill in the air; but when I reached the office, that girl I dreaded so much was nowhere in sight. On top of that—as if to prove that good things really do come in streaks—the clerk K——— gave me 1000 yen more than usual. (They never gave me the full amount I asked for.)

I left the place in record high spirits and made my way on light feet down Mount Yake. . . . As soon as I could begin to see the shopping district, about halfway down the hill, every sign and decorative bunting from the jumble of shops below drew my eyes as if by some tremendous force, and I could feel the money in my pocket leaping and squirming like a fish just pulled out of the water. . . . How many years had it been since I'd had this feeling, of money in my pocket that was actually mine to spend? During the war you couldn't use currency to buy goods at all, and after the war my family had fallen into poverty. . . . Before I knew it I was back in the mood of another period and, imitating the style of a dissolute student, I tossed my cigarette away just like Lloyd Nolan and whistled a few bars of ragtime.

I would have dinner, see a movie, stop for tea, and then

buy some sweets to take home to my parents. . . . . Without my particularly having thought about it, this plan sprang full-blown into my head.

Almost immediately upon entering the street of shops I came across a combination restaurant/coffee shop. . . . . I could already feel the spoon in my hand dipping into a bowl of soup as I rushed toward the entrance. But about one foot from the door, as if my body had somehow sensed a hidden trap, my feet reversed themselves and took me right back out to the street. . . . Strange things do happen. Try as I might to go back there, my legs refused to obey, and I ended up walking past the place altogether. I came to another restaurant. But here as before my body veered off in the other direction. . . . . Whenever the real brass doorfittings, the white tiled floors, or the backs of so many chairs lined up in neat, quiet rows came within my line of vision, my body shied away, like a wild beast that cannot approach light. This was repeated again and again until before long the sheer presence of a restaurant was enough to distress me and I couldn't so much as walk a straight line down the street.

What had come over me? Without money, I had walked this street with composure; now, I was completely unnerved. . . . Gradually losing my confidence in the glowing visions I had so recently entertained, I finally resolved that, if I couldn't bring myself to enter a restaurant, at least I could buy a sausage from that store where I always stared at the display window, climb the hill to the foreigners' compound in Yamate, and eat the thing in the raw, one big mouthful after another, while taking in the view of the harbor—somehow that seemed more my style anyway. So thinking, but fiercely determined to see my hopes realized this time, I purposely bypassed the butcher shops in the area and headed straight for that particular store. The result was disaster. For some inexplicable reason the polished glass of the display window startled me with a clear reflection of my own face. This was a worse blow than a zero on an exam. My face looked like a gourd, with its drooping folds of yellow green flesh; my eyes and eyebrows sagged, my mouth

hung open. . . . I had known I probably looked pretty deca-
dent most of the time when I stood staring into this window,
but it was supposed to make me look tough. This was the face
of an idiot.

I gave up on the sausage. Any interest in the things
around me was gone by now. The only thing left was to walk.
So, with mounting agitation, I walked. Eventually I came to a
corner dessert shop with a large sign advertising traditional
Japanese sweets made with sticky rice cake. This sign evoked a
certain recklessness in me. Ever since I was little I have dismissed this kind of dessert, but at this point that soft, white,
insensible mass, totally without art save its sweetness, seemed
to suit me perfectly. I parted the white cotton curtain in the
doorway and stepped inside. What should loom up in front of
me larger than life but the face of that girl from the prefectural
office.

Damn.

I turned and pelted out of the shop. . . . Those terrify-
ing eyes of hers had put me right back in the Reparations division.

In the panic of the moment my mind went blank. . . .
Looking back on it, it seems obvious that she was the one who
ought to have been scared, loafing in a place like that during
what must have been working hours——I had nothing to be
afraid of at all. In spite of which it was me who had panicked,
while she was unperturbed.

I had worn myself out with so much walking. My good
spirits gone, all I felt now was loneliness. The things I noticed
now, standing in the middle of the street, were a wig on a hairdresser's sign that looked like the hair of a corpse, or a thread-
bare overcoat stuck on the eaves of a thrift shop, its gyrations
in the wind recapturing at moments the shape of the man who
had once worn it. . . . There was nowhere for me to go. I was
wondering if I should give up my plans and go back home,
when——

"That's it . . . ."

——suddenly I remembered a certain old woman. . . . Going to her might be just what I needed.

Last month, too, I had been exhausted as I made my way back home from the Yokohama office. Heading for the station, I had dragged myself as far as the foot of the Bridge of Tears when I came upon a row of shoeshine women, four or five of them, lined up in front of a brown building facing the canal. I started. The one in the middle was calling to me. . . . An old shoeshine lady had raised her hand and was beckoning in my direction. I looked around. There was no one. The only person in her path was me. . . . Though I've used the word "beckon," the woman had made only a vague gesture with her hand, but it was enough to stir something deep inside me. She sat on her haunches in the sun with a towel wrapped around her head, smiling. But I didn't stop. To have my shoes polished by an old woman, on top of everything else, would have been too much pleasure for one day.

. . . What luck that I should have thought of that old woman just now. My shoes had gone for half a year without being polished a single time, but I set off now with urgency, and a new sense of purpose.

The old woman was bent over, apparently dozing. She didn't even notice when I walked right up to her. Without a word I deliberately thrust one foot forward; the woman abruptly looked up. It was a disquieting moment. She was younger than I had thought. As she went to pick up her brush first thing, I said, "Aren't you going to wipe it down with gasoline first?"

The woman looked up. "Would oil be all right?" she asked in a troubled voice. "From the occupation camp?"

Once again a strange feeling came over me. I had only meant that I wanted her to take a little time over it, so I said, "Go ahead," and sat down on the one-legged iron stool, placing my foot on the platform. A spindly willow tree waved its naked branches in a breeze that rose off the canal. . . . At last I had found a place where I could relax, I thought, and my tension was suddenly released through my seated loins.

But I was in for a surprise the moment the woman started to work. Her method of shining shoes, which was new to me, involved scraping the caked-on dirt from the shoe with a piece of string held taut between her hands. This was done, moreover, with incredible force. I tried hastily to stand up, but with my trunk locked in plaster my body was not free to respond, and I very nearly toppled over, stool and all.

"Please hold still," the woman said. I rose out of the stool and leaned hard on my kneecap with both hands, but when she started in again with the cord my foot began flopping back and forth on the wooden platform. . . . By this time I was ready to call the whole thing off. Where the cord had cut through the thick dust caked onto the shoe leather, it had left a series of red stripes, but I could live with that, it was only a shoe, after all.

The woman simply would not let me go. Gripping the wooden platform between her trousered thighs and pressing against my shin with her forehead, seeming in fact almost to lick the dirt off that restless shoe, she polished away. As she did so I could see down the nape of her sunburnt neck to a red undergarment. . . . I had obviously asked for more than I could handle, and though I was trying my best to enjoy it, I had really had my fill by now. But the woman kept producing cloths and brushes one after another, giving a quick swipe here, a gentle caress there, until it seemed there would be no end to it. . . . Though it was a cold wind that blew off the dark water of the canal, her forehead glistened with sweat. The shoes already sparkled so brilliantly that I could scarcely believe they were on my own feet. For some reason this depressed me.

When the woman finally finished I was so weary I hardly even noticed she had stopped. I asked how much I owed her; she told me twenty yen. The figure was dismayingly low. I wanted to leave a little extra, but didn't know how to go about it, so I ended up giving her just what she'd asked.

Buying the return ticket at the station always takes something out of me. When the chit marked for the K——— coastline is passed to me through the dark window, a certain resignation—like that of a dog leaving his master's house to go back to his own miserable little hutch—settles in.

There was scarcely a soul inside the station. . . . I felt dejected. But in a different sense than usual. Climbing the steps to the platform in the cold left behind by the departing sun, I could still feel in my thighs the warmth of a moment ago. . . . It would be some time before my train arrived.

I walked alone from one end of the long platform to the other . . . on my feet, the shoes whose glossy shine reflected the pleasure of an entire day.

Rain
(Ame)

*E*ven for a rainy season it had been unusually wet. Though you wouldn't know it from the rainfall totals, it had been coming down steadily day after day, almost without letup.

"Three days in a row," I muttered to myself. There was a heavy object attached to the inside front of my raincoat, pulling the hem down in front and the collar taut against my neck in back; warm raindrops kept rolling along the collar rim to drip at the base of my throat. ——This constant drizzle was more than I could bear. There was a novel I had read once, a story about a man who squandered his life in a romance with some unremarkable woman, but queerly enough one detail that stuck with me was that the main character had been the son of a cleaner. Considering that a man who does laundry for a living spends all his waking hours, year after year, immersed in a cloud of steam from his iron and surrounded by the smell of drying clothes, it seemed not at all implausible for a person born into such a family to come out with a less than resolute sort of personality. As I recall, the famous criminal K———, who terrorized Japan after the war with a rash of murders in which he would invite a woman shopping and then kill her, came from a launderer's family himself; when you think about it, there's something menacing, some strange atmosphere of fevered passion, that seems to seep out through a cleaner's window, brightly lit as they always are late into the night, and hover over the place making the air there thick and murky. ——The more I thought about it, the more likely it seemed that the unrelenting rain might account for my own bizarre behavior of the past three days. I would have to come up with some daring project, some single ambition with which to pierce my body and soul to the quick. For three days now I had been wandering around town like a fool carrying a hatchet in one hand. I had decided to become a burglar, you see. I say 'like a fool,' but I don't mean to make fun of either my motives or my decision. At the time I had no job, no home, and not even enough money for trainfare to my parents' home in the countryside: there was really no other choice. Besides, I figured the actual work of a burglar could hardly be much of a challenge. If I avoided all the elaborate scheming and plotting typical of detective novels and stuck with a straightforward approach, everything was sure to go smoothly. With an initial resolve and enough persistence to carry it out, the work itself ought to be ridiculously easy.

I originally planned to threaten my victim with a certain knife of mine. I was convinced that this alone, if handled right, would bring about the hoped-for results. But after making one round of my targeted neighborhood I got the feeling this wouldn't do the trick after all. Entering a movie theater in Shinjuku on the way, I thought it over and decided that a weapon of intimidation ought to look like a proper weapon. So from the movie theater I went straight to a cutlery shop. I intended to buy a dagger, one with a birch handle and a blade that shone a dull blue. But as soon as I caught sight of a row of small hatchets designed for chopping kindling wood, I decided to go for one of them instead. I handed over my last 400 yen for it. This was the article I now carried under my raincoat.

The next day I again made the rounds in D_____ town, my targeted neighborhood. But the result was the same as on the day before. All I ended up doing was making repeated comparisons between the gates and walls of a score of houses. But what really depressed me was that, when I decided to start over and had gone back as far as Shinjuku, I walked without thinking into the movie theater that was showing the same film I had seen the day before. More than my own inexcusable carelessness, it was the sight of the same images playing across the same wide screen that really gave me a shock. For some reason I was instantly gripped with terror. I knew then that I was a doomed man. Not only would I fail as a burglar; I would fail at everything I tried. From here on, no matter what good luck might come my way, no matter how easy a road to success might lie open in front of me, I was doomed to falter over some trifle and let the chance slip away from me. . . . The picture on the screen showed a wide expanse of blue ocean. I tried to get up from my seat several times, intending to go back to D_____ suburb. But every time I went to stand up it was as if a wave

surged out from the screen and rolled over me, and I kept falling right back into my seat. I ended up sitting in that clammy,
broken-down chair until the end of the picture, unable to move.

Today, the third day, the sun had set before I could drag
myself out of bed. Since I had carried the hatchet around the
whole day before, now when I stood up I got an ache in my
left thigh as if someone were jabbing needles into me. If anything, though, this pain became something of an inspiration. I
may not have had anything to show for all the walking I had
done the day before, but in its own way the sheer determination not to let this pain get the best of me managed to rouse
my spirits.

In front of the D_____ town train station was a semicir-
cular pond, the heart of a similarly shaped park from which five
streets led out in the shape of a fan. The five streets corresponding to the ribs of the fan were connected by a network of
smaller crossroads. I singled out the avenue in the middle, running straight ahead from the station, and resolved to enter the
house at the bottom of that street. I had decided that, rather
than weigh every factor, it was more important to concentrate
on carrying out whatever I made up my mind to do.

A low iron gate hung ajar in the middle of the ivy-cov-
ered stone wall. Beyond the gate a massive and imposing pine
spread its branches; beyond that I could just see the front door,
set into an English style brick entryway. A small green car was
parked in the shade of the tree, its wet roof glistening in the
rain like the back of a giant beetle. I made my way up the path,
crunching gravel underfoot as I went. It seemed an eternity before I reached the door. On the stone patio were two doormats,
one of iron and one of woven hemp. I deliberately avoided them
both. I rang the bell. Then, to be ready to flourish the hatchet
on a moment's notice, I unbuttoned the front of my raincoat,
grasped the handle with my right hand, and waited for the door
to open. As soon as I heard the lock turn, in an instant I had
forced my body through the crack between the door and the
jamb, left shoulder first. A sudden smell of mildew made me
shudder, and there before me stood a grey-haired, aproned

woman, bowing. I gripped the hatchet and took half a step forward.

"Oh!" A soft cry escaped the woman's lips as she raised
her eyes. But the uncanny thing was, her expression radiated
nothing but peacefulness and calm. She looked to be about fifty.
There was actually a hint of a smile on her face, which was now
so close to mine that even her light dusting of powder seemed
glaringly white. I involuntarily relaxed my grip on the hatchet
handle under my raincoat. Just then the woman's eyes went
wide with surprise and she said an astounding thing.

"Why, if it isn't the man from the electric company! In
that case, why don't you step on around to the back door . . ."

The woman broke off midsentence with a peal of laughter, apparently overcome with the humor of her own mistake.

For a moment I was stunned. By the time I snapped out
of it I was standing on the doorstep outside the entryway. I took
two or three steps toward the back door and then I was suddenly overwhelmed with a feeling of total foolishness. The
woman's laughter still rang in my ears. Despite its apparent
spontaneity, some quality in that laughing voice had commu-
nicated gentility—there was something shiny about it, as if it
had been scrubbed clean with soap—and this left me completely defenseless.

Should I really pretend I was from the electric company
and go into the house as she had bidden me to?

I toyed with this notion more out of curiosity than desperation. From the direction of the kitchen I caught a whiff of
the sweet, heady smell of boiling meat; they must be making
some kind of soup. But no sooner had I started to walk to-
wards it than I heard a sudden burst of laughter, presumably
from the maids and houseboys, which filled me at once with
dread and self-loathing, and I promptly turned on my heels and
ran for the gate.

I ran blindly until I came out at a small park. I had made a note of the place before. There was an enclosed spot in one corner that afforded cover on all sides, behind some bushes that fronted the road. . . . Before I had even reached the place, I heard the first raindrops on the leaves overhead; gradually I began to catch my breath.

I sat down on a bench at one end of a pond, full to the brim with muddy water. But this time I was tormented by the question of why I should have been such a coward back there. Who was that woman who had answered the door, anyway? The lady of the house? Then did her apron mean she had guests coming on short notice, I wondered, and was bustling about with last-minute preparations? If that were true, then when I happened to come to the door just then she had mistaken me for her drop-in guest. . . . I was sure the whole household was having a good laugh about me by now. But I couldn't work up any hatred for them because of it. In fact, my memory of the woman's laughter was indescribably sweet. I knew it was silly, but I was starting to picture her as a genuine innocent, a person so pure of character that she would show equal graciousness to burglars and guests alike.

The soup in that kitchen had sure smelled good, though, I mumbled to myself, and I stood up to go. But a stab of pain shot through my right thigh and I fell back onto the bench. I hadn't noticed anything while I was running, but the hatchet I was still carrying under my raincoat must have banged me there repeatedly. Maybe I was imagining things, but at this thought my whole thigh felt suddenly warm and wet. Was I bleeding? The exposed blade of the hatchet could have torn my pants and made a gash somewhere in my leg. Trembling, I took the hatchet out from under my wet raincoat to have a look. The blade lay across my lap like a thing asleep, gleaming dully in the fading light of the rainy dusk. There was no trace of blood, not a nick on the blade.

Though I was relieved, I was irritated with myself at the

same time. Everything in the world seemed stupid and infuri-
ating, including me. D_____ town, with its placards hung on
every house like little botanical labels; the laughter of that old
woman, still ringing in my ears—stupid, all of it. Whatever had
possessed me to read a stupid thing like "purity of character"
in her, I was sure I didn't know. But my own stupidity was the
worst of all. Looking at the hatchet on my lap, I thought again
about the panic I had felt while running away just now from
that house. Hadn't that been closer to the desperation of a little
boy who's been left out of the game than to actual fright? One
thing was sure: the mere voices of the household help had
frightened me more than any prospect of being arrested and
sent to the police.

   I would have to start all over from square one. I just
couldn't leave it like this.

   Following my earlier reasoning, I tried as much as possible to avoid setting up a "plan" ahead of time. The way I figured, if I did try to slap together some kind of scheme, the first
thing that didn't go according to my calculations would ruin me.
So, abandoning the idea of breaking into a stranger's house, I
hid out instead in the branches of the corner thicket to wait for
a victim.

   But for some reason, as soon as I started waiting the traffic
going by the place mysteriously fell off. Of course I had purposely chosen a secluded spot, but at this rate I was beginning
to doubt whether anyone lived there at all. Not a soul walked
by. . . . Since I was without a watch I'm not sure exactly how
much time passed, but I'd say I was there for over an hour,
crouching in the bushes in vain.

   Maybe I shouldn't have let myself fall into a passive,
waiting position.

   As I mulled this over I looked across the blank face of a
wall of *ōya* stone barring the view across the street. To one side
of it was a concrete wall, and on the other side stood another

one of stone, topped by a grassy enbankment—honestly, it was as if someone had purposely put them there to try a man's patience. . . . So where was everybody? Surely this was where I had passed that old American woman yesterday, out in the rain walking a dog in a little raincoat; and the day before that I was sure I'd seen a young woman walk by here alone. Was there some awful jinx on me so that for this one day not even a lone puppy dog was to go by?

My boredom finally got the best of me and I stood up half out of my thicket, when suddenly I caught sight of a man coming straight toward me.

Damn. Had he seen me?

Quickly I fell back to my knees. If I had been spotted, it would be better to stand up boldly, but I thought there was a fifty–fifty chance I hadn't been. Though he was heading straight toward me he was still fairly far away, and the light was behind me. . . . On the other hand, there was the man's formal, traditional clothing—a crested kimono over a divided *hakama* skirt, with white tabi socks and wooden clogs; it clashed strikingly with everything in the surroundings. And then, as if I hadn't already had enough surprises, he completely threw me by turning straight into the park. He was mumbling under his breath as he started down a path that passed within six feet of where I was hiding. His head was shaved bare, and seemed to wobble back and forth on his thin neck.

"It's not right, simply not right. . . . I'm sorry, but it's just not right. . . ."

As he repeated these words the man shifted a white bundle he was carrying to the hand that held his umbrella, turned to face a clump of trees, and proceeded to urinate.

"It's not right, it's simply not right. . . ."

Somehow it seemed that he was talking to himself. He looked terribly precarious, standing there holding the bundle and the umbrella with one hand while hitching up the front of his *hakama* with the other, and it made me nervous just to watch him, but I was to be more exasperated still when, after he was through, he continued muttering to himself and showed no sign of going away.

"It's not right—people in this town talk a good line but all they really care about is themselves—whatever happened to religion? What happened to faith? I tell you, this is not right."

Could the man be a Shinto priest? Maybe his bundle was full of oracles and paper charms for selling door to door. If so, there ought to be grounds for a certain camaraderie between us. Instead, his mumbling only irked me the more.

"Here's a fellow with seven children and nothing to feed them—it's just not right, people around here think it's nothing to do with them and won't give a penny to help."

How long was he going to keep this up? Glancing away, I saw a plump, middle-aged woman in a black raincoat walking down the road in front of me, her eyes on the pavement. Here was my chance. I had only to jump out right now and wave the hatchet at her and she was sure to drop her purse and run. . . .

But it didn't take long for it to dawn on me that with that bungling priest here my hands were completely tied. In fact, I'd been wanting to relieve myself for some time now, but had had to keep still because of him. I wondered if I should attack him first; but somehow after listening to his diatribe I couldn't do that either. It wasn't that I felt sorry for him—not in the least: it was rather that simply letting that sullen, under-the-breath muttering fall on my ears had depressed my spirits, sapped my energy, and killed whatever will I may have had to act.

Before long the muttering broke off. But any sense of relief I felt was short-lived. Turning back toward him, I was startled to see that he was bent over a lunch box, eating. At this sight my last hopes were dashed. In the same moment the tension I'd lived with these past three days went slack, and I was sharply reminded that I had had nothing in my stomach since morning.

I was furious with this man. He ate noisily; I could distinctly hear him crunch on a pickled radish, or cough down some crusty piece of cold rice with a scratching sound in his throat like a chicken swallowing its gravelly feed. I very nearly leapt out of the bushes, tore the lunch box from his hands, and hurled it into the mud-filled pond. But just then a gruff voice boomed out of the darkness behind me.

"You there."

It was a policeman.

"Hullo, you there, what are you doing in here. It says in plain letters right out front, nobody's allowed in the park after dark. . . . Come on, let's get moving. If you don't get going I'll have to . . ."

The man made no reply; he only turned around once. He continued to work his chopsticks the whole time as if he were under a spell. . . . "Oh brother," said the policeman, and he turned and went away. The man carried on with his meal, completely oblivious.

I stood up and came out of my thicket. I stopped directly behind the man, and stood awhile watching him eat. I could see the jaw bone that jutted out from either side of his thin neck moving ceaselessly as he chewed. The longer I looked at the exposed crown and the deeply sculpted back of the man's bald head, the more murderous I began to feel. A musty smell of radish pickles seemed to seep from the wrinkled skin just visible above his collar. I could wait until the moment he finished eating, and then plant my hatchet right in the middle of that clean-shaven head. Soundlessly I unbuttoned my raincoat. This time—this time I'd really do it. But just then the man started mumbling again.

". . . I can't go back like this . . . I can't go back like this . . ."

Go back where? What did he mean, "I can't go back?" Chances were he was fretting about not having brought in enough money today. But to me this thick, low voice, seeming to crawl along the very earth, suddenly conjured up powerful images of the darkness of both my ancestral village and my family home, and I felt my grip on the hatchet start to go limp.

After a brief letup, the drizzling rain must have started falling again. I could hear droplets hitting the leaves and grass, and something cold struck my cheek. I took the hatchet firmly in hand once again and inhaled loudly. But the man went on as before, his lunch box and chopsticks in hand, muttering over and over to himself the mournful words. "I can't go back like this, I can't go back like this."

A View by the Sea
(Umibe no kōkei)

*T*hrough the side window the water in the Bay of Kōchi shone a flat leaden grey. Inside, the small taxi was as hot as a steam bath. When it passed the jetties a swirl of white silt from a coal refinery, spun upward by the wind, passed in front of the car's windshield like a drawn curtain.

Shintarō stole a glance at his father Shinkichi in the next seat. Sunburnt neck craned forward, Shinkichi was gripping the back of the driver's seat for support. His temple was a blur of dark splotches, and his rigidly profiled cheek was creased as if to suggest a smile. It had been a year since Shintarō had last seen his father's face. He noticed three whiskers his father's razor had missed, one on his adam's apple and two under his temple, that had grown almost half an inch. The eyes were too small for the large head and were the color of old glue, and they shone feebly as the eyes of an unfortunate would.

"What's her condition?"

"What was it the telegram said, 'critical'? . . . It doesn't look like it'll be over right way, not tonight anyway, but I imagine it's just a matter of time." Shinkichi answered slowly, like a cow chewing grass, leaving a white bead of spittle at the corner of his mouth.

"Oh." Once his father had spoken Shintarō replied only perfunctorily. He rolled his window most of the way down, but the evening breeze that wafted in off the calm surface of the water brought only hot air with it and didn't seem likely to affect the temperature inside the taxi. He rolled up his shirt-sleeves, the cuffs of which were beginning to stick to his wrists, and tried repeatedly to conjure up the clean feeling of changing into dry underwear. . . . Suddenly a stench like rotten fish scraps being boiled struck his nostrils.

A flock of chickens, covered with white dust to the tips of their combs, crossed right in front of the cab with a tremendous clamor. Crude plankboard huts that looked ready to topple any minute huddled roof to roof along the road. They had come to the *buraku,* the outcaste village. Just beyond the *buraku* the road would level out and fork off in two directions.

This was just where the driver had turned on the radio last year. Shintarō had been sitting in the front seat of the large old cab, with Father and his aunt in back on either side of Mother. The trunk held one set of bedding. . . . The badly tuned radio had blared out loudly as soon as they passed the *buraku*. Some comedy routine was on, and in the bursts of laughter he could hear a particularly shrill woman's voice. ——Turn it off! he opened his mouth to say, but the words didn't come. Instead the driver lifted his black-gloved hand with a flourish and gave the steering wheel a vigorous tug. Bright red flags hung in front of tea houses on either side of the narrow road they had entered. Shintarō panicked.

"This isn't it, this is the wrong road."

The driver hit the brakes and turned his dark glasses toward Shintarō with visible displeasure. Shintarō's father and aunt leaned forward from the back. His mother's face was reflected very small in the rear-view mirror, smiling. She hummed along with the popular song the woman from the comedy routine had started to sing.

"You said K____ Beach, didn't you? Well, that's where we're going. . . ."

The driver's irritation echoed through the taxi. Shintarō's father seemed about to say something but Shintarō raised his own voice to restrain him.

"Not exactly. It's close to K____ Beach. But you have to turn off just before."

People began to gather around the cab. Brightly colored bathing suits of red and blue hung from the eaves of the house next to a tea shop. The driver clicked his tongue.

"Well, when you sit here and say K____ Beach I think you mean K____ Beach. . . . Which way do we turn? Right or left?"

"Left. But in any case I'm afraid we're going to have to go back a ways. . . ."

"Back? Where are you going that you have to go *back?*"

Where *are* you going, Shintarō muttered to himself. He

thought he knew perfectly well why he couldn't answer out loud. He couldn't let his mother know their destination. But was that really it? If that were the only problem, why hadn't he, say, taken the trouble to write out a detailed map and give it to the driver the night before, when he had gone to reserve the cab? The car's engine rumbled as if to express its driver's impatience, but the crowd around them only grew. It was a group of summer guests; they all flocked around, peering inside the stalled cab as if at some drowned corpse.

They certainly couldn't park the car where it was and get out. So Shintarō whispered into the driver's ear,

"You know Eirakuen? We have a little business there."

"Eirakuen?" said the driver in what had to be a purposely loud voice. There was an uproar around the cab. The driver shut off the radio and turned slowly to face Shintarō. Pointing a finger at his head he drew two or three circles in the air and drawled in an affected Osaka accent, "One of those, huh?" Then he yanked recklessly on the steering wheel and jerked the cab around to go back the way they'd come. Shintarō could feel his previously suppressed uneasiness erupt suddenly into an undirected anger.

Now, a year later, he couldn't remember what that had been about. Maybe it wasn't extroverted anger at all, maybe it was just panic. This much, at least, was certain: thanks to that little incident he had been forced to see just what he was doing as clearly as in a picture. He had said to his mother, "Let's go up to Tokyo together." Let's go back to Tokyo. But first let's spend a nice day with Father and the relatives at K_____ Beach. There in the dim electric light of the tea room just off the entrance hall his mother had suddenly come to life at his words, and had started hastily wiping the floorboards at the step up into the house. . . .

The taxi climbed a hill; they were already on hospital land. Rows of cherry trees lined the sloping road on either side.

"A lot of people come up from town to see these cher-

ries in the spring, you know," Shintarō remembered a young
attendant telling him when he had first visited the hospital to
look it over. Certainly they were splendid. At their peak the
blossoms would cloak the entire slope. Still, Shintarō couldn't
imagine this place as a bustling site for blossom viewing; it was
too ordered, it didn't have that haphazard quality that flower
viewing seemed to call for. Rather than what the attendant de-
scribed, Shintarō imagined a forest of cherry blossoms in full
bloom, abandoned to silence. Each cherry tree, each trunk shiny
with sap, seemed to have sucked up an invisible "madness"
from the very earth that was now being spewn out in the form
of pink blossoms. . . . In the middle of the slope the road divided again; a signboard reading "Eirakuen Women's Ward"
pointed to the left. The car pulled over the top of the slope in
one motion, and suddenly a vast field opened up to view. There,
on a U-shaped bit of level land enclosing a small bay, stood a
brand new white concrete building. It looked like a painted scene
from a fancy chocolate tin. This was the hospital.

"Well, what do you think? Being in the country and all,
I suppose it's not exactly up to date; I mean they hardly do any
brain surgery or anything . . . but from here that ward sure is
pretty."

The boy who had boasted of the cherry trees on the slope
had said this too when Shintarō had first come here. Even
Shintarō, who had been skeptical about the story of tourists
coming to view the blossoms, had had to agree that the place
was beautiful. In fact, the beauty of the picture-like scene seemed
to call for no explanation at all. But when he thought about it
later, he realized the young attendant's words could also be taken
to mean that the facility itself was hygienically clean. If so, the
boy was right again—in that sense too this hospital was unquestionably superior to the ones that Shintarō had looked into
near Tokyo. The taxi cautiously descended the steep, winding
road down the mountain face.

A light was already on in the ward entrance. The sea,

calm as a lake, yawned out from the edge of the parking lot, and though touches of fading sunlight remained here and there, it was already past lights-out for the patients, who had all gone inside.

"Should we check in on her?" With that seeming trace of a grin still on his face Shinkichi looked up at his son.

"Alright, let's go," Shintarō answered irritably. ——What else was a son who had come to see his dying mother going to do?—— But as they walked down the long, unlit hall behind the attendant with his flashlight, Shintarō suddenly began to feel as if the whole thing were a pretense. Did he really want to see his mother or didn't he? What was the sense of visiting someone who had already lost consciousness anyway? Wasn't he walking along the hall at a fast clip like this just because he thought this was what a son was supposed to do?

"It's this way, sir."

The attendant gestured with his flashlight. Shintarō had started for the opposite stairway, and he had to stop now to right his overturned slipper.

"She's been moved over here. . . ." The boy spoke in an impersonal, businesslike tone, and went on ahead. When Mother was brought here the family had specifically requested a bright room on the side facing the sea. When had the staff moved her? But there wasn't much point in asking now. They went through an iron door, beyond which a sweet, rotten odor hung in the air. Private rooms for intensive care patients lined both sides of the hall. Stout iron grating and a thick metal screen covered every window; silence seemed to emanate audibly from each one. An animal fear grew in Shintarō with each step. As their guide's flashlight swung carelessly from side to side, faces floated into view, pressed to the screens, their glittering eyes fixed on the three men. At only one room, on the left side, was the door ajar.

"This is it."

The attendant's feet in their ragged tennis shoes came to

a halt. Inside a room with only one tatami mat on a wooden floor, Shintarō's mother had been laid out on a thin straw mattress and quilt.

"How are you, Mrs. Hamaguchi?"

Bending over her pillow, the attendant spoke in a jarringly loud voice. Rectangular blocks of moonlight slanted in from outside. Mother's face, illuminated by the flashlight, was grotesquely distorted, bare skin and bones. She had lost nearly all resemblance to her old self. The attendant held the light right next to her face and lifted one eyelid with his finger. The grey pupil never moved, as if fixed on some one invisible point.

"Mrs. Hamaguchi, Chika Hamaguchi? Your son's here from Tokyo. It's your son, the one you always talked about."

Having practically shouted this into her ear the attendant turned his eyes to Shintarō. He looked like a salesman making a trained animal perform for an audience, looking up for an assessment.

"Why don't *you* try saying something? Who knows, she might wake up."

Feeling compelled by the boy's businesslike tone, Shintarō leaned in closer to his mother. A smell of decay—sweat, body odor, secretions—stung his nose. Yet somehow breathing in the stench put him at ease. It was as if inside and outside came into a sort of balance when that heavy, sweet-sour air penetrated his lungs. Now he could make out in his mother's gaunt features the unmistakable outlines of the face he remembered. Her once babyish forehead had turned the color of coarse tea and was etched with deep vertical creases; her cheeks, formerly as round as a child's rubber balls, were completely hollow, as if the flesh had been scooped out from the inside; all her false teeth had been removed, and her mouth with its sole remaining front tooth gaped open black as a cave. Further, all the flesh from her once ugly double, even triple chin had vanished totally; it looked as if her chin were directly connected to her heavily wrinkled throat with no jaw line at all. But all these features now gradually brought back to him memories of the parts of her face he used to know. . . . Yet that didn't mean he felt like saying anything to the mother he saw here. Rather, the stronger his awareness that the figure before him was indeed his mother, the more awkward Shintarō felt about opening his mouth to speak to her.

Before long the boy grew visibly irritated.

"Mrs. Hamaguchi, it's your son! Don't you understand, your son's come," he shouted into her ear; but shaking his head he made a face to show his disappointment and muttered, "Well, it can't be helped, she just doesn't seem to understand." With that he took hold of both of her hands and began to pump them up and down. Two gaunt, bony wrists appeared from her cuffs.

"That's alright, . . ." Shintarō said, smiling for no particular reason. "That's alright, please, just let her lie there quietly."

Indeed, Shintarō did not understand why he was smiling. His mother had a fever of nearly 104°, and had apparently been in a coma for over ten hours; yelling in her ear and jolting her body seemed only to exhaust her more. She lay on her side, as limp as a rag, her chest heaving violently. . . . It was probably improper to smile at such a time. Yet it wasn't even that he was amused. He just felt the area around his cheeks starting to quiver, as if with the physical impulse to smile. What could it be?

Shintarō suppressed the smile. But he still felt uncomfortable. Putting a cigarette to his lips out of habit, he remembered that smoking was forbidden in hospital rooms. But to put it back after he already had it out was a bother.

"Have one yourself?" As an afterthought he held out the pack to the boy.

"Thank you," the attendant answered briefly. He pattered out of the room, shortly to return with an empty glue bottle for an ashtray. Shintarō's father Shinkichi appeared behind him.

Shintarō faced the boy once more and struck a match. Judging from the face that rose up in the circle of firelight, from the whiteness of the cheeks, he guessed that the boy was very

young, perhaps even a minor. The three put their heads together to light their cigarettes off the one match—and in that
moment Shintarō felt the eerie silence that filled the whole ward
come lapping in all around them.

Shintarō was disgusted by the way his father smoked.
He held the cigarette in his thick fingertips and put it to his
puckered lips, and as he sucked in the first breath he made every
muscle from his lungs to his adam's apple bob excitedly up and
down, like a suffocating fish. After he inhaled the smoke he
narrowed his eyes and sat motionless, gazing off into space, as
if waiting for it to penetrate to the farthest corners of his body.
. . . Any heavy smoker looked forward to a cigarette. But when
Father smoked, nothing else existed—if anyone tried to talk to
him while he was inhaling he couldn't even respond.

More than anything else, the patients in the hospital were
starved for tobacco. That was why the ashtrays in the attendants' room or the doctors' office always looked newly cleaned.
Given half a chance, the patients snatched up every half-smoked
stub. When they did get their hands on a cigarette, though, they
weren't given any matches; but they would laboriously rub
stones together or climb up to the ceiling and short a wire, anything for a light. "Fact is these patients will think up things no
ordinary person would ever dream of—we can't take our eyes
off them for a minute."

Taking in the attendant's words without really listening,
Shintarō sat remembering the house on the Kugenuma coast
where he and his parents had once lived. It had been the first
year after the war had ended. Father came home from the south
in a military uniform stripped of insignia, carrying a strange
leather backpack, and began the life of a prison camp inmate in
one corner of the property. He dug up the whole garden to plant
barley, millet, and various vegetables, never setting foot outside the gate, in terror of contact with the outside world. Inside
the backpack, which he claimed was made by an army tailor in
his prison camp, he had stuffed a lot of bizarre items—a rice

bowl which doubled as a washbasin, a star-shaped mosquito net, and so on—all of which he valued as treasures. Every day, over and over, he would examine the contents, pulling them all out one by one with great care, gazing at them, and taking a long time to put them back. This accomplished, he would fit a "home pride" taken from his mess tin into a hand-carved cigarette holder of water buffalo horn and blow out the foul-smelling smoke, grudgingly, a little at a time.

A grimy bamboo tube was another of the treasures. Inside it were little black things the size of sesame seeds. These, he claimed, were spice and tobacco seeds. He planted them in the garden plot and sure enough, just when the "home prides" were beginning to run out, they began sending out luxuriant green leaves. Father plucked two or three from each plant, setting them out on the veranda to dry, and as soon as he estimated that they were cured, he filled his pipe with them and, as always, inhaled greedily, one breath at a time, sucking the smoke down to the depths of his chest with his eyes dreamily half closed. But two or three days later he was sick in bed, his weathered forehead covered with ashen sweat. His appetite, always unusually hearty until now, dropped off completely, and he vomited every couple of hours. Shintarō's mother sold off most of the few clothes the family had left to call a doctor. For a household with no income, this was grocery money meant to keep them all alive for a number of weeks; but there was a dark brownish stuff that looked like blood mixed in with his discharge, and they couldn't very well let it go. . . . As it turned out, the doctor never came up with a diagnosis, and within a week the patient healed on his own. When they later figured out that the cause of his illness had been an overdose of the homemade cigarettes, the family's reaction was less relief than anger, or even amusement.

"You must be about ready to turn in, aren't you?"

The attendant had put out his cigarette. He sounded more friendly now than he had a while ago. But when Shintarō was informed that another room had been prepared for him off the ward, he didn't feel like getting up from where he was, and he said so. At this the attendant seemed to stiffen once again.

"From the way she looks now she'll be fine tonight. If anything happens I'll call you. . . . You must be quite tired if you've come straight from Tokyo." His tone implied not so much consideration for Shintarō's welfare as a strong message to leave.

"Would I be in your way? I'm really not sleepy at all."

That was true enough. More to the point, though, standing up seemed like such a nuisance.

"No, it's no bother."

The boy directed his flashlight to the patient's face once more as he answered, and he squatted beside her pillow for a time as if lost in thought. It was obvious from his pose that in fact it was a bother.

"Do they lock the door from the outside?" Shintarō asked, thinking of the time he had visited a friend's wife in an I_____ City psychiatric ward. The attendant answered right away,

"No, we don't lock Mrs. Hamaguchi's room anymore."

A mosquito hummed near Shintarō's ear. He thought of asking if he couldn't get some mosquito repellant incense, only it occurred to him that if tobacco were prohibited, incense would be too, so he decided not to ask. The attendant stood in the doorway looking down at him, flashlight in one hand, and Shintarō, leaning back against the wall, spoke without getting up.

"That's okay, I'll watch over this room tonight. You might as well get some sleep in your own room."

The attendant moved his lips as if he wanted to say something, but then closed his mouth again. The fluorescent light in the hall showed half of his pale face. It struck Shintarō for the first time that his words had somehow hurt the boy's feelings. But what had he said? ——It was then that Father suddenly stood up in the pitch black corner where he had been sitting in silence and said loudly,

"That's enough, Shintarō. Let's get some sleep."

And he walked ahead out of the room.

For an instant Shintarō felt himself rebelling against the harsh words. But immediately he understood why the attendant and his father had been so irritated. . . . They thought I was trying to act like a "filial son," didn't they? He sensed in his father's stiffened back as he marched off in silence down the hall the sort of strength of one who, when a latecomer shoves into the front row, wordlessly shoves right back, and hard. At the same time, he felt a voiceless groan come flooding in at him from behind those little, barred windows all along the hall. While the attendant gave a quiet satisfied nod, Shintarō pushed his feet into the slippers and followed after his father.

Shintarō was wakened the next morning by the light of the sun as it rose over the ocean. His room was right over the entrance, and its wide-open window faced the sea. This was one inlet of the bay of Kōchi; its single island was surrounded by a small spit of land, and the water, calmer here than lake water, lapped black and heavy against the stone wall just below the window. The whole sweep of the sky was red, and the foliage that completely covered the spit and the island was such a deep green that it looked almost black in the red light.

After he looked out the window Shintarō lay back down. The berth of tatami on a wooden frame was clean and comfortable enough, but with the morning sunlight streaming in the whole room was bright red and Shintarō couldn't sleep. Still, his body felt sluggish when he tried to get up, and he didn't want to do that either. The night before last Shintarō had been out late at a bar in Shinjuku with a friend. A short fellow in big dark glasses had been saying something to his friend. They were in high spirits and had their arms around each other's shoulders, laughing, displaying more affection than they needed to. Somehow Shintarō ended up fighting with the man. Before he knew it he was gripping a piece of a broken glass in his hand. Minute splinters had scattered across the counter; a frowning woman said something, and then other women bent over and busied themselves with something on the floor. The short man, who had wound up sitting on the floor, stood up and wiped his glasses. Seeing the benevolent smile on his face when the man took off his glasses, Shintarō felt his cheeks whiten in self-loathing. He went outside. His friend followed behind him, and the two went into another bar. There a big woman in a black dress sidled over to sit down beside him. "Hey, want to go out Sunday?" he had said, and the woman, nodding yes, had moved her large breasts closer. When he got back home, toward dawn, the telegram informing him of his mother's critical condition was waiting for him. . . . He had passed the next day pulling together money for the trip. That evening, just when everything was ready, he remembered his date with the woman, and called the number she had given him. The woman accepted the change in plans with an almost disappointing nonchalance. Of course, when he thought about it, it did sound like exactly the sort of excuse people made up in such situations—my mother's sick and it doesn't look like I'll be able to make it Sunday. . . . Shintarō was amused to think that his mother should be interfering in his love life even from her deathbed. Indeed, he couldn't remember how many times his plans had been upset at the last minute on her account.

Not that Shintarō paid much attention to omens and such. Besides, while the events of the night before last may not have been typical, they weren't that unusual either. He just remembered that he was tired of it.

The light streaming in had lost most of its earlier redness, becoming ordinary bright morning sunlight. But even if he closed his eyes tight he still couldn't sleep—that much hadn't changed. He looked over at the bed next to his; his father was curled up with his back to Shintarō, fast asleep. It was a sturdy back, thick-necked, square-shouldered. People had always said that Shintarō looked like his father. They said he was a carbon copy, from facial fatures to physical build. Mother herself was always lamenting the resemblance; her husband displeased her to a surprising degree. For dozens of years now she'd been telling anyone who would listen—and especially her only son, Shintarō—that Shinkichi's personality was not to her liking. Thousands of times he had heard how disgusting his father had looked in his pale blue crested kimono on the day of their wedding. "After all, I was married off without ever having met him, you know. When I saw this round-headed bald man come shuffling up to me the day of the ceremony, I thought, my goodness, this wedding is so countrified they've even invited the temple priest along, and believe me, when I found out that was the bridegroom I nearly ran off right then and there." Father came from a locally respected family line, but that was in Y_____ Village in Kōchi Prefecture; Mother was the daughter of a bank employee, Tokyo-born and raised in Osaka. Discontent over that gap between them had probably contributed a great deal to Mother's distaste for her husband. Anyway, it was undoubtedly his mother's influence that had made Shintarō also detest his father. For Shintarō had been taught to find everything about his father repulsive, down to the most trivial detail. . . . He had come to feel ashamed of his father's profession, for instance, one day shortly after one of their moves, when he and his mother were seated at the sunken table in their new home, in a tea room just off the kitchen. An errand boy came in through the service door, and Shintarō's mother received him from where she sat at the *kotatsu*. For some reason the boy asked, "Your husband is a military man, isn't he?" Perhaps because the Manchurian Incident had just started and children's magazines and comic books were full of war stories, the serving boy wanted to know everything. What was his rank? How many sabers did he have? And finally he asked, "Is your husband in the cavalry?"

"Not exactly," Mother answered.

"Oh? Then what is he?"

A veterinarian, Shintarō was about to say, but Mother's hand grabbed his leg under the *kotatsu*. "Yes, indeed," she said, her tone suddenly cold, and she glared at Shintarō in silence.

In that moment Mother's shame was transferred directly to
Shintarō. The incident planted a stinging pain of humiliation
inside him, like the pain of her nails clutching his leg. At the
same time, his mother's embarrassment over such an insignificant matter hurt him deeply. From that day on, whenever
Shintarō had to specify his father's occupation for school records or anything, just writing the word "serviceman" made him
uncomfortable, even until the elimination of the professional
army after the war.

Shintarō had apparently dozed off without realizing it.
He woke with a start when a sound of footsteps came to a halt
outside his door, and he sat straight up in bed. It was the attendant from last night; he had already opened the door and
stepped inside. He looked different than he had the night before. Downy unshaven hair was beginning to grow around the
mouth on his narrow, fair face, whose age Shintarō still could
not guess. His puffy eyes shining blankly from behind rimless
glasses, the attendant awkwardly wiped off the bedside table
and set an aluminum tray on it with a clatter. He had brought
them each a breakfast: a bowl of soup, a small plate of pickles,
and a tin of rice. Apparently they were meant to eat the rice
straight from the tins.

Shintarō had been on edge ever since the boy entered
the room. Was this business of bringing breakfast something
special, or was it a routine service for visitors? Somehow it
bothered him not to know.

He asked if this was what the patients ate.

"Yes," the attendant answered curtly. He took the lids
off the rice tins and turned them over, filled them with over-
steeped green tea, and said only "enjoy your meal" before hur-
riedly leaving the room.

At first Shintarō didn't have any appetite. When he picked
up the container, though, he was suddenly ravenous, and he
ended up eating almost all of the rice from the heavy tin. The
rice was damp, and smelled sweet and metallic when he chewed.

Now and then he felt a hard, cold grain scratch the inside of his chest on its way down.

But with a few bites yet to go, Shintarō set the box down. For when he looked up at his father, slowly lifting a mouthful of his own rice, which was still only half eaten, a vague anxiety came over him. . . . Father always took his time chewing. Shintarō could clearly see the movement of the muscles below his wide, balding forehead as he thoroughly ground up one mouthful at a time. Unaware that a piece of seaweed from his soup dangled blackly from a corner of his dry lips, he just kept his mouth moving; his adam's apple, along with the two or three longish whiskers, would jerk once to show that the food was finally starting on its way through his esophagus. He worked with the methodical accuracy of a machine processing some kind of material, the devotion of a domesticated animal executing its duties. . . . Then Father suddenly looked up. Their eyes met.

"Aren't you eating?" he asked, peering at Shintarō as he sipped on cold green tea from the lid.

"No. . . . This is already more than I usually have."

"Oh." There were beads of sweat on Father's nose and brow as he took another swallow of the tea. A few grains of boiled rice and some black husks had settled to the bottom of the lid. "The rice here's pretty good. High quality strain. You probably can't tell the difference, since your generation grew up on the kind they rationed in Tokyo, but . . ."

Half of what followed was unintelligible, as Father was realigning his false teeth while he talked. No matter; it probably wasn't very important. Maybe he wanted to talk about how Shintarō had chosen to live alone in the city, leaving his parents in the country. That sort of talk wasn't going to get them anywhere now.

Shintarō lay down on the bed, figuring he might be more comfortable that way. It didn't work. The white glare of the ceiling hurt his eyes, and a smell of varnish burned his nose. As the angle of light shifted, the room got hotter. The sun was already high above the sea, casting a yellow glow on the calm surface of the water. Patients were visible from the south window, on their way out to the playing field. ——By turns Shintarō felt that he and Father ought to be going down to the room pretty soon, and then decided that it was better to wait until someone came for them. Yet when he did hear the sound of tennis shoes in the hall, an indefinable anxiety surged through his chest. He realized that the only time he had actually been relaxed was while he was eating breakfast. That was why he'd been able to eat so much.

The doctor came a little before nine. When Shintarō answered the knock and found a man carrying a stethoscope on the other side of the door, he blurted out, "Is it all over?"

The doctor seemed perplexed. Then suddenly he laughed.

"No, no, I'm just on my way to see how she's doing. Come along?"

He told the two of them that he had just come back to the hospital yesterday to relieve the doctor who had been on duty before him. They rotated in six-month shifts from the main hospital in Kōchi city. Shintarō thought he could get to like this doctor. When a smile broke across the man's dark face, with his two front teeth cutting a clean line across his dry lower lip, something in the expression suggested a frank, open disposition.

The doctor walked down the hall at a good clip, the white uniform clinging to his tall frame. To the patients who stopped and greeted him he responded briefly, calling out, "Still here, eh?" or slapping a shoulder. His bearing made Shintarō think of the captain of some high school sports team. He seemed like the type who would have a slogan like "Authority Without Force" pasted up over his desk. ——So Shintarō thought, watching the patients who had gathered in front of the kitchen scatter the minute they caught sight of the doctor coming their way.

When the three turned a corner at the kitchen, a pale

green steel door came into view ahead. Beyond that was the intensive care ward. A man in white shorts with a bandage wrapped around his neck pushed the door open with his shoulder. The odor of pickled vegetables that had wafted to them from the kitchen gave way to the sweet-sour smell of yesterday, which now pressed heavily upon them. The hallway suddenly became dark and narrow, and faces peered at them from behind the rows of barred windows on either side. At every step Shintarō felt his joints going weak all through his body.

One chubby young woman was milling about her room naked, humming an indistinct tune; a dark-skinned man bowed again and again to the wall; an old man was sprawled out on the floor reading a book: but as the footsteps approached they all flew to the window bars. Maybe it was the way the color of the walls reflected the light, but the look of the patients' greenish faces made them seem like so many reptiles.

Mother was sleeping as before, with her mouth wide open. Her close-cropped white hair lay across her sallow forehead and cheeks as on a broken clay doll.

The examination was perfunctory, as Shintarō had expected. Having glanced over the chart that the attendant had brought, the doctor only opened the patient's shirt and applied the stethoscope lightly in two or three places. Then he stood up.

"Temperature?"

"102.4."

"Pulse 92 . . . otherwise nothing unusual?"

"We gave her one vitamin shot last night before the guests arrived."

Following this simple exchange with the attendant, the doctor turned to Shintarō and smiled. "You must find it hot here, coming from Tokyo."

The smile was friendly. Shintarō shook his head and replied that it really didn't bother him, but then, since the doctor was already heading out and Shintarō wanted to talk a while longer, he asked what sort of an illness his mother had developed. Perhaps he would get some honest answers from this man.

"Well now, that's something we don't understand too well ourselves," the doctor said, putting his hands on his hips and arching his back. "One thing's for sure, this kind of case has multiplied since the war. . . ."

While every other part of the body remained healthy, it seemed, the brain cells alone deteriorated. The problem had become more common as medical science had made progress in lengthening life. Today more cases were reported in America than anywhere else. So the doctor told him. Shintarō was a little disappointed. He had hoped for an explanation as clear and explicit as a set of rules for an athletic meet. Such a concrete explanation, he figured, would conversely make his own role more abstract, more removed.

"By the way," the doctor asked, "how old is your mother this year?"

"What was it, fifty- . . ."

Shintarō stopped short and tried to cover his ignorance with a nervous laugh.

The smile vanished from the doctor's face. Flustered, Shintarō continued, "Fifty-eight or nine, maybe, at full count."

But now the doctor seemed completely uninterested in the answer. The smile that before had exposed his white front teeth was now shut tight in disapproval, and the dry skin stretched across his sharp cheekbones gave his profile an unapproachable, wooden look. The attendant's eyes shone from behind his glasses. Shintarō became aware that he was in a real state of panic. . . . It wasn't because he hadn't been able to say offhand how old his mother was. No—the bewildering thing was why the doctor had asked him in the first place, when a glance at the chart would have told him. As this thought raced through his mind, Shintarō recalled the face of another doctor he had met the year before, when he first brought his mother to the hospital.

That doctor had been older than this one by some years,

with a round, fair-skinned face. The whole time they were together his wet lips were parted slightly in a perpetual smile,
and he spoke quietly in a Tokyo accent. As they walked together through the halls he spoke to Shintarō in general terms
of the hospital and the disease. ——"As you know, we're
speaking of a protracted illness, and hardly any of the patients
here are handling all their own fees. Most have health insur-
ance. Trying to stay within the limits of the coverage, it's all we
can do to provide room and board, so clothing is, as you can
see, . . ." he said, as if apologizing for the patients' clothes. It
was true; frankly, many of them had covered themselves with
tattered rags, not even whole enough to be called clothing. But
they did seem clean; from close up he could see they were more
sanitary than they looked at first. When he remarked on this
the doctor looked pleased and, shaking his head, replied ami-
ably, "The hospital certainly appreciates the patronage of patients who have a good person like yourself behind them,
agreeing to accept responsibility for all the fees." Shintarō felt
uncomfortable accepting this praise, so to change the subject
he asked, "How many people are there in the country with a
disease like my mother's?" The doctor replied with the amiable
smile still on his face.

"I have no idea. In other countries they bring people to
an institution right away, old people included; but here—call it
belief in the family, or a case of underdeveloped individualism—most of them are kept at home and never sent away like
that. Especially since it is the nature of the disease to afflict older
people for the most part . . . as in your mother's case."

All of a sudden Shintarō felt as if the hallway in front of
him had stretched out infinitely, and for an instant his feet
stopped moving.

Shintarō was dizzy with confusion. He didn't know what
had caused it. All he knew was that the green door to the room
where they had just left his mother seemed to be cut off from
the long hallway, cut off from the yellow varnish and white walls
and green window frames, and getting infinitely distant and

small . . . and that all the while there rang in his ears the echo of a soft, sweet, light voice, like a musical instrument, repeating the words, individualism . . . belief in the family . . .

Just now, as Shintarō stood before the attendant and the dark-complexioned doctor with his mouth shut tight in ill humor, that confusion had come back to him. Or rather, it had been there the whole time, cloaked in Shintarō's surroundings, watching out for an unguarded moment in which to rear its head again.

"She's sixty," the dark-skinned doctor said wearily. "That's still young for a patient with her disease."

"How old are most people when they get it?" Shintarō asked, much relieved to pick up a new thread in the conversation.

"That I can't very well say." Again the doctor shut his mouth in displeasure.

A neurologist at a university hospital had once explained the disease to Shintarō, saying that when people who had exercised their brains relatively little—farmwives, for example—reached a certain age, their brain cells began to deteriorate rapidly. But that explanation didn't seem to apply in Mother's case. True, being a housewife had undoubtedly demanded very little of her. Even when her husband Shinkichi wasn't overseas he tended to be out of the house most of the time; Mother had had her livelihood guaranteed, and had mostly passed her days alone with her son. Yet it wasn't as if her life had involved no thinking at all. Shintarō thought a more likely reason was the combined blow of the drastic differences between the easy life before the war and the deprivation following it on the one hand and, on the other, the physiological imbalances which menopause induced at the same time.

But even if he tried to bring up the subject now with the doctor standing before him, he wouldn't be able to get the doctor to discuss the real reason for Mother's illness, and it would be no good even if he could. The doctor's question about Mother's age had just been something to say. It hadn't been meant to comfort him, nor was it a courtesy. It had just been a sign that it was time for them all to leave the room. Yet for Shintarō the exchange had turned into proof of the inexcusable fact that he was a man who did not even know his own mother's age. The doctor left the room in silence the same way he had come, his white coat flapping, and Shintarō had no choice but to silently watch him go, his consternation unresolved.

For some reason, ever since he was a child Shintarō had thought of his ancestral home with dread. Flipping through a photo album he would suddenly come upon a strangely dark, shadow-filled picture. His grandmother sat in a black kimono on a Chinese-style chair in the center, with lots of uncles, cousins, and aunts lined up stiffly in two rows to either side. All the women held their hands together in front of them, hidden in their sleeves. The male cousins about Shintarō's age wore long, triangular capes with tabi showing beneath the hems of their kimonos. They all looked eerily old-fashioned and poor to Shintarō, but at the same time a dreadful atmosphere seemed to advance threateningly toward him from the photograph.

News from Grandmother came often to Shinkichi's house. In her letters she would always add a remark like, don't go in such-and-such direction today, there's an *inugamitsuki** there.

"I can't very well stop going in the direction of the office every day just because of something Grandmother says," Father would usually mutter, and after a quick once-over he would fold the letter up and put it back in the envelope. But Shintarō's mother would pull it out and read through it again, grumbling and looking displeased. . . . Thinking back now, it seemed likely to Shintarō that his grandmother's actual intent in those letters was to press for a little spending money. But the silent war her letters always caused between his parents was dimly linked in Shintarō's memory with that fearful word, *inugamitsuki*. And when he looked at all those relatives from his ances-

---

*A spirit believed in Japanese folklore to avenge lapses of filial piety.

tral home lined up in the photo, he murmured the word *Inu-gamitsuki!* to himself.

When he was a little older, in fifth or sixth grade, Shin-tarō's ancestral home became distasteful to him in yet another way. About two months after his father had been transferred from Hirosaki, Shintarō entered an elementary school in To-kyo. At school he began to realize that he spoke differently from everyone else. He noticed that whenever he started talking the others all became quiet and listened to his voice. He tried to copy the way they spoke, but that only made him self-con-scious, as if he had one too many tongues in his mouth. Since he started inventing lies to skip school at the same time, Shin-tarō was convinced that self-consciousness about one's speech was at the root of all lying. It had been a terrible burden to have to speak differently at home than at school. A college-aged cousin who came to visit them after he had started using his carefully cultivated new accent remarked, as though he were praising a trained parrot, "Oh, I see Shin-chan's talking like a Tokyoite now?"

Two other families who lived in Shintarō's neighbor-hood in Tokyo were from the same village. As if they had worked it out ahead of time, these families seemed to take turns trekking back to the village repeatedly in the course of a year. It was almost painful to watch the preschool children with their little packs strapped to their backs, toddling along behind the last of the baggage-laden group; but their father explained in his country dialect, "If you don't show these youngsters the province now, they'll abandon it altogether before you know it"—as much as saying to Shintarō and his family, "We don't want them to turn out like you."

Why were they so attached to their native village? Just what did it mean to abandon it? Was it some sort of crime? Every time he saw the members of that family Shintarō was beset by a childlike bewilderment. For him, "ancestral home" was an abstract concept, always accompanied by a disturbing uneasi-ness—the feeling that somehow, without realizing it, he had made a promise that he couldn't possibly remember. . . . But hearing the words "abandoning one's ancestral home" made him feel certain he was guilty of something underhanded.

The confusion Shintarō had felt in front of the doctor and the attendant at his mother's bedside had a great deal in common with this other bewilderment of his childhood.

That day Shintarō decided to sit in the room at the foot of his mother's bed until dark. He reasoned that he would be most at ease there. As on the night before, the attendant let Shintarō know that he was in the way. But it wasn't as if the boy would have been satisfied if Shintarō waited in the room by the sea where he and his father had spent the night, either. As long as the attendant was going to be disgruntled anyway, Shintarō decided he might as well stay beside the patient. At least this way there was some return on his long trip to see her.

The entire room, which he estimated to be nine feet by nine feet, was painted a pale green. Since the ceiling was too high for the room, and since thick concrete walls surrounded it on all sides, Shintarō felt as if he were sitting inside a tower or a chimney. Only a three-by-three area in one corner of the wooden floor was reinforced with a slab of polished synthetic stone, on which a toilet had been installed. The toilet was set up so that the attendant could turn a faucet out in the hall to flush water through it. Apparently the reason the faucet had to be put on the outside was that otherwise the patients would turn it on themselves and drink the water out of the toilet. But it looked like Shintarō's mother had not used this one for a long time, if ever: the white porcelain was dry; grey dust had settled in the bottom; and the whole thing was covered with a layer of yellowed newspaper. Next to the toilet was a stack of old, faded rags, tied in bundles with red cloth cords. These, Shintarō later discovered, were his mother's "diapers."

Shintarō sat on the floor, his back to the wall. Had he stretched his legs out straight they would take up the space where his mother was lying, so though it hurt to draw them sideways, he accustomed himself to it and didn't mind after a time. Naturally the room was bleak, but at some point Shintarō no longer found it inhospitable. Somehow he came to feel as if he had been living there for a long time. He even had a fleeting notion of building a room like it for himself some day. After all, being imprisoned on the one hand meant that on the other hand one could live without lifting a finger. That didn't seem like a bad way to pass a lifetime. . . . Part of the base of the six-inch thick door was cut away at floor level. The patient's food was pushed through here at meal times. Obviously the meals didn't amount to much, but they were probably nutritious enough to sustain a person in a basically sedentary existence.

As the lunch hour drew near, the ward came to life in what sounded like preparations for the meal. A voice called out from the distant kitchen, and here and there in the ward, which had been quiet until now, various sounds could be heard. Someone got up and folded a blanket, while someone else padded barefoot around a room; there was the sound of stretching, and of what might be dry, expectant swallows—all these merged with the clattering of utensils, the creak of the cart's axle and rubber wheels, the sloshing of soup in the kettle and over onto the wooden floor, and the voices of the food servers, attendants and regular patients as they called back and forth. Altogether it struck Shintarō as having the same eerie, ominous quality as the rustle of leaves in a storm wind.

After a time, the mixed sounds of footsteps and cart noises came down Shintarō's hallway. The attendant showed his face at the door.

"What would you like to do about lunch? Shall I take it to the same room as this morning?" he asked brightly. It was the first time today Shintarō had seen him looking so cheerful. Though he didn't want to spoil the boy's good mood, Shintarō answered, "I'm not eating." He was about to explain that he normally ate only two meals a day, but the attendant had already disappeared, so he let it go. True, he wasn't hungry; but more than that, he didn't want to get up and leave the room.

He hadn't been hungry this morning either, and he'd still been able to eat a lot once he got started. If he had decided to eat now, he probably could have; but whereas this morning he hadn't been able to relax unless he was moving his mouth, that was no longer necessary.

The afternoon heat was sweltering. As the sun began to stream in through the window there was no place in the little room to escape. Shintarō tried to think of a way to put up a sunshade of some kind across the window, but there wasn't any place to stick a tack. So much moisture had collected on the concrete wall that the paint itself seemed about to melt and run. Because of the heat, perhaps, one of the patients was seized with spasms, and the man next door had been shouting continuously for some time.

"Attendant, attendant! Dinner, dinner! I'm hungry, I'm . . . Attendant, attendant!"

The voice was weirdly like the cry of some huge bird. The hoarse croaking carried through the hallway, repeating the same few words over and over in a strange accent that Shintarō couldn't place.

"What's all this racket? As if you didn't just eat dinner! Quit yelling, put some clothes on, and sit up straight now. If you go on screaming the attendant'll come and bawl you out again."

It was a middle-aged woman talking from the window of a room across the hall. Her voice only aggravated Shintarō more, though. Apparently the patients did this sort of thing to compete with each other in making a good impression in front of the attendants. In the room next to the middle-aged woman was an old man. The men's ward was off the right fork of the cherry-lined road, but the serious cases were put in the private rooms of this ward. One could not begin to tell by looking what this man's trouble was. He always lay on the wooden floor, wrapped in a blanket as if he were cold, his forehead drawn as though in an effort to endure great pain. He was the only one who did not get up and look out through his window bars every time the attendant came down the hall. All the rest of them called out their own style of greeting or offered their reverent obeisances. Indeed, the reason they had frightened Shintarō with those staring faces when he first set foot on the ward was that they had mistaken him for a new attendant. This occurred to Shintarō one day as he stood at the urinal, and while he found it amusing he hadn't exactly felt like smiling.

Mother slept on. For some reason one of her eyelids stayed half open, the ash-colored eyeball directed at Shintarō. She had lost all vision half a year ago, though. When a big fly with a shiny, dark green body buzzed dully into the room and settled near her encrusted eyelid or in the area of her gaping mouth, the muscles of her face didn't even twitch. As proof that she was still alive, though, the sound of her violent, rhythmic breathing continued.

Outside the window was a playing field that faced the sea. As the window was small and the wall thick, Shintarō's view was severely limited. All he could see from where he sat was a section of ridgeline and one face of the mountains that surrounded the hospital on three sides. Now, however, the sunlight filled the whole window, making it so bright he couldn't even look in that direction. Sometimes Shintarō heard the echoing shouts and laughter of the regular patients; when he got up to look, he saw them dashing barefoot across the blindingly bright field at mad speeds, gripping bundles of laundry under their arms. The sight, clipped by the square window frame and glittering in the sun, made him think of a single frame of movie film. From the hospital room it looked like a piece of a scene snipped from another world.

The fly persisted in hovering about Mother's face. When Shintarō brushed it off and swatted it with newspaper he squashed it, leaving a spot of blood on the floor boards, but the next one or two already crawled around her open mouth. In a way, Shintarō was actually grateful for them. Swatting flies was one constructive thing he could do. As he brought the newspaper up to another one that had alighted on the floor, Shin-tarō was suddenly reminded of himself on a summer day three years back, walking down a street in Tokyo. Walking in the smoldering heat down a dry, bleached street that stretched endlessly before him, wondering dazedly how much farther he had to go . . .

Shintarō had already spent a number of days walking around the city by then. His family had just been given one month to move out of the house at Kugenuma, and they had no idea how they were going to come up with money for mov-ing expenses, or where they would live afterwards. For the moment, the only choice was for Mother and Father to stay with Father's family while Shintarō found a room in Tokyo. But in-stead, for some reason they started scheming to get a govern-ment housing loan and build a house in Tokyo for the three of them. Mother had heard talk somewhere that there was a man who knew an official in housing finance, and that if you asked this man you could get a loan with no problem; Shintarō had accepted the task of going to see him. As it turned out, the man worked in a firm with the unhelpful name of Yotsubishi Indus-tries. He was short, with a small face and small hands. His one hand was bound in a soiled bandage, and perhaps because he made an effort to look up into Shintarō's face, dark wrinkles appeared on his brow. The first thing this man asked Shintarō was how much money he had on hand. Sintarō answered, quite truthfully, that he didn't have any now, but said that in a month he'd have X-thousand yen. The man listened with his head cocked to one side and then said, "Well, that should do it. Let's give it a try."

The first place the man took him was a fairly large bank. Their business here finished in short order. After a mere two or three words at the teller's window the man gave an ex-tremely deferential bow, roused Shintarō from the sofa where he had been sitting, and left. He explained on the way to the next place. "You see, you're dealing with bureaucrats, and with

bureaucrats you have to bow low. If you just humble yourself
they'll say yes every time." In fact their destination was not a
government office. This time it was a real estate agency. Apparently another man here also had contacts in government finance. This new man got on a bicycle and led the way to yet
another place while the other two followed on foot. But the official he had in mind was not at the office when they arrived.
So ended the first day. The next day the Yotsubishi man took
Shintarō back to that office. Again their man was not in.

"When it gets like this you have to persist," he said.

The two decided to wait near the receptionist's desk. After
about ten minutes one of the office girls came over to inform
them that meeting with personnel at the department was not
permitted, so would they please leave. The man replied gruffly,

"Who said so? Give me his name please."

The girl answered that it was someone named Y_____.
Whereupon the man, having barely said "thanks" to the girl,
called out loudly, "Mr. Y_____!," opened the door, and barged
through. Shintarō, pulled forcefully along in his wake, followed him in.

The Yotsubishi man talked quickly at the official, bringing up a number of subjects. All in one breath he managed to
touch on the weather, how happy he was for this meeting, even
how large his family was—all the while bowing deeper with
every word. The official's thin, stubbly face reminded Shintarō
of an elementary school teacher he had once had; but this man
kept looking off to the side, hiking his pants up to his knees
and letting them fall again, craning toward the next desk to follow a chess game. . . . After chattering on by himself for nearly
thirty minutes the Yotsubishi man finally concluded, "Well, we'll
be by tomorrow. . . . ," then bowed and left the room. He told
Shintarō that from here on out they really had to get persistent;
if they could just make some kind of connection with this
Y_____ fellow, they'd be able to borrow the money. Yes, maybe
so, Shintarō said, pretending to agree. The man nodded as if
satisfied with this and asked Shintarō if he had any money on

him. If he did they should take Y_____ out for a drink tonight.
Shintarō didn't have enough to mention. Well then, the man
replied, they should wait until Y_____ left work and ask where
he lived, or, if that failed, follow him home. After that Shintarō
must have gone into a daze. . . . The next thing he knew he
was by himself, crossing a street where the streetcar ran in front
of the government office. The Yotsubishi man was on the other
side, standing in front of a red signboard in a pedestrian safety
zone and frowning at Shintarō while he waited for a trolley to
pass. After Shintarō dodged trucks and buses to get across, the
man looked up at him with some indignation and scolded him
for his lack of assertiveness.

"And basically you don't know how to bow right, either.
If that's the way you're going to bow, I'd be better off without
you. . . . In fact I wonder if you even care whether you get
this house built at all. This is a house we're talking about, mister, a house. And whether or not you get to build that house
is being decided right now." At the end of this brief lecture he
looked up at Shintarō, his black eyebrows glistening with sweat.

There was nothing Shintarō could say, for it was true—
he had not the least intention of building a house. So why was
he walking in the blistering hot streets with this man? ——True,
he didn't plan to build a house. But not because he thought the
man at his side was something of a shady character, nor because he didn't want to waste his time on an effort that was
doomed for lack of money. The simple truth was, Shintarō didn't
want to live with his parents anymore.

But in that case, why had he done all that walking? The
following day too, and the day after that, Shintarō followed the
man into the streets again in the heat of the day. Stop and talk,
take a bow, ask directions, bow for yet another stranger—they
went through the same motions over and over until the sun went
down, when Shintarō would go home to Kugenuma exhausted, sighing with relief that another day's efforts had passed
safely in vain. . . . His mother would come to meet him, looking anxious. "No good?" she'd ask, and Shintarō, shaking his

head to indicate as much, would unaccountably feel genuine disappointment.

When the sun went down, the flies left. Mother's face dissolved like the walls around her into a thin, inky blackness, in which only her forehead loomed round and white. Father arrived, saying, "I'll take a turn now." The expression reminded Shintarō that there really wasn't any particular need for anyone to sit at the patient's side at all. Nonetheless he got up obediently and walked outside.

As always, the view of the ocean was picture-perfect. The waves were unusually calm; the small, round island on the surface became a floating black shadow, with the spit stretching out to the right like a woman's arm. To the left the lights on the wharf twinkled brightly.

Here was the absolute embodiment of the concept of "scenery": there was no room for anything else. It wasn't a scene you could look at for very long. Without moving from where he stood, Shintarō watched some patients who had come out for a walk. Lingering in the afterglow of the sunset, they too melted into the scenery. A Japanese boat with its lamps alight approached from across the bay, carrying hospital employees. Apparently it was time for a shift change; nurses' caps bobbed about on deck. When the patients ran down to the water Shintarō suddenly remembered these were not normal people—and for an instant the thought shocked him.

Shintarō did not understand what that shock meant. Was it surprise that he could have been so deeply engrossed in the landscape? Or was it that he had only now sensed that madness really lurked in these patients? Leaving the question dangling, Shintarō turned his attention to his surroundings in an attempt to puzzle out the enigma that was his mother.

He drew a picture of her in his imagination, standing in the twilight with her arms folded. There were many expressions familiar to him from childhood that went with that pose. There was the way she looked that day they climbed together up the long stone staircase to his grade school teacher's house to apologize for his bad report card; her expression when she greeted a son home unannounced from boarding school for summer vacation; her expression the time she paid him a surprise visit in his army sickroom to tell him their house had burned to the ground in an air raid; her face the day before they had had to leave the house at Kugenuma; and the way she looked on that summer evening last year at her brother's house in Y_____ Village, senselessly pacing back and forth by herself between the gate and the doorway. . . . With this melancholy landscape for a backdrop, it wasn't hard to recall all those faces. But when he tried to go beyond them, to figure out which might be linked to his mother's insanity, Shintarō only became confused.

Without a doubt, the happiest hours for Shintarō and his mother had been those between the end of the war and his father's return in May of the following year. True, Shintarō did nothing but loll about, still bedridden from the tuberculosis he had contracted in the army, and his mother wasn't getting any younger. But in spite of it all the war was over. His mother could tend her son's bedside, and Shintarō himself was finally free of the roll calls and orders and incessant regulations that had pursued him even inside the hospital. The summerhouse in Kugenuma that his mother's brother had leased them was more comfortable, both the surroundings and the house itself, than their own house in Tokyo, now destroyed, had ever been. Mother would spread her mending out on the sunny winter veranda while Shintarō lay in bed, gazing out at the garden and wondering when the pale brown roots would begin to sprout. The two of them carelessly supposed that peacetime meant just this kind of a life, this and nothing else. When the telegram arrived—"Returning Tomorrow, Shinkichi"—it was as if they were going to greet a husband and father who was coming back from a mere pleasure trip. But the next day Shintarō stood in the entrance and watched his father who, when their eyes met, could only say "hey there" and look down, embarrassed, clumsily removing his tight-fitting military boots; it was then that Shintarō felt his first vague misgivings.

It had been ten years since Shintarō had slept under the same roof as his father, who had been stationed overseas in one place or another since the beginning of the China Incident. Things were awkward. He seemed less a father than a distant relative. It was as if some old relation had dropped in for a visit on his way to the capital. Instead of changing as the days wore on, this impression grew into a feeling that the guest was overstaying his welcome. When the family sat around the dining table, Shintarō and his mother ended up siding together in silence against Father. Father, emptying his second bowl of rice, would cock his head to show he was perplexed and say, as if thinking aloud, "Hm, and I still have all these vegetables left over. . . ." He would lift his bowl, steal a glance at Shintarō and Mother, and, as if ashamed of his own hands, sheepishly draw it back empty. By now Shintarō was too old to make a big show of being filial. He didn't even have it in him to overcome his own increasing self-consciousness enough to call Father by his respectful title and tell him he should feel free to help himself. An uncomfortable silence grew up between father and son as a result. . . . Shintarō had had to think a lot about how to address his father. He seemed to remember he used to say "Dad," but that must have been in his childhood. What a relief, he thought, if they could just call each other by the neutral words for "parent" and "son"—but things didn't work that way. He remembered the nickname "Onchan" from the Tosa dialect and decided to try that. This was one day only a month after Father had moved in. As usual, the three sat awkwardly around the supper table, Shintarō complaining to his mother about some trifle or other—when suddenly Father flung his chopsticks at him. "Watch how you speak to your mother!"

This unexpected outburst from Shinkichi turned out to be Shintarō's salvation. One sentence had made it clear that he could not call his father by a derogatory nickname like "Onchan." Moreover, it established at least one standard for his behavior as a son.

It was only after Shinkichi's return that Shintarō and his mother really began to experience Japan's defeat. Until then they had groundlessly assumed that they could continue living off their monthly pension indefinitely. In fact, as a fatherless household they continued to receive a stipend every month, even after the war, until Shinkichi came home. But as the days passed they realized their assumption had been mistaken. It became clear that the hopes they had placed in Shintarō's father were completely unfounded.

Shinkichi spent nearly all of every day in the garden. Coming up into the house only for meals, he dashed back to the yard almost as soon as they were finished eating, and whatever it was he was doing, he would not come back in until dark. Even on rainy days he wouldn't stay inside; before long he had worn out the family's only raincoat.

"What in the world do you suppose your father intends to do?" Mother would ask Shintarō out of Father's hearing. But Shintarō could not have answered that question to save his life.

Shintarō took on some translation work for fashion magazines and the like, but what work he could manage while bedridden at home brought in only enough income to support himself. Yet this was the family's sole source of cash. Within three or four months, all the valuables in the house had been sold off and the money converted into food, but still all Father did was spend his days in the garden, digging up the yard and turning it into a plaything—more a flower bed than a field. Mealtimes between the three of them continued to be tense. Father got over his reticence about passing his bowl back any number of times for refills, but by now Mother had begun acting like a landlord dealing with a tenant who hung around without paying his rent. She would offer him his rice on a tray with slow, exaggerated politeness, and then rudely snatch the tray back. For his part, Shintarō tried to cut his own food consumption to a minimum, hoping to set an example in "rice economy." But this little demonstration met with absolutely no success. Contrary to his intentions, Father began to eat more and more, giving his sole attention to the garden work that was the cause of his growing appetite.

Finally one day Shintarō's mother said, "Today, there is no rice. There are no potatoes. This is all we have for dinner," and she set on the table a pot full of dripping black juice—nothing but boiled potato vines.

"All right, I get the message," Father said. "I'll go back to Y_____ Village and see what I can arrange. Fifteen bushels or so should be enough rice for three for a year, shouldn't it? I'm sure we can manage that somehow."

These were the first words Father had uttered since his return that acknowledged his responsibility as head of the household. His family's home in Y_____ Village had been standing for over two hundred years, but it had plenty of rooms; and though the estate had been whittled down in the land reform, it still had field acreage beyond comparison with their little garden plot. Furthermore, there was always the possibility of veterinary work in the country. Now, however, Shintarō's father loathed this work for some reason, and it was Mother, who had previously taught Shintarō to be embarrassed by the profession, who pinned her highest hopes on it. "Vets in the country really rake it in, you know. Farmers think more of cows and horses than they do of people—they say when an animal gets sick the farmer won't think twice of going 200 miles with a load of rice or rice cakes to pay for a diagnosis." . . . But within two weeks these hopes were completely crushed. When Father returned, all he brought back was a crate with one chicken in it, and except for telling them how crowded the train had been, he didn't say a word about how things had gone in his home village. ——Oh, the ride was terrible. We all had to stay put, you couldn't even get up to go to the bathroom. There were people sitting on the overhead luggage racks, and some even tried to sit right on the heads and shoulders of the people who had seats. I wouldn't have been surprised to see a baby smoth-

ered in its own mother's arms in that crowd!—— Even now there
was fear in Shinkichi's eyes as he recalled it. He took off his
white coat, which was covered with footprints. But what really
impressed Shintarō and his mother was the chicken that Father
took out of the crate he had so carefully carried home. The bird
had barely let out a single shriek when it suddenly flew off the
veranda into the garden. What was more, it had laid an egg in
the basket—and it was still warm.

The next day Father earnestly began building a chicken
coop in one corner of the garden. First he used their ration of
firewood as building material, but soon he switched to regular
logs, and he ended up with a magnificent structure that looked
more like a picture-book version of Lincoln's log cabin than a
chicken coop. Shintarō and his mother whispered together in
front of the finished building.

"He does mean to fill this up with chickens, doesn't he?
Surely he doesn't think he's going to sleep in there with them?!
——Do you suppose he's maybe a little off?"

"I'm sure I don't know what he intends to do. I just
wonder if he didn't have an argument with his brother back
home."

. . . Though it had been several days since he'd come
back, when asked about how things had gone at his family home
Father would just stammer and look around at nothing in particular, like a student who had forgotten his homework. In idle
moments between spurts of work on the coop, he stared trans-
fixed at the chicken. He had tied a rope to one of its legs, teth-
ering it like a dog on a leash, and mostly it scratched the ground
with its claws in search of food. At such times Father's eyes
gradually came to look just like the chicken's. The bird, having
survived the long trip from Tosa on a packed train, in a cramped
little basket no less, had completely settled in here, and every
three days or so it laid an egg in the grass in the garden; but
the morning after the coop was finished, they discovered it inside, dead. The mark of a cat's claws could be made out on the
back of the chicken's bloodstained neck. Father stood awhile in

the coop cradling the stiff bird, and then, at the wellside in back, he slowly began to pluck out the feathers with his stubby fingers.

If anyone showed signs of insanity it was Father, not Mother. Especially then. Mother was still all right then. Yet it was possible that the major events leading to her later deterioration were already being set in motion.

Shintarō was frequently startled awake at night by his parents arguing in their room across the hall. From his mother's high-pitched whine he gathered she was crying; the low rumble of Father's voice interspersed with hers sounded inexplicably ominous to him. One night, after this had gone on for several nights running, Shintarō slept undisturbed by the familiar arguing. The next morning he saw that his parents were sleeping in separate rooms. Father's bedding was spread as always in the front room, but Mother's quilt lay twisted like a dead snake in the tea room next door. Shintarō, averting his eyes, had a sudden sensation of his mother's body heat within him. It was from that time that Shintarō started feeling repelled by her. Especially when she would come and sit dumbly by his pillow in the daytime while he was in bed. As far as she was concerned it was probably just an unconscious habit. But Shintarō at such times could not help but feel the "woman" in her. He imagined her fat, shapeless body bursting open and gushing out any moment, like liquid flooding from a cracked bowl. As he lay there he felt as though his cheek might flush from her body heat, and his eyes turned involuntarily toward the garden. But there his glance fell on Shinkichi, chopping away at the grass roots with his hoe or resting before the deserted chicken coop, and Shintarō realized with a start that he was spying on his own father.

The death of their only chicken had not crushed Father's ambitions for good.

That winter, Shintarō's uncle sent a letter informing the

family that they would have to get out of the house. The place had originally been his summerhouse, but now he said the factory he managed needed it for employee housing.

The news came just after Shintarō's family had sold off the land in Setagaya where their own house had burned down. Once again there was talk of returning to Kōchi. But it wasn't at all clear that Father's family would take them in. His absolute refusal, ever since the day he had come home with the chicken, to say a word about what had happened on his last visit, could be taken as a sign that help might never be forthcoming again. If so, they had nowhere to turn. So Mother wrote back to her brother, telling him it was doubtful that they would take the whole family in at Kōchi and that Shintarō was sick besides and couldn't get around very well, so couldn't he please let them stay on at least until Shintarō could travel. Everything she wrote was true. But there was a more important truth left out: they just didn't like the thought of going back to Kōchi. At least, she didn't. When Father had asked, "Well, shall we raise some more birds and try living on here a while yet?" she had been the first to jump at the idea.

The plan, then, was to scrape some money together and go immediately to buy up chickens. This decision was based on a fragment of information Mother had picked up somewhere, that according to the new law, a landlord could not arbitrarily evict his tenants if they were making their living off the rented property. She had gone so far as to find out that the land within their gates was registered as farmland. In other words, just as the tenant farmers had gained title to the land they worked, once her family was raising chickens in the backyard they need no longer fear being kicked out.

"If these farmers think I don't know anything and try to put something over on me, they'd better watch out," she said, inflated by her newfound knowledge. So, insisting that it would be quite impossible to collect as many chickens as they would want from the farmers in the neighborhood, Mother and Father set out for Ibaraki Prefecture, where one of Father's former subordinates lived. It was almost the first time the two had stepped through the gate together since before Father had gone abroad.

No one realized until afterward just how rash this scheme was, for they were all thinking along completely different lines. Mother's sole intention in running a poultry farm was to hang on to the Kugenuma place. Father just wanted to raise chickens. Shintarō didn't care one way or the other. The sight of the old couple setting out through the gate in high spirits, their arms and backs weighted down with bamboo baskets of all shapes and sizes, struck the son as absurd and pathetic, and made him vaguely uneasy. The only thoughts that came to him as he lay feverish in his sweaty quilting were fantasies of various unlikely ways to commit suicide, and daydream scenarios for carrying them out.

Mother and Father came back on the third night. The spectacle of the two old people bound head to foot with baskets full of chickens was absolutely horrifying. They had shaken every last penny out of their pockets to buy twenty birds, but in their obsession to wrangle as many chickens as possible for their money they had apparently overlooked the problem of how to get them home. . . . Father's army uniform and Mother's old-fashioned work suit alike were plastered with bird droppings, and where their arms and legs were exposed their skin was a mass of scabs.

"Water, water" Father cried out as soon as he was inside the gate. He had to let the chickens out and get water to them as soon as possible. Without a word, Mother unfastened her baskets from her shoulders, collapsed on the tatami, and didn't budge again.

As if the chickens alone weren't more than they could manage, the two had had to carry feed for the trip home as well. About noon the day after they arrived, when his mother finally woke up, Shintarō heard several times all about the exhausting journey—how they had had to hide from government officials, chase after birds that broke loose along the way, ride ferries and

trollies and trains one after the other. But one look at the exhausted pair had told him as much. And that was only a fore-
taste of the real hardship to come. Just what a blunder this
scheme had been was something they would appreciate better
and better as the days went by.

Until the wooden chicken coop was finished, the birds
were screened in under the veranda. Two had died on the way,
and one more followed the next day, so now there were seventeen altogether. The family's first miscalculation was that no
one had considered the cost of feeding seventeen birds. Father
had figured the potatoes he could get from the garden plus the
scraps from the kitchen would take care of them, but a little
experience took care of that theory. Even supposing he had
known how much food a single chicken needed, simply mul-
tiplying that by seventeen would not have given him an accurate estimate of the amount needed to feed seventeen of them.
Seventeen birds penned up together squabbled continuously,
and about half their feed ended up scattered outside the screen
or trampled into the ground. Futhermore, while the kitchen
scraps might have supplied enough protein for one bird, seventeen birds would need leftovers from more than seventeen
houses. So the bulk of the money left from the land sale was
quickly spent on chicken feed. The second miscalculation was
to expect a chicken in such conditions to lay eggs. The only birds
that lay during the fall and winter molting season are the first-
born of that year or those under excellent care. But the ones
that the farmers had parted with had been mostly old and weak,
or else physically inferior to start with.

Now Mother began to see the birds as her enemies—and
at the same time to despise her husband more than ever. She
was convinced that he had tricked her into raising chickens. She
said that her husband cared for nothing in the world except
keeping chickens, that even though he had known all along that
they would lose money he had cleverly tricked her into buying
them. "Ever since I've known that man he's done whatever he

damn pleased, with that innocent look on his face the whole time. As if he didn't know how much other people were suffering." . . . To top it all off, the chickens kept fighting under the veranda. At first the family wondered if it was a shortage of feed; but no, that wasn't it; they simply squabbled incessantly, even without any apparent provocation. The weakest one was always picked on by all the rest. When that one had been completely disposed of, they chased the next weakest. Sometimes the very leader of yesterday's offensive, if it happened to develop a boil on its leg or some other wound, would suddenly find itself the victim—its feathers would be torn out and its comb chewed to pieces until it couldn't even stand up. The wild screeching of the victim, and the sound of its head banging into the underside of the veranda in its desperate attempts to get away, pierced the floorboards from below—depressing sounds one could never get used to. Mother would cry out as if in reply, "Oh, I can't stand it! I can't stand it! Look at your father—he's starting to look like a chicken himself!"

There were times when Shintarō could see what she meant. When Father was eating, gulping down his cornbread with his strange, possessed-looking brown eyes open wide, he did look like a chicken throwing its head back to swallow some piece of food stuck in its throat.

Shintarō stood atop the stone wall, looking at the sea. He had been there for quite a while; the sky had gone completely dark a long time ago. . . . The black surface of the ocean swelled with heavy-looking water, drenching everything around it with damp, warm air. But Shintarō was strangely cold. Whenever he started to move his legs or arms an icy chill shot all the way through him, as if the wind were slicing through a tear in his clothes. Maybe he was tired from standing for so long in one position. Then too, there was something chilling about not being able to see another soul.

A while earlier some of the patients had been out. Shintarō had spoken with one of them. It was the first time he had talked to a patient, or for that matter to anyone, other than his mother, whom he knew to be abnormal. But there had been no feeling of strangeness, of a significant "first." If anything was strange, it was that it had all seemed so natural.

Shintarō had been about to throw a cigarette butt into the ocean when a woman who was talking loudly with another patient nearby came running over and said, "Wait, give me that cigarette."

Shintarō was taken aback. The woman's voice, belying her appearance, was that of a young girl. Judging from the sun-blackened face and faint smile she might have been over forty, but clearly that was the voice of a girl in her twenties. Her kimono, ragged almost beyond recognition, was barely held together with a red cord sash. Shintarō threw the butt into the ocean and offered the woman a fresh cigarette.

"No thanks," she said, looking back and forth from the cigarette to Shintarō. "I don't want one. I don't smoke. It's for my friend."

She was clearly lying. "Go ahead. I'll give you another one for your friend. You smoke this one," Shintarō answered, and at length she reached for it. He struck a match for her; the woman cupped her hand carefully around the flame. After one puff she turned toward her friend with a laugh, then turned back to Shintarō and asked if he were a visitor. When he answered that he'd come to see his mother, the woman suddenly opened up.

"What's your mother's name?"

Shintarō told her.

"Oh, Hamaguchi. . . ." Suddenly her face took on an expression of respect. "Mrs. Hamaguchi was one good lady, that was one good lady," she repeated.

Shintarō laughed—he couldn't help recalling that the woman was not exactly in her right mind. At this the woman blushed and blurted out,

"Well, she was. A good lady's a good lady. You got to say so. That's why I still do her laundry. There never was such

a good lady, singing songs all the time like that, cute like that.
. . . It's just too bad, I mean really too bad, letting such a rare
good lady die."

As soon as she got this out she turned and, holding tightly
onto both a fresh cigarette and her partly smoked one, ran back
to her friend.

Something about the way she looked reminded Shintarō
of the army. Every institution must have people like her. A
friendly second-year private would look out for newcomers in
all sorts of ways, but eventually you'd notice that he would occasionally help himself to a little something from their personal
belongings. Similarly, Shintarō imagined, his mother must have
learned some secrets about how to get along at the hospital from
this woman, the general rules of life here. In new surroundings, not knowing some insignificant detail can cause a great
deal of hardship. On that score Shintarō could certainly be
grateful that someone like her had been at Mother's side. On
the other hand, as he pictured his mother joining hands and
singing with these women in the twilight on the grounds, it
seemed to Shintarō an extremely gloomy sort of recreation.

Mother had been especially fond of singing. Even after
coming to the hospital, when she had lost all trace of other
memories from her past, they said she could still sing all the
words to a long song straight through. Shintarō remembered
one set of lyrics that had plagued him since childhood. It went,

> Have you forgotten the past,
> When you were small and knew no wrong,
> When you would cry and Mama would hold you?
> Like the rain on the rooftops in spring,
> Like the dew in the garden in fall,
> A mother's tears never dry between prayers for you.
> But do you ever know it?

It had been her theme song, you might say. She was apt to sing
it countless times in a single day. It was probably partly a ha-

bitual, unconscious thing. But to the listening Shintarō, its very unconsciousness underscored the oppressiveness of the mothering emotion behind it. Thanks to that overbearing pressure, Shintarō as a child had sometimes felt as if he had to ask his mother just exactly what she expected of him—what a mother was, what a son was. . . . But the experience just now with the mad woman who had pestered him for a cigarette had suddenly shown him, he thought, what that emotion of motherhood signified. Finally, what bound mother to child was sheer convention. The only thing was, this convention itself had a nature of its own.

Hearing the low moan of a fog horn out at sea, Shintarō stood up to head back for his room and get some sleep.

The next morning, like the day before, Shintarō was wakened by a roomful of red sunlight. And like the day before he dozed again until his breakfast arrived. But unlike yesterday he felt at ease, and he realized he was gradually coming to feel at home here. Breakfast this morning was not brought by the attendant with the fair complexion, but by a short, fiftyish woman in an apron. As she set out the dishes she inquired after his mother. When Shintarō had answered, she too said, "Poor thing, she was such a nice lady," and proceeded to tell them that until recently she had been a patient here herself.

"What—" Shinkichi said, looking up. "Then, you're completely over it now?"

Yes, the woman answered, she had recovered, but since there was no place for her to go she stayed on and helped at the hospital; her family was on the K_____ Coast where they used to operate a restaurant, but while she was in the hospital the store had been sold. As she talked, the woman put her hand to her hair and looked out the window toward the sea. Unquestionably something of the proprietress lingered in her pose. Though she didn't wear any makeup, her hair had been smoothed with an oil whose perfume was so pervasive one might think it had seeped through the lid of the food tin and into the bean paste itself. But Father seemed to have taken an interest in her, and he continued to speak to her, groping for a topic. He asked her if she had any children, and what her favorite food was. "I used to hate boiled food myself. But ever since I had to eat army cooking at the front I can eat anything," he said. The woman answered without interest, still looking out the window, "Oh, were you at the front? We're indebted to you then. My cousin was a soldier too, private first class, but he was killed." "Where, in Manchuria? When did he die?" Father asked, then pursed his lips as he watched the woman with a gleam in his eyes. But the woman had forgotten what she was saying. Or maybe she hadn't caught his mumbled question.

Shinkichi was considered agreeable wherever he went. Among relatives, colleagues, college friends—everywhere it was the same. You could even say he had lived until now expressly to earn the reputation. In short, he had no other special characteristics worth mentioning. Even when he had been on active duty his bearing had been more appropriate to a retired officer who had put on a uniform just for the day. By now no one could tell that his background was in the professional military. Which was not to say that some other occupation came to mind. Chika, standing at the gate one day to see her husband ride off to work on horseback, had said,

"What a way to mount a horse. That's not mounting the horse, that's crawling up it. I'd be ashamed if even the neighbors saw that. Why such a weakling ever joined the army I'll never know. Why didn't he become a priest, at least that would've been more like him."

As the battle front extended across the continent, though, she changed her tune. "It's only because that man's in the army that we make a decent living. Suppose he'd been working for a company, he'd be lucky just to be kept on till retirement as a clerk."

Shintarō had no idea whether his mother's estimate of his father was accurate or not. He had only a vague notion from the way she talked that people did not find a man like his father attractive. Especially not women. Now, as he watched the woman who smelled of hair oil standing there with her eyes on the scene out the window, not responding to his father, Shintarō was reminded of what his mother had said.

Unable to keep the conversation going, Father kept his puzzled look fixed on the woman for a while, but eventually the gleam in his eyes dimmed to a dull grey and he looked down, as though resigned, to resume eating his meal. Shintarō suddenly felt he was witnessing, in this picture of his father, the classic defeated male, and in the plump, fiftyish woman standing at Father's side, the prototype of the heartless female. . . .

Shintarō had little appetite again this morning, but he felt compelled to eat what had been set before him. What was the source of this sense of duty? Was it the mingled odors of aluminum and hair oil emanating from the rice in the tin? The fact that an identical meal was being shoved in the little slot under every door down the corridor? Or the necessity of averting his eyes from his father and the woman in front of him? Whatever the explanation, Shintarō felt he had to eat, and he managed to finish almost all the rice, soup, and pickled vegetables. Afterward, though, his stomach just felt heavy; there was no sense of relief.

Already the day felt as hot as noon. It occurred to Shintarō that there must be a lot of big flies buzzing around Mother's bed by now. The thought of combatting flies sent a strange surge of energy through him, and, leaving his father still eating and the woman waiting to clean up after them, he left for the ward by himself.

When Shintarō came to the covered walkway leading to the intensive care ward, the man with a bandage around his neck who had been by the door the day before now stepped in front of him, blocking his way. Something about this man had been bothering Shintarō since yesterday. The neck bandage already suggested it, but also from the grey, close-cropped hair and whittled-out cheeks Shintarō gathered that he was an ob-

stinate, hypersensitive type. His was a face you'd often see
among domestic warrant officers in the army. They might never
reprimand anyone out loud, but after an event they would secretly rate each person's behavior and keep track of it all in a
notebook. . . . The man stared at Shintarō's face, then frowned
and shook his head. Shintarō had no idea what that was supposed to mean, and he could see no particular reason to defer
to this person, so he pushed past him and went on to the room.
There he came across the spectacle of his mother having her
diapers changed. This chance event actually brightened Shintarō's mood for a moment. When the attendant came out carrying the diapers, Shintarō bid him a cheerful "good morning." The woman he had given the cigarette to last night stuck
her head out from a door at the end of the passageway, took
the diapers, and ran off to the well. Shintarō laughed. He decided it had only been an expression of embarrassment he had
seen on the bandaged man's face. But the next moment, when
he saw the figure of his mother amid the shadows beyond the
doorway, Shintarō thought he knew what it was the man had
been trying to communicate. She was almost completely naked, laid out on her stomach with her head twisted around to
face the door, her wide-open eyes staring straight at him.

"Wait there until we finish treating the bedsores, please,"
came the attendant's voice from behind, as if the boy had been
pursuing him. In the same instant, Shintarō made out the dark-
complexioned doctor and several nurses inside the room. He
realized that he was becoming extremely agitated. . . . The iron
door at the end of the passage was half open, and from where
he stood Shintarō could see what was going on outside. The
regular patients had gathered to work the pump by the well;
they seemed separated from him by an unnatural distance, almost as if he were looking at them through the wrong end of
a pair of binoculars. ——"It'd be better for you to be out there,
you know," warned a voice from the room again. Shintarō in-
stinctively moved closer to the door of the room.

Mother was lying on the floor at his feet. Her head was

still twisted to face the door. Her body was startlingly bony, and whenever the doctor would pull gauze from one of the sores with his blunt tweezers her back contorted painfully. The sores covered both buttocks and her left shoulder; the one on her left hip was biggest, about six inches across. "She's got herself a pretty bad one there," the doctor muttered as he lifted the pus-soaked bandage, dangling the heavy thing from his tweezers like noodles from chopsticks. Beneath this first strip yet another piece of gauze poked up from the open sore. A bedsore of this size clearly indicated that Mother's heart was weakening. With the heart's function impaired, blood stopped circulating in the area pressed to the bed, and the body began to rot there like fruit. When one bedsore developed more could be expected to follow. . . . The doctor gave Shintarō this explanation as he applied fresh gauze.

"Ow!"

When they rolled her over, Mother's violent breathing was suddenly broken by a sharp cry. It was the first time this visit that Shintarō had heard his mother speak.

"What's the matter?" the doctor asked, as if to a child who had just woken up. He turned to Shintarō. "I think she's come to. Don't you want to say something?"

Shintarō could not speak. As he knelt down close to her face, he tried to think what to say. He panicked like a man who gets up behind a podium and faces the commotion of the audience only to find that his mind has gone blank. Mother's eyes were still directed toward the ceiling. But gradually tears began to spread over her grey eyeballs and dilated pupils, and when her eyes were full teardrops formed and ran down her dry temples, over skin the color of coarse tea.

"We'd better lay her on the bed," the doctor finally broke in impatiently. As the nurses stood up to carry her to the mattress, Mother's blind eyes began to roll back and forth in obvious agitation and fear. One nurse put a hand out and took hold of Mother's shrunken arm. But the arm was rigid and trembling.

"Ow . . . Ow . . ."

They picked her up as if she weighed nothing at all, and laid her down gently on the straw mattress.

"Ow, ow . . ."

Mother continued to cry out until the open sores adjusted to the mattress. Her chest heaved as her whole body worked to draw in short, violent breaths between cries. A nurse told Shintarō to take his mother's hand. He did as he was told. The fair-skinned attendant spoke to her as he had on that first night.

"Mrs. Hamaguchi, Mrs. Hamaguchi, it's your son. Your son's holding your hand now."

But Mother just kept crying, "ow, ow," between gasps for air. As Shintarō stood there, feeling the incredibly tiny, soft palm of the wrinkled hand he held within his own, he was conscious of a vague memory just outside his grasp. But while he was still fishing for it, the attendant's voice broke his line of thought.

"It's your son, your son . . ."

Mother's breathing began to calm down a little. She closed her eyes. Footsteps sounded outside the room, and Father appeared; he came in and sat down beside her. At this her cries of "ow . . . ow . . ." gradually subsided until she was only muttering softly as if half asleep. Then, in a hoarse, low voice, she said it.

"Father. . . ."

Shintarō felt as if something had just slipped out of the palm where he had been holding onto his mother's hand. Father wore the same faint smile as always, as he looked down at his now peacefully sleeping wife.

The room was hot, as usual.

White light glared from outside in the little window pane;

before long the sunshine would inch its way across the floor. Shintarō stayed where he was, leaning against one wall and staring at the other. . . . . All the walls in the ward were painted pale green. So were the window sills and the iron bars and the metal screens, all of them. No doubt this was due to someone's notion that the color green has a calming effect on the human spirit. The wall seemed to have been painted over many times; here and there he saw blisters in the paint, and what looked like brushmarks. The thick, bumpy places had worn pale and lost their shine, but around them were patches that were glossy as new. It was probably the light coming through the little window that gave the whole room a dirty yellow cast. The length of the wall, about a foot up from the floor and again two or three feet higher, was blackened with smudges, forming a blurry pattern of double stripes; these must have been the places most often touched by the patients' hands and bodies. How much time and energy would it take for so much grease and grime and oil to soak into a painted surface that way?

Shintarō sat with his back against this wall for so many hours every day that the sheer weight of it seemed to be passed on to him. Where his shoulder blades touched the wall he could feel the weight of sand, gravel, and iron bars through the smooth surface of the cement. It seemed like more than half a year since he had come to this hospital. Only the hard resistance of the wall to his back when he shifted seemed new since yesterday. The fact remained that today, yesterday, or any day before that, everything in this room was the same. Beyond Shintarō's knees Mother slept on, her mouth always open; the air in the room was laden with that pungent sweet-sour odor; and from the next room came the same neighing cries. "Attendant, attendant! I'm waiting, I'm waiting! My lunch, my lunch, I'm waiting! Attendant . . ."

Shintarō was fairly sure that it was yesterday he had thought of tying up a blind in the window to block out the sun. With the light shining in, it wasn't only the heat that Shintarō couldn't bear, but also the fact that he could see straight into his sleeping mother's mouth. It had been hanging open for so many hours now that the tongue and the palate and the whole upper throat were completely dry and cracked; yellow columns of saliva and mucous had dried there, and no amount of swabbing with wet cotton would remove them. In any case, because of a middle-aged woman he had run into on the way, Shintarō remembered quite clearly that it was yesterday he had gone out to buy the shade.

They had met near the bottom of the slope with the rows of cherry trees, just over the crest of hills that surrounded the hospital on three sides. A woman holding a black parasol stood there alone, evidently not doing much of anything. Despite the sunshine beating down, she had propped her parasol on the ground like a cane, and stood stiff as a fencepost herself in a perfectly straight skirt. Shintarō sensed intuitively what she was doing there. She must be on her way back from committing a relative to the hospital.

The prospect of walking past her bothered Shintarō. She would probably say something to him. He was not about to turn around and go back, however. This was his first breath of fresh air outside the hospital. The smell of leaves, the smeall of ocean, the smell of earth were all so magnificent—and out here the sun that poured over his whole body felt so clean. If he could just quit thinking about his mother he could almost be in a true picnic mood. . . . But as he had feared, when Shintarō came near the woman, she turned and spoke as if she had been waiting for him. She asked if this road led directly to the K_____ Beach bus route. When he answered that it did, she twisted the ridge of her Japanese sandal into the dirt and told him she had just come from committing her daughter.

"She cries. She cries awfully. It's the only thing wrong with the girl."

"Girls that age cry when they're first put in a dormitory too, don't they?" Shintarō said, recalling what the attendant had said to him last year when he had committed his mother.

"Oh, I don't mean now—just now she's been put to sleep with an injection. But at night she cries. Every night she cries."

Five years ago the daughter had lost her sight. Since then

she had been in a constant state of depression and had cried all
the time. Shintarō tried to pay attention to the story. The more
he heard, though, the less believable it seemed. The woman had
probably left out the part that implicated herself. But once she
had everything she wanted to say off her chest, the woman
pulled herself together in short order and began to walk. She
breathed heavily, and beads of sweat collected on her narrow,
weathered brow.

The girl, seventeen this year, was now in the room next
door.

"Where am I? I don't know anyone here—where am I?"

Last night after supper Shintarō had heard muttering to
this effect, and shortly afterwards, just as her mother had said,
the girl began to sob. Low at first, then gradually higher, . . .
until before long her voice was transformed into a rhythmic,
distant sound like the murmuring of a mountain brook.

As the sun moved to the west, the light penetrating the
room grew more and more intense. Shintarō stood up and decided to try his hand again at hanging the blind. . . . He would
try fastening it with a string to the window's iron bars. This
was the same method that he had attempted yesterday and failed
with miserably, but there was no other way to do it. The bars,
planted straight up and down in the cement window frame, were
round and slippery; furthermore, he couldn't coordinate his
fingers very well with his arms extended to the top of the window. Once tied, the string quickly went slack and fell under
the weight of the blind. It was the same story every time. Finally, after many tries, the blind happened to catch at an angle
between two bars, about a third of the way down, and Shintarō decided to leave it there. . . . Even that was enough to
make the room surprisingly dark. Now there were only irregular splinters of light, in fragments twice the size of a hand,
scattered across his sleeping mother's stomach. But now, when
he went back to his spot to sit down, the sweet-sour smell began to fill the airless room.

No matter how long Shintarō lived with it, the stench was

awful. It was completely unique in his experience, certainly not the smell of rotting flesh; it was more like a combination of cat urine, rotton onions, and boiled fish scraps. At first Shintarō had wondered if it wasn't an odor characteristic to any captured animal, man or beast. Now he knew it was partly from the medicine they used to treat the bedsores. . . . The unbearable stench reminded him of the open sores and pus-soaked bandages spread across his mother's body. At the same time he recalled the word "Father" that had escaped her lips. It had been such an unpredictable event that he found it almost unbelievable.——Since then, Shintarō had felt a certain disappointment, but a corresponding sense of relief too: after all, with that one word a burden of thirty years had fallen from his shoulders. But he had felt no deep emotional response. All he retained was an impression that it had been quite peculiar. He seemed to remember that the fair-skinned attendant had glanced his way, a wry smile on his sparsely whiskered mouth. A moment later everyone in the room fell silent. The nurses gazed at the old couple with typical female sentimentality. Shintarō likewise found himself looking at the two of them. Mother's unseeing eyes turned in Father's direction. Father looked down at her, smiling. Both faces were severely sunbeaten and aroused a kind of claustrophobia in Shintarō. The deep creases running from Father's cheeks to the corners of his mouth seemed to glow, perhaps because of the angle of the light; and Mother's eyelids were red since she had just been crying. Someone sighed. Just then there was a loud sneeze. It was the doctor. He pulled a handkerchief from under his white coat, blew his nose with a dry sound and commanded "Let's go"; then he strode out of the room, stooping just to clear the doorway. The place suddenly became lively again, as the nurses came to and ran out after the doctor. . . . For a time Shintarō sat dazed. Nothing made any sense. Or rather, heat and fatigue had done away even with his desire to understand, yet had left him with a fuzzy sense of uneasiness. ——Why had the doctor purposely sneezed so loudly? He could think of a number of possible explanations now. For one thing, the man had probably felt that he ought not to stay in any one room for too long, since he had sole responsibility for the whole corridor. He might also have wanted to avoid getting involved in an emotional drama between patient and family. And it was quite possible that he thought the sentimentality of the scene would arouse the resentment of the other patients. . . . But aside from all that, Shintarō sensed that the doctor simply didn't like his family very much. He had already decided that the doctor did not like him personally; but now he thought he saw a certain suspicion, a certain skepticism concerning the whole family, reflected in the doctor's eyes.

Even after the poultry scheme had completely backfired, Father continued to spend all his time in the garden. Mother did a number of odd jobs. She took in neighbors' ironing, helped the black market broker, rented out part of the house to a beautician/masseuse, whom she even assisted by washing the customers' hair or clumsily massaging their shoulders and buttocks, and so on. Naturally none of these efforts met with success, and the family's livelihood was exceedingly precarious. The only thing that moved forward was their eviction. . . . The property had already passed from their uncle's hands to a third party. The uncle had shown up one day with a big grin on his face, introduced a ruddy-faced companion as "my friend," and then departed alone. The man he left behind was their new landlord. This new owner sought possession of the house in various ways, in response to all of which Shintarō's mother—with more new information that she had picked up God knew where—was always thinking up strategies of resistance. "Don't try to tell me that man's really our landlord," she said furiously. "He's working for Kōzō, no doubt about it. Probably fronts as a lawyer. Your uncle can't talk to us himself so he hires this fellow to do his dirty work. Well, does he think we're going to fall for that? It's just the sort of thing Kōzō would do, you know. That uncle of yours has always been a sneaky one." From that time on, though, her expression began to change. Her eyes glittered unnaturally, as if there were another set of eyeballs inside them, and darted about incessantly like the eyes of a hunted criminal.

Getting through each day was like trying to patch rags together. Mother left the house early in the morning and struggled in after midnight on the last train, carrying bundles of saccharine or m.s.g. on her back. She would put her head down on the *kotatsu* and fall asleep right there. The disorder in the untended house eventually got completely out of hand. The bedding was left out on the floor for the better part of a year; things pulled out of closets were left on the tatami or in the alcove until the whole room was buried in underwear and socks and miscellanea; then, once the cupboards were empty, everything would be stuffed back in at random, like junk being tossed on a pile. There was a saw in the dish cupboard, and leftover cornbread and dirty dishes would tumble out of a closet. Layers of spider webs hung from the ceiling, and cotton fluffs and dust balls were always billowing about, making it look as if a fine mist had settled on the room. Father stood in the middle of it all, putting a few more pine needles on the fire in the charcoal brazier to boil fish scraps for chicken feed, always straightening his own war treasures on top of the kitchen shelves with a bizarre diligence that was a throwback to barracks discipline. A mantle of fatigue lay over the entire house; the details of daily life turned chaotic and stuck to each other all out of order, tumbling by in an oppressive, feverish stream.

Occasionally one of the relatives who had not yet stopped talking to them would ask, "How long do you plan to keep this up? Why don't you go back to Y_____Village and have your family take you in?" Indeed, no one in the household could say why. Except that they had not heard a word from Uncle Genkichi, head of the family in question.

In the beginning their "landlord" showed up every month to blast them with threats and abuse. But soon it was every other month, and gradually the intervals widened until by the end they had not laid eyes on him for half a year, when one day quite unexpectedly he came by, poked around the chicken coop as though he had nothing better to do, and then sat down hesitantly at the end of the veranda. "I'm sorry to do this to you," he said. "I'm afraid I've come to dislike this job"; then, after one more glance through the house, the man went away.

About a week later, the postman, who rarely stopped anymore, delivered a brown envelope. On the back was a row of characters in black spelling out, "Yokohama District Court."

Shinkichi and family were being sued for illegal occupancy of the premises.

Mother panicked. It was loo late to go out and solicit any new "information." Naturally she went right away to ask for advice, but all she was told was, "This is a real trial, madam. According to the law you'll have to request the services of a licensed attorney." As it turned out, the man who had been her source had also been informed of this action ahead of time by the new lawyer representing Kōzō. He told her that he could not involve himself in the case beyond this point, and offered to introduce her to a colleague. It was decided that Shintarō would accompany his mother to the office of this colleague.

On the appointed day Shintarō felt weak. He had barely begun to walk when he had to sit down by the side of the road. It had been a year and a half since he had last gone anywhere at all, let alone on foot. But his fatigue was not exclusively due to illness. He simply did not want to go. Ordinarily the last thing Shintarō wanted was to turn out like his father; but at the thought of going to a strange house in a strange place to meet a strange man, Shintarō began to appreciate why his father hated to go places and never asked people to help him find work. Mother was frightened too, having been personally named as defendant in the letter of suit. She was convinced that this event branded her for life, and she thought she would soon be on the books as a criminal. "What of it—I'd be better off sleeping in a jail somewhere than I am now anyway," she said, walking briskly on the balls of her feet.

Shintarō had always imagined a lawyer as a person with a round, pudgy face. On the other hand, this one was also a member of the reform party, which would indicate a thin, pallid face. But when they arrived at the door of an alley house in Setagaya, one that had survived the fires, the man who answered had no particular characteristics at all. He was just an ordinary middle-aged man, with greying whiskers and a dull complexion. Perhaps that was why Shintarō felt more relaxed at he sat across from him. They had been ushered into what was supposed to be a Western-style room off the entranceway. The floor was tatami, six mats in size; between the man and his visitors was a narrow low table, like a child's writing desk, covered with a brown cloth; a fake-marble clock called attention to itself atop a small bookcase. The depressing smell of bathroom deodorizer seeped into the room from somewhere. Staring up at a stain on the ceiling, Shintarō asked off-handedly,

"Have you lived here since before the war?"

"No, I was in Manchuria. I'm staying with my brother at present," the lawyer replied, as if he had often been asked.

Shintarō remembered all the worn-out canvas shoes that had been strewn on the concrete floor of the entranceway and realized he should have known how large a household was living here; he fell silent. The lawyer too said nothing, but sat quietly running his fingertips with their close-trimmed nails over the brown cloth on the table in front of him. Mother handed him the letter. He turned to the first page and glanced at it briefly, then folded it in half and set it back down on the table. Shintarō's heart sank. It's a lost cause, he thought, before the lawyer had said a word.

Mother began to explain the situation. She spoke in a subdued, deferential voice, making liberal use of those roundabout turns of phrase peculiar to women's speech. The lawyer's fingers, which had been resting on the tabletop, began to fidget again.

"This kind of case is a headache."

At the lawyer's words Mother looked up, startled. She wasn't half finished yet. She had just come to the part about how her brother had made a lot of money during the war, while she had given him all kinds of moral and material support.

"It's no use." The lawyer spoke with deliberate emphasis.

"What do you mean?" Mother asked.

"I'll be frank with you. You are occupying another person's home. Perhaps you did pay rent, but I assume you are aware that at today's prices fifty yen a month wouldn't even pay for cigarettes. I don't care how much the law has changed—this will never be acceptable. I think you should leave the house as soon as possible and have the suit dropped. The longer the case drags on, the more expensive it will get, and all those expenses will be your responsibility. . . ."

Mother looked as if she were in a stupor. This was totally different from the advice she had always heard in her consultations at Kugenuma. Her face was still lowered, but even so it was obvious from her reddening temples that Mother was blushing. Raising her eyebrows and hanging her head so low that her chin almost sank into her throat, Mother began again, in a low voice, this time going over the hardships of their daily life. But the lawyer, still toying with the old tablecloth, looked away the entire time. Mother went on. She explained how fifty yen was what she and her brother had agreed upon, and how given the cost of living right after the war it had certainly not been unreasonably low. She told how her son Shintarō still had the tuberculosis he had contracted in the army and was not yet strong enough to work; how when their house had burned down in the air raids she had been away helping her brother evacuate his family and possessions. She was just explaining that the fire had been put out at the house right behind theirs, and how it was not unlikely that if she had been home she would have been able to stop it herself, when she added, "My husband was a military man, you see, sir, and Kōzō wanted to use that connection to get on good terms with the army, so whenever something came up he would call on me . . ."

At this the lawyer's fingers suddenly stopped moving. "Your husband is a soldier?"

"Yes, sir," she answered triumphantly, "Major General in the army, sir."

"Oh, a career military man, I see, a Lieutenant General.
. . . Well, you had it easy during the war then, didn't you? I'd
say your present hardship is simply fair turnabout, wouldn't
you? . . . I, at least, do not care to lift a finger in this case. You
may request the services of another lawyer or do anything else
you see fit, but I'm afraid I can not answer any more questions.
My earlier advice to you still stands."

Shintarō felt the blood rising in his cheeks. He didn't
really know why, but he supposed it was from embarrassment.
But a moment later Shintarō burst out laughing. Even after they
had left the lawyer's house he could not stop laughing. ——It
felt to Shintarō as if he had just met up with a long-lost ac-
quaintance. They were walking along the bus route now, past
a row of charred, blistered barracks where Father had been stationed as the regimental veterinarian when Shintarō was small.
He had been right there, cringing forward on his horse as if
from cold, clinging to the mane for dear life. But it had not even
been necessary for the lawyer to know about all that. For him
it was enough that this suspicious supplicant had been a career
military man, and a Major General at that. (The lawyer had been
off by one rank, but surely that was inconsequential.) And it
had been ages since Shintarō had been humiliated about his father's profession. Father had been home for four years now. In
those four years, the family had completely forgotten that they
had ever lived off his salary. Shintarō had convinced himself
that, since the profession of "career military man" had been done
away with when Japan was defeated, he could forget all about
it; only the lawyer's stare just now had finally brought it back
to him. His shame was like that of a kid who had wet his pants
and had to stand there with his thighs smarting, feeling the
urine spread down his legs. ——What's your dad do? Come on,
tell. ——Isn't a "veterinarian" a guy who sticks his arm up a
horse's ass to see if it's sick? ——Don't go near that kid, you
might get some horse disease.

The doctor's sneeze had reminded Shintarō of that lawyer's cold stare. Of course, there was no comparison between

the two. The lawyer had refused the family's case; the doctor had taken over from a colleague and was graciously looking after Mother. But why was it, then, that Shintarō got the feeling from both of them that they thought he was a suspicious character? . . . One evening Shintarō had been watching the doctor play catch with some patients. The patients cheered when the lanky doctor missed the little ball. The doctor laughed and called out, "No problem!" Then he picked it up again and threw it back with an exaggerated gesture. But when he saw Shintarō's head in the hall window, the doctor stopped smiling suddenly, threw two or three straight balls, and disappeared into the ward.

Shintarō might be making something out of nothing, of course. His first impression of the man with the neck bandage, for example, had been grossly in error. True, the man had silently blocked his path the day Shintarō had been heading for the room where Mother was being treated for bedsores; but as it turned out, the man was always silent. Whenever Shintarō walked down the hall he followed wordlessly with broom and dustpan, sweeping up behind every passerby. There had been another misunderstanding the day Shintarō put up the window blind. Frowning, the man had watched Shintarō's clumsy efforts, and Shintarō thought he was going to tell him to stop. But he didn't. He merely shook his head jerkily two or three times, absorbed in watching this other person at work, and then he padded softly away. Since then Shintarō had felt that the bandaged man was looking over his shoulder all the time. It even seemed possible the man knew Shintarō had given a cigarette to a patient. One day when Shintarō had been sitting at Mother's side, stretching his legs out and smoking a cigarette, the man's face appeared between the iron bars in the window. Shintarō made up his mind to get up and go over to ask if he had something to say. When he did, the man got a look of panic in his eyes and violently waved Shintarō back. . . . Maybe he's a deaf-mute, Shintarō considered. But no; he had seen the patients and attendants talking with the fellow hundreds of times. The man would fold his arms, cock his ear toward them, and nod self-importantly or shake his head. . . . The man began to move his mouth painfully. For the first time Shintarō noticed a glass tube protruding from the bandage on his throat. He was holding up an electric fan, and said if Shintarō needed it he could borrow it for a while.

At first Shintarō hesitated. Partly he was embarrassed at his own misjudgement of the man, but there was also a fleeting moment when he felt as if he didn't understand anything anymore. A second look at the man showed sagging yellow skin, colorless, deep-set eyelids, and above them, sparse, greying eyebrows. The eyes were ashen and expressionless. ——Could those be the same eyes that reminded me of a domestic warrant officer?—— Shintarō wondered. He could not imagine that this man would be one to lavish kindness on a stranger. Not to imply, of course, that something evil motivated his offer. . . . Finally, Shintarō decided to accept it. For one thing the big, black, old-fashioned fan looked too heavy for the bandaged man. The glass tube protruding from his neck quivered with every breath. Shintarō thanked him and hastily took the fan in his own hands. But as soon as the man had handed it over, he trotted off again down the hall to the far end of the ward to return with a long cord. Sure enough, there were no outlets in the rooms. The man hooked a number of extension cords together, then crawled under the desks in the office looking for a plug. His very silence while working made his preparations appear energetic and thorough. Asked if it wasn't hard for him to breathe, he merely shook his head from where he was on all fours. As soon as the man saw the fan start up in Mother's room, before Shintarō even had a chance to thank him, he had gone into the corridor and disappeared.

What was Shintarō to make of this fellow? . . . Sitting in front of the fan, Shintarō could not relax. He had never liked fans. Also, it didn't seem fair to the patients shut up in the other rooms that only this room should have one. On the other hand, he couldn't just turn it off. He began to realize that, bad as it was, in this heat he was undeniably better off with it than without. . . . Shintarō still felt tense that evening when he came across the bandaged man again.

This time he was working on a boat that had been hauled up onto the stone embankment at the water's edge. The belly of the upturned boat and the bandage on the man's neck both shone white in the fading light. He was busy making repairs, apparently cutting away leaky spots and plugging up the holes. As soon as the man had a free moment, Shintarō called to him. The man looked up. When Shintarō thanked him for his help that afternoon, the man suddenly said out of the blue, in a croaking voice, "You shouldn't put a sick person in a place like that."

Shintarō was a bit startled. Partly it was the voice, which was clearer than it had been that noon; but the words themselves shocked him. The man went on. "In summer it's hot and there're mosquitoes all the time, and I don't have to tell you how cold it gets in winter. Even a healthy person would die if you left him in a place like that. . . ."

Shintarō groped for an answer, then said at last, "But I'm sure the doctor and attendants do the best they can." The man emphatically shook his head and proceeded to tell Shintarō things that made him really start to worry. The staff just served time there, he said, and were irresponsible in the extreme; that wing of the hospital in particular was blatantly ignored, since that was where they put the patients they thought were beyond help; people said it was all over when a patient was moved there, but sooner or later most of them were sent there to die. He said all this without giving Shintarō a chance to get a word in edgewise.

"See those people over there? They may be doing all right now, but before long they'll all be taken in there to die," he said, pointing to the patients scattered across the dark playing field. They made even Shintarō think of so many ghosts in a graveyard. Trying to change the subject, he asked about the dome-shaped island in the sea before them. It was the classic island, completely overgrown with dark, lush foliage: something you might find in a fairytale picture book. The bandaged man said it was uninhabited and had recently been bought by a travel agency that had erected a shrine there, supposedly to the "God of Romance," to attract tourists; but for the holiday tomorrow all the patients from the hospital were to go there, and they would bring back the offerings.

Shintarō said that was amusing. "But how do you get there? Do you swim out, or take that boat, or what?"

"How do you get there? Oh, different ways. They say the island and the mainland used to be connected, a long time ago, and even now at low tide you can walk over if you're careful."

"Really? It looks awfully deep from here."

"Oh, it is deep now. The tide's all the way in. . . . At low tide you can see the pilings though. They breed pearl oysters here, you know."

"Pearls?" Shintarō asked absently, looking out over the sea before him. But the black water only seemed to rise, little by little.

Weariness showed on the bandaged man's face. Perhaps he had talked too long. Looking again at the glass tube in his neck, Shintarō suddenly remembered that this tube was one thing the man had never spoken about. He had probably had surgery for cancer of the larynx or something. That would explain why he sympathized with the plight of the patients here. . . . Yet Shintarō had to admit that he still didn't know anything about him.

The two decided to head back for the ward. "Good night," the man said hoarsely, almost in a whisper. Shintarō replied that he was going back to his mother's room. At this the man abruptly looked away. There was a coldness to the gesture that contrasted sharply with his behavior up until then. Shintarō, not knowing what was the matter, walked beside him anyway back toward the room. The man picked up a ring of keys at the office. He stopped at the door to the first of the private rooms that lined the hall like so many animal cages, and with a practiced motion he unlocked the door, stooped slightly, and crept into the dark room. Shintarō almost cried out. So this was where he lived. Though his symptoms were minor, he was another of the insane.

About two months after Shintarō and his mother went to see the lawyer in Setagaya, war broke out in Korea. The period of a little over two years that followed, up to the time they left Kugenuma, was probably the family's sunniest time after the war. The trip to the lawyer's house apparently gave Shintarō the push he needed, for after that he was able to leave the house without developing a fever; he got part-time work with a textile company, bringing in a stable monthly income, and at the same time he managed to take on large translation jobs. Father found employment in the file room at the Occupation's military hospital. The day Father brought home his first paycheck, Mother bought saké and sweets, and while pouring saké for Father at the dinner table she bubbled, "It sure is nice to have a salary coming in, isn't it. Almost like old times."

They were able to hire a lawyer, too, and on easy terms, thanks to an introduction from a former classmate of Father's. Through his efforts the suit had been dropped and the matter was being settled out of court. . . . Everything had started to go beautifully. But it was just at that point that they began to notice aberrations in Mother's behavior. At the store she would mistake one of their hard-earned 1000-yen bills for a 100-yen bill, and come home without the change; the next time she might be given extra change, and she would broadcast it to the neighborhood, saying, "Look what a good shopper I am!" She had always been irreverent and fond of pranks, but the way she acted now, as if nothing were out of the ordinary, suggested that this was no joke. She grew terribly absentminded, and would wander through the house muttering to herself and darting her eyes back and forth as if she were possessed—all the while looking, of all things, for the coin purse that was right in her pocket. Possibly because she was overweight, she waddled around like a toddler, her rounded calves peeking out between the top of her socks and the hem of a kimono that was too short for her; when she started to run she often tripped and fell in the street.

"You're so unsteady on your feet it makes me nervous just to look at you. At least when you walk around you could try to watch what you're doing," scolded Father, who by now had even accustomed himself to going out into the world in a business suit.

It was certainly evident that Mother was shaky. But it never occurred to them that it might be because of a nervous disorder. As they saw it, Mother had finally won a little release from years of hardship and now could not stir herself to do anything. Her excessive grumbling, though, and her quick temper, the way she flared up over nothing and then burst into tears—this did seem strange; but they thought no more of it. She said that the neighbors insulted her, not responding when she addressed them; as she repeated this again and again she got more and more worked up until she was red as a drunkard, her eyes bloodshot; then she stood up stiff as a rod and said breathlessly, "Oh, my head aches. The left side of my head aches. A blood vessel is going to burst, I just know it. I'll be paralyzed. What'll I do now, I'm going to be paralyzed!" As she cried out she pounded her head with her own clenched fists.

Shintarō and his father had been edgy lately too. Each had become irritable for his own reasons since the two had started going out and earning money. Father got annoyed with Mother for being so slow to serve meals; Shintarō whined about the food being bad. Father's job had strict hours, and if he were late he would lose a full day's wages, or, if worse came to worst, the job itself. As a result, Mother watched the clock constantly, and at ungodly hours of the night she woke up with a strange cry and leapt out of bed.

On the whole, though, it was certainly a more peaceful existence than what they had known before. The surviving chickens in the coop were laying eggs; Father tended the backyard garden for amusement in his spare time. And Mother mostly lay in her dusty bedroom, remembering the taste of some candy she had eaten long ago, or something Shintarō had done as a baby, sighing and chuckling to herself.

It was not exactly that they had forgotten about it, but somehow no one seriously believed the day would come when the family would be forced to leave the Kugenuma house. They had lived there for seven years now. That was longer than they had been in any other place, including their own house. It finally hit home that they had only one more month to stay the night Shinkichi came walking slowly through the gate and up to the veranda, lunch box in hand, and blurted out, "I was fired today."

They had known from the start that the job would not last long. If the fighting passed its peak and the front line were stalemated, the number of dead and wounded sent back to the hospital would naturally decrease. Still, they were unprepared for the layoff when it came. . . . Though it was not through any fault of his own that Father had lost his job, still he looked ashamed, and sat staring vacantly into the garden. Mother's eyes turned red again; she muttered disconnectedly to herself, pacing meaninglessly, restlessly back and forth from the gate to the house, as if she hoped to find something she had lost there.

Shintarō too felt a certain disappointment and panic. But on reflection that was an odd reaction for him to have. After all, everything was turning out well for him; he had no reason to be pessimistic or anxious. If Father had kept his job after the family moved out, the three of them would have had to share a single rented room—a miserable prospect, suffocating even to think about. They would have still less to live on than they did now, Mother would have to do her cooking in a neighbor's kitchen, and the friction inside and out would be unrelenting. On top of that, they would soon spend all the money they were to receive as compensation for being evicted. Then Shintarō would be completely trapped. It was potentially a blessing in disguise that Father had lost his job when he did.

But the next day Shintarō's parents seemed to have forgotten Father had ever been fired. Father was hard at work feeding this spring's flock of chickens, while Mother watched with her hands in her pockets, looking contented. What could they be thinking? What did they plan to do now? Shintarō thought of how the two of them had had secrets back when Shinkichi first came home from the war.

"Listen, there's nothing to worry about," Mother said out of the blue several days later. "We can get a loan from a finance corporation and build a house of our own, can't we? Mr. K_____ next door says a relative of his will even lease us the land for free. . . ."

Shintarō could tell from the look in her eyes that he shouldn't even try to argue. So he obediently went to meet an employee of the finance corporation, thinking thus to let the issue settle itself. . . . It was possible that Mother had already completely lost her senses by then. But thinking back now, it seemed to Shintarō that things had happened so fast during those days that he hadn't had a chance to notice. It was Father's eccentricities if anything that had preoccupied him. With the deadline for the move only days away, Father spent all his energy making bizarre boxes out of the wood from the disassembled chicken coop. He said he was going to put the birds in them to ship them to Y_____ Village in Kōchi. He had already finished a number of boxes. Since there were few valuables or furnishings in the house that were worth what it would cost to ship them, these chicken crates made up the bulk of the family's baggage. The day they went to ship them, the stationmaster told them with some surprise that he had never handled anything like this before, and that they would have to butcher the birds or sell them or dispose of them some other way. Shintarō agreed that this was the sensible thing to do. The trip from Fujisawa to Kōchi took a week by freight car, three or four days even by passenger train. For the leg from there to Y_____ Village you had to figure at least another day. Mailing live cargo that far in the sweltering heat of late August was not merely risky, it was positively futile. Just to be sure, Shintarō asked how many of the ten-odd chickens might be expected to survive the trip. Wrinkles creased the old employee's weathered face as he answered without a moment's hesitation, "They'll die to a bird, that's a fact." Father smiled throughout this exchange but said nothing. He poked his finger between the side boards of the odd looking boxes, making airholes for the chickens inside, who occasionally let out strange clucking sounds.

On September first, the day the family was to leave the house, a sort of holiday excitement charged the atmosphere. People from all over the neighborhood dropped by, both to say goodbye and to see what a legal eviction was really like. While Shintarō and his father were busy packing suitcases and bags, Mother, who hadn't yet done anything in the way of preparation, spent her time as if she were on her way to the theater, nervously pulling her tickets out of her purse and looking them over. The next thing they knew she had gone around back to peer into the shed or look at the pump beside the broken well.

"Quit dawdling! Hurry up, before the bailiff gets here!" Father yelled irritably. If the bailiff came while they were still on the premises it would mean they had broken the arbitration agreement, and he was afraid that then they would not be able to collect their eviction payment. But at 11:30 a.m., thirty minutes before the noon deadline, they were finally ready. The truck carrying the family of three and all their worldly goods drove off with an ominous rumble. Mother sat on the luggage rack between Father and Shintarō, her greying hair blown about by the wind until it was plastered to her damp forehead.

The plan was to spend that night with relatives in Tokyo, and to set out the next morning for their respective new lives—Mother and Father to Kōchi, Shintarō to a rooming house outside Tokyo. Shintarō went first to the room he would be renting to drop off his luggage, and when he came back to the relatives' house that evening Father was waiting idly alone.

Mother had wanted to go around to some places on the way to say goodbye, he explained, so they had decided to come separately.

"I told her to be back by dinnertime, but I suppose she's stopping to gab at every house along the way. These people with no sense of time . . ." he said, trying to appease the relatives, who had decorated the table for a farewell party. But after dinner Mother still hadn't come. The children who were sent to the station to look for her came back without her, reporting that the man at the station had said he had seen no one of that description. For the first time things began to look ominous. With Mother hating the idea of going to Kōchi as much as she did, it was not inconceivable that she had suddenly taken it into her head to run away. . . . A little past eleven, heavy footsteps were heard and Mother's voice sounded in the entrance.

"I got lost on the way, and a nice man brought me right to the gate," she said cheerfully.

Since getting lost on the way to a house she had visited quite often sounded unlikely, the family assumed this was just an excuse for her tardiness. The next morning, though, before the rest of them had a chance to catch their breath, she startled them again.

"Oh no! We're missing a suitcase. It's the little alligator trunk. I wonder if that man stole it from me last night."

Sure enough, a small suitcase of Mother's was gone. The family's post office savings book and cash, which admittedly did not amount to much, had apparently been lost with it. But as the assembled relatives began to panic about it she burst out laughing, and now she said,

"Oh, forget about it. Since I've decided to stay right here in Tokyo I figured I wouldn't be needing that suitcase anymore. So last night I gave it to the nice man who brought me here."

Now they finally began to realize that Mother was not normal. One could not rule out the possibility that she was just trying to distract attention from her mistake, though. She had always been one to pull little stunts like that. . . .

"Look, it's all right, I'll just stay in Tokyo. I'll stay right here with Shintarō. Father, you go to Tosa by yourself. M_____, T_____, all my friends tell me I should stay," she repeated all the way to the station. She was still at it when they reached the Shinagawa stop.

"Don't be ridiculous. Hurry up or we'll miss the train," Father said, yanking at her sleeve.

"What?" Mother's eyes went wide with bewilderment. She looked distrustfully down at the tracks beside the platform.

After seeing his parents off at the station, Shintarō set out immediately to retrace the path Mother had most likely travelled the day before. He stopped at the police station, the central railway station, every place he thought she might have been, always asking after the suitcase—but it was nowhere to be found. He couldn't turn up even a clue. For the moment he at least had to notify the post office that the savings book was missing; that meant a trip back to Kugenuma. Just one day away and he would have to go back. But Shintarō didn't really mind. He was used to this kind of wasted effort—in fact, he was nervous when he didn't have something like this to do. . . . When he got off the train, though, for some reason Shintarō didn't feel like going straight to the post office, and he headed instead for their old house. A strange feeling of nostalgia came over him as he walked. It seemed like ten years since yesterday when he had ridden the truck through these streets. As he neared the house, familiar scenes came into view: a fence, a garden glimpsed over a wall, trees; he felt his chest tightening. Finally the gate was in sight. Shintarō heard someone calling his name, and he turned. It was the neighbor, Mrs. K_____.

"You've come back for this, I suppose? I was just wondering how I would ever get it to you."

To Shintarō's surprise, what Mrs. K_____ held out to him

was the little alligator suitcase he had been looking for. Apparently the family had left just this one article behind them in the house yesterday. For a second Shintarō was crestfallen. But almost immediately he was swept with indescribable fear. Since the lock on the old, worn bag was broken, it had been tied shut with cord from the outside; when Shintarō got it open and looked inside, both the postal savings book and the money that he was positive had been put there were gone. The only thing inside was a sickle they had used to cut twine, its long handle lying diagonally in the suitcase. That was all. The saw-toothed blade still had bits of yellow twine caught in it, and it glistened blue-black like some frightful reptile. The sharp tip had cut through the lining. Shintarō was terrified. . . . It seemed as if the disorder of his mother's mind were flooding from this dilapidated suitcase, trying fiercely to overwhelm him.

One day not more than three months later, Shintarō got a strange and unexpected letter in the mail. It took him a while to figure out that it was from his mother. Crooked characters of irregular size were scattered all over the envelope, and the stamp had been pasted on the back to seal the flap shut. When Shintarō cut the seal, what the envelope yielded was either mostly blank pages or ones where every second or third word was messily crossed out, with rows of characters that looked like nothing more than random ink smears. When more or less deciphered and pieced together, this was how it read:

> dear Shintarō
> how have you been since we saw you last I went to
> see a crazy-doctor the other day but it looks like
> there's nothing much wrong with me Father is rais-
> ing chickens again he spent a lot of money on a
> rickety second-hand bicycle that he takes to get feed
> every day seems stupid since he only makes enough
> on the eggs to pay for the feed in spite of every-
> thing he's convinced he runs a model poultry farm
> and is always boasting that he'll become a village

leader but the peasants say you can't make money
on eggs and refuse to take him seriously Father
doesn't speak to anybody here not a single word
even to your uncle your aunt is a terribly bad bad
person she's mad all day long the other day she
chased me with a stick she hits me with sticks she
tells me to take my clothes off and makes me stand
by the well naked and beats me I want to go to Tokyo let's live together in Tokyo right away I'm
writing this letter in secret it will be another problem to mail it they don't let me just go to the post
office whenever I feel like it I'll have to get somebody to mail it for me hope it gets to you somehow
       Mother

Another letter came from Father about the same time, saying
first of all that every single chicken had arrived safely; that the
birds were laying eggs every day; that he was tilling the fields
for Shintarō's uncle, who had lost his tenant farmers; and that
on rainy days he took books out of the storehouse to read—in
short, that he was leading a sensible life, literally making hay
while the sun shone, and getting along fine with the relatives.
About Mother, all he said was, "She is frequently hallucinating
of late; the sight is a painful one."

    Mother, Father: Shintarō didn't know which one to be-
lieve. Only one thing was clear: both letters depressed him.

    It had been a week now since Shintarō had come to the
hospital. He knew it was a week, because his aunt from Y_____
Village had told him so when she came up to see Mother. Apparently she had been the one who had told Father to send the
first telegram asking Shintarō to come. Seeing him now, she told
him, "Your father is quite a man. He really is. When all this is
over I hope you'll take good care of him."

    Shintarō nodded and replied that he thought so, too. He
knew his father had suffered. His aunt went on and on: the
reason she was so late in coming was that she just couldn't leave

her husband, he yelled at her all the time but he couldn't really get along without her, but when she suggested they make the trip together he said, "Makes me sick to go to a place like that, I can't keep my food down," and absolutely refused to come along, in principle you'd expect him to take the lead when his own brother's wife was the one having difficulties. . . . Shintarō thought his uncle was quite right. "I know how he feels," he answered. At this his aunt laughed. "What, do you take after your uncle?" Shintarō said maybe he did, in some ways.

Once she was there, there wasn't much Shintarō's aunt could do anyway. Mother slept on as before; the attendant gave her an occasional injection of vitamins or camphor, but the others only sat keeping watch. In the patchy afternoon light that managed to get in through the windowshade, Shintarō sat thinking of the office where he worked. His boss, a man with chronic indigestion, always grumbled that the company didn't appreciate the work of the P.R. department, and never would. At the time Shintarō had left to come here he had merely shown this man the telegram, not divulging anything about the nature of Mother's illness or the name of the hospital; the boss was undoubtedly complaining by now about the irresponsibility of his subordinates. But Shintarō could do nothing about it. Until this matter with Mother was resolved, he could hardly get up and leave.

Shintarō's aunt started up again, telling him how good Father had been about looking after Mother while they were staying at her house in Y——— Village. Why, if you let her out of your sight for a minute she'd take off, when she took off it'd be to some stranger's house a mile or two away, there was no way to look for her, of course she couldn't do any housework so all the washing and cleaning fell to Father, she couldn't even take a bath alone, he had to get in and bathe her. Shintarō had heard all of this last year when he had paid them a visit at Y——— Village. But the nuance was different this time. Last year there had been a stronger implication that his aunt was also one of the burdened. "Shinkichi was amazing, just amazing. All that hardship and not a word of complaint. The only thing he ever said was that it was hard to have her keep waking him up all the time on those cold winter nights when she had to use the outhouse, having to go with her every time and wait outside until she was through. He only mentioned it once."

What a picture, Father standing still in the cold by the outdoor toilet listening for Mother to finish—Shintarō could imagine his suffering. Then again, it seemed to epitomize the man's whole life.

On the other hand, Shintarō positively could not imagine the woman before him doing anything like stripping his mother and beating her with a stick. Clearly this was one of Mother's paranoid delusions. So Shintarō thought, looking now at his aunt's simple face as she squinted in the light. After all the trouble she had been put to, to have Mother secretly write such things about her and send them in a letter off to her son was really the last straw. . . . About half a year after his parents had moved to Y_____ Village, letters from his aunt, his father, and other relatives had begun arriving periodically at the house where Shintarō was staying, asking him to come to the village sometime. Shintarō always wrote back explaining that he was not allowed to take time off work, or that he lacked the financial means to travel. It was true: at the time it wasn't easy for him to come up with money for a train ticket to Kōchi, and he might well have lost the job he had finally found if he asked for several days' leave so soon. But even supposing someone had given him the time and the money, Shintarō didn't think he could have brought himself to go. Mother's illness had nothing to do with it. Quite bluntly, it was too much trouble. It seemed such a waste. . . . Over twenty rough hours on the train, crossing the Inland Sea, crawling through who knew how many tunnels in the Shikoku mountains, all to take a look at two old people and go back the same way: it was all he could stand just to think about it.

But the final reason Shintarō couldn't bring himself to go

back to the village was that, whatever his aunt and father might say, he could not be persuaded that his mother was deranged. It seemed to him that her behavior was a ruse, for one thing. She was staging a little show to get him to come, or maybe she was doing these things deliberately to irk the relatives because she didn't want to stay in Y_____ Village. That was how Shintarō saw it. Or perhaps he had some vague notion that she physically couldn't be mad, since no one in the family line had gone crazy before. . . . No, somehow, somewhere deep down, he stubbornly continued to believe that his mother was sane. It was ridiculous, of course. But there was nothing he could do about it.

There were other instances like this where Shintarō's behavior toward his mother seemed strange even to him. One was the way he kept that incoherent letter tucked away in the back of his desk drawer all this time. Shintarō was not generally in the habit of keeping things he received in the mail. Even if he did set something aside—thinking it might prove useful some day, or saving it as a keepsake—it always got lost eventually. But that one letter he could not throw away. It may have been partly that he was nervous about a stranger getting hold of it. But weren't there ways around that?—Surely he could have burned it or something. Yet he had no desire to do anything like that. Quite the contrary, every once in a while he still impulsively took the letter out and engrossed himself in it again. At twilight, after spending his whole day off shut up in his room, Shintarō fixed his eyes on those distorted characters dancing across the stationery, which was grey and ratty by now. Sometimes he didn't even hear the loud chiming of the clock downstairs. . . . He had probably reread that letter hundreds, no, thousands, of times. By now it was all clearly etched in his head: what was written in what sort of characters on what page, even the feel of the violet-ruled paper and the color and permeability of the ink. Then for what conceivable reason did he go on reading it? He was sure it was not affection for his mother. His emotion was more what one might feel for a snake in a glass cage, when one suddenly recognized in it a kindred soul. ——— Then again, it could be that through this letter he sought to probe his mother's madness. That would mean that his purpose in reading and rereading the letter was, at bottom, to refute the notion that his mother was truly mad.

. . . Whatever the explanation, Shintarō had not believed it when he had received the news last summer that Mother was going to have to be hospitalized. He thought it was just another ploy, an excuse to call him down.

The family house at Y——— Village was surrounded by a whitewashed earthen wall, and in front of the house sprawled a pine tree many hundreds of years old, its huge trunk stretched out nearly parallel to the ground. The moment he caught sight of it in the dusk Shintarō simultaneously felt relief and apprehension. Most of the wall was in shambles; the pine could barely hold up its own weight. Moss or grasses had taken over most of the weathered tiles on the vast roof, which made Shintarō think of a temple—the whole building looked ready to cave in any minute. His father and aunt met him at the gate. He followed them inside, and as soon as he set foot in the dim, earth-floored room off the kitchen, a voice sounded from out of the darkness beside him.

"Why, Shin-chan, you've come back!"

It was Mother.

Shintarō froze, absolutely shocked. He had expected her to look different, but nothing had prepared him for such a drastic decline. On reflection he realized that the face he had been picturing was the healthy one of more than ten years ago. Even when they left Kugenuma she had already looked essentially as she did now. Mother was smiling. Leaning against the wall in one corner of the earth-floored room, two front teeth showing through her grin, she seemed to Shintarō like a bashful little girl. At this he fleetingly thought again of her as she had

been when healthy; but one glance made it clear that she was
not normal now. Shintarō shuddered when she advanced toward him, without even knowing why he was afraid.

As he got used to seeing her, she seemed more and more
like her old self, though. "If this is all, she's not so bad, is
she?"—"No—looks like she's calmed down a good deal since
you came," Shintarō and his father were saying the next afternoon, when they overheard Mother and Shintarō's aunt laughing together over something amusing. . . . The four of them
ended up taking a walk up the hill in back to the Hamaguchi
family cemetery. Inside the house grounds, surrounded by
woods, it had been dark, and a cool breeze had been blowing;
but as soon as they stepped outside, the sun was so brilliant
that everything seemed to blaze white, even through shut eyes.
Out on the path between the rice paddies the air was heavy
with the smell of ripening grain. Mother seemed to be short of
breath and lagged behind, so Shintarō stopped and turned
around. She narrowed her eyes as if to beckon to him, then
smiled as she said into his ear in a near-whisper,

"There's something strange going on. It's your father.
He's been meeting a young girl by the temple and going off
with her."

Shintarō laughed. "What makes you think that?"

Father, in the slacks from his worn-out army uniform and
a pair of canvas shoes, walked on ahead with Shintarō's aunt,
unaware of their conversation.

"What makes me think that?" Mother's eyes flashed.
"There's no 'think' about it. It's getting to be every night now.
When I tried to follow him he said 'get out of my way!' and
tried to push me right down in the field. What a dirty trick,
after all the years of poverty and suffering I went through for
him in Kugenuma—now he pulls something like this."

Shintarō had no way to calm her. The sun blazed on, and
there was no shade anywhere. So they started walking again.
Mother's fit seemed to subside; before long she resumed the
pace and looked as if nothing had happened. But when Shin-

tarō saw that she seemed to be short of breath again and stopped a second time, she started up anew. Her voice grew gradually louder, her eyes fixed on one point in space, and the veins stood out on her temples as her breathing got so violent that her chest heaved.

"Curse you, you old bastard!" Her shout echoed into the distance.

"Are you sure she's all right? Maybe we'd better turn back," Shintarō called to his father, who had stopped but was still facing forward.

"We're better off going . . . it's worse at night," he answered, and with that he took the lead and started up again.

The next day, Shintarō and Father went by themselves to the hospital. Mother had been examined at the main clinic in the city shortly after coming to Kōchi. Now when they said they wanted to have her admitted, the doctor remembered her; his fair face broke into a smile as he said, "I'm sure it's quite a challenge taking care of her at home." His voice sounded velvety to Shintarō, even seductive. Shintarō gathered from the doctor's tone that he had suggested hospitalization from the first, but that until now Father had refused. While the other two discussed procedural matters, an attendant showed Shintarō around the building and grounds. It appeared that the doctor and attendant were trying to be polite. But after they had made the arrangements to bring Mother in the next day, as Shintarō and his father were about to leave the room, the doctor called them back, had them stand outside in front of the ward, and aimed a brand-new-looking camera at them. The summer sun glittered on their heads; they could hardly bear waiting for the shutter to click.

It was evening when they got back to Shintarō's uncle's house in Y_____ Village. For some reason, ever since they had left the hospital Shintarō had been too exhausted to talk. But when he passed through the gate to where his aunt was feeding the chickens beside the coop and saw his mother standing vacantly behind her, a new tenseness immediately overcame Shintarō's exhaustion. . . . Mother stood with her lips pursed, apparently seeing no one. She brushed past Shintarō without acknowledging his presence at all and began pacing mechanically back and forth between the kitchen and the gate, muttering to herself. Shintarō couldn't help being reminded of some animal penned up in a cage.

That night Mother slept peacefully. Maybe it was because at dinner they had told her they would be going back to Tokyo the next day. Once in the night Shintarō heard something bump against the sliding door of his parents' room and wondered if she was having another attack; but over Father's thick drowsy voice he heard Mother say, "I'm going to the bathroom," and the door slid open. . . . When he realized the footsteps in the dark hallway were advancing toward his room, Shintarō was so terrified he thought his blood would run backwards in his veins. A shadow fell across the dimly visible *shōji* screen before him.

Just then, "No, no. The bathroom's this way, it's the other direction," he heard Father say.

"Really? Did I go the wrong way?" came the unexpectedly meek reply, and this time the footsteps receded off in the direction of the bathroom, where the cedar door creaked open.

From then through the next day, everything went off as planned. Aside from their confusion over how to tell the taxi driver where they were going. . . .

Mother had looked bright and cheery since morning. The closer they came to the hospital, the more composed her bearing and her words became—it was almost as if she were getting her senses back. Strength returned to her eyes that had always stared off into space; she focused clearly, and the people around her had some sense of where she was looking, what she was thinking. Until the driver switched off the radio and turned the cab around, Shintarō had been worried that at any minute Mother might go into one of those fits of hers that seemed to start up when she stopped moving, but the look on her face reflected in the rear-view mirror, eyes closed, was one of repose such as he had not seen there for years.

When the cab turned off the little street lined with tea shops and started up the mountain road, the inside of the car suddenly sank into silence. Mother, who until then had been singing along spiritedly with the comedians on the radio, now looked straight ahead, her face enveloped in the green-black shadow of the trees streaming by outside the window, her mouth shut tight. . . . At this rate her "sanity" became a cause for concern for Shintarō. Wasn't it possible that she had suddenly come back to her senses, figured out exactly what was going on, and decided to accept her fate nonetheless? He should never have asked the doctor's advice. (The day before, at the hospital, Shintarō had asked him how to go about bringing a patient in. The question seemed to dampen the doctor's spirits. "Oh, people try different things. As they say, a little white lie does have its uses," was all he had answered—essentially avoiding the issue.) Recalling the doctor's fair skin and velvety voice as he had stood there aiming the camera at Shintarō and his father just before they left, Shintarō felt remorse beginning to gnaw at his insides.

"My, how lovely!" Shintarō's aunt cried out.

The cab swung toward the panorama of sea that had suddenly unfolded, and began a zig-zag descent as if down the side of a mortar bowl. The ocean reflected a clear blue sky, and the white buildings, like sugar cubes on the green slope, seemed to grow as they drew near. Shintarō suddenly felt as if these buildings had turned into living creatures since yesterday, as if they were stretching their huge bodies out full length toward him. . . . As yesterday, the doctor came out to the gate to greet them with a smile.

"Yes, now, which room shall we give Mrs. Hamaguchi?" The doctor had Mother take a chair in his examining room, and spoke to her as to a child.

Shintarō was startled. Did the doctor think she had consented to come here? Today the light from the bright window

showed the faintest red shadow of facial hair on the doctor's
smooth, white cheek. . . . Mother remained silent. They could
only wait; he had asked "Which room shall we give Mrs. Hamaguchi?" but it wasn't at all clear that it was up to them.

"Please wait here. I'll go and check on the room assign-
ments."

The doctor left, wafting a delicate smell of disinfectant,
and suddenly the room seemed deserted. . . . Bare but for one
sturdy varnished table and five or six wooden chairs, the place
had none of the furniture or equipment that one would see in
an examining room in a regular hospital or clinic. There could
be no mistaking it, though. It had that certain gloom peculiar
to examining rooms. . . . Just then a tiny sigh cracked the
strained silence in the room.

"So, I'm to be locked away after all, am I!" Mother sput-
tered, as if she were forcing the last air from her lungs. . . .
She sat in the hard chair as if she had flung herself down, her
body looking more shrunken than ever in the dark striped kimono Shintarō's aunt had given her, her sunbeaten face turned
stiffly aside to avoid their eyes. Overwhelmed by this outburst,
everyone in the room sat looking at the floor, unable to move
a muscle in the tension, when the doctor strode briskly back in
and said,

"Well now, Mrs. Hamaguchi, your room is all ready. Will
one of the relatives kindly come along? We can't excite the other
patients by having a big crowd in . . . and it's terribly lone-
some for the patient being admitted if everyone leaves at once."

Shintaro's aunt raised her face and looked back and forth
from Shintarō to Father, nominating Shintarō with her eyes.
Father looked positively drunk, flushed red from the neck up,
his head swaying dizzily to and fro. It was decided: Shintarō
would go. He stood up.

To reach the appointed room they had to pass through
countless corridors, climb up and down countless sets of stairs.
——Perhaps he had walked these halls and stairs the day before. But there was a completely different feel to the place to-

day. ——Shintarō thought he was staying relatively calm. But the doctor, walking up ahead, seemed to be purposely letting the distance between them stretch to frightening lengths, or pulling back so close that Shintarō almost bumped into him. . . . At the far end of one of the long corridors, which were partitioned by a number of fire doors, was a large tatami room. It was the sort of room you saw everywhere, the like of which most of humanity had slept in at least once. Judo halls, third-class sleeping quarters on a ship, the main building of any temple, the banquet hall of a Japanese-style inn . . . Shintarō himself had stayed in rooms like this in the service, whenever his division was transferred.

"The matting is fresh, and the window looks out over the sea . . ."

The doctor's voice was suddenly ringing in his ears, and Shintarō realized he had been daydreaming. . . . Sure enough, the air smelled of green tatami, and the sea and the sky shone white through the eastern window. Still, Shintarō thought the doctor had said yesterday that they were giving her a nice little single. When he asked about it, the doctor did not directly address the issue. "Oh, that," he answered, "there are more people down here she can talk to . . ." Shintarō didn't have the energy to press him any further. From the moment he had stepped into the room everything around him had gone fuzzy, and he felt absurdly as if his own body was about to disintegrate and fly out into space.

"Why don't you say something to your mother?" the doctor whispered, drawing his pale, silky face close to Shintarō's.

"Yes . . ."

Shintarō stood awhile and thought, but by now there was nothing he wanted to tell her. . . . The doctor leaned in closer as if to hurry him. "Anything will do, anything," he repeated. "Anything that'll help the patient feel better will do; just say something."

The doctor smiled. Mother stood in front of Shintarō, her

brown face turned toward the room. He could see stray white hairs, a lot of them, on the wrinkled nape of her neck.

"Mother, you hurry up and get well now, all right? Just bear with it here until then. . . . When you're better we'll come right away and get you. We'll go to Tokyo then."

Shintarō was beginning to feel tongue-tied, and as soon as he had said this much he was ready to get out of there as fast as he could. But the doctor whispered to him again. "Now pat her shoulder or something."

Shintarō did as he was told, placing both hands awkwardly on her shoulders. He could feel them small and bony under his palms. Mother turned around and looked at him out of the corner of her eye. A rush of strength filled his hands where they lay on her shoulders; he pushed her forward slightly. . . . Shintarō walked to the door and turned back one last time. In that moment, he actually felt for the first time like saying something. Mother looked so small, sitting tense in the middle of that cavernous room, her eyes darting back and forth.

The next instant Shintarō was standing in the hall. A crowd of patients he hadn't noticed before had surrounded the doctor and were calling out, "Doctor, when do I get out?" — — "Look, I'm already well . . ." —— "Doctor, I want to talk to you."

"OK, OK! I hear you," the doctor laughed, making fluttering motions in the air with his hands.

At that moment Shintarō saw, over the heads of the doctors and patients, the door to his mother's room going shut. . . . The pale green steel door closed slowly. A green bolt clicked into place. And Shintarō realized that everything he knew had just been cut off from him before his eyes.

It was already pitch dark. A faint white glow lingered in the outline of the window, distorted by the clumsy shade, but that was all. There was no such thing as the peace of evening in this place. As soon as darkness fell, all kinds of silent sounds began to fill the ward. . . . The seventeen-year-old girl next door who was admitted the day before had been sniffling and sobbing until a moment ago. As usual, the attendant had given her a shot of sleeping medicine. She was asleep by now, of course, but Shintarō could still hear the weeping—it was as if that voice had permeated the very wall, and touches of it echoed yet. The neighbor on the other side, the woman who was always calling for her lunch, had also been given a shot tonight, but that was because she had been so excited with all the commotion in Mother's room earlier that she had gotten completely out of hand. She had been doused with water and had run distractedly to the back of her little room, setting up a cry which also still hung on the air over in that direction.

Around three o'clock the next afternoon, Mother's breathing visibly weakened. . . . Shintarō's aunt had just left, saying, "If I go now I'll get back to the village just in time to fix dinner." She had probably not even reached the bus stop. Shintarō and his father had a minor argument over what to do. Father insisted they call her back; Shintarō disagreed. The attendant was on Father's side. "Why, it's a shame, her coming all this way to visit and then leaving right before the woman dies." As it turned out, it made no difference anyway. By the time they had finished arguing, the bus had already left, and Mother resumed normal breathing. The doctor and nurses who had been called in by the attendant left looking disappointed. The doctor was visibly displeased as he walked out of the room; but by now Shintarō could sympathize with the man's position. . . . Didn't that displeasure, after all, stem partly from an awareness of his utter helplessness toward his patients? Anyone would find it exasperating to have a job that held him responsible for countless situations where all he could do was surrender.

After the doctor and staff had left, Shintarō went out and sat down on the stone steps outside the ward for a smoke. One of the patients came over, bowed respectfully, and began to offer his condolences. Shintarō looked up to see a whole crowd of patients whispering together, looking his way. It was clear they all thought his mother had just died. Shintarō felt embarrassed and somewhat guilty, and started to get up to go back to the room, when he heard a voice behind him.

"I knew your mother wouldn't pass away yet."

Without even turning around Shintarō knew it was the man with the bandage wrapped around his neck. The man came over to the steps and sat down next to Shintarō. ——At this hospital, he said, the only time a doctor goes into an intensive care patient's room off schedule is if the patient is dying.

"But I said to myself, this doctor is wasting his time again. People always die at low tide, see. Nobody ever dies at high tide. Ever. Now what can you do with a doctor who doesn't even know that?"

"Is that so?" Shintarō said politely, wondering why this man bore such a grudge against the doctor and the hospital. He was still baffled remembering how the man had let himself into his own cell-like room. ——He must have decided to pass the rest of his days, which were undoubtedly numbered anyway, here in the hospital. But if so, it made a mockery of the whole idea of "free will." In the end all "free will" meant for this man was being able to open the door to his own prison.

Shintarō had finished his cigarette and was about to go back to the room when the voice behind him told him the low tide tonight would be past eleven, and that he might as well get some rest until then. Shintarō was more grateful for this advice than he had been even for the fan, but unfortunately he was not the least bit sleepy, so he told the man as much and went back to the room.

How long had it been since then? Shintarō lifted his eyes and saw that a fragment of night sky was peeking through the window. He had fallen asleep; the strange dream he had just seen came back to him now. ——-Dark, pitching water surrounded him completely. He was on top of something rocklike. Air rising from beneath the water occasionally rushed hard by him, and he realized with a start that it was not a rock he was riding, but the back of some hard-shelled animal, a sea turtle.

In the dream he remembered how his mother had taken him to the ocean when he was little and taught him to swim. He opened his eyes as she had told him to do, and there beside him was her big, black corpse, the image rippling in the green water. . . . How long had he slept? With the uneasy feeling of the dream lingering in his head, Shintarō suddenly remembered that the bandaged man had said, "People always die at low tide." An awful premonition flashed across his mind. ——What if Mother had died before his very eyes and no one knew. . . . As quickly as the thought came to him, he shuddered and moved to look at Mother's face. Even in the cool night air the smell hit him sharply, and he heard her steady, if weak, breathing. —— Saved, he thought. Just to be sure he went to check the clock in the office. Ten past two. If what the bandaged man said was true, the hour of danger had passed. So, she had safely weathered the crisis one more time. The very next moment, though, Shintarō thought of having to go through another day like every one he had spent at the hospital so far, and his heart fell.

Shintarō spent the remaining hours of the night in this contradictory cycle of disappointment and relief. As nearly all of his attention became concentrated on his mother's breathing, after a while he started to feel as though his own breathing had synchronized with hers. At length he noticed that morning had arrived. . . . The sun began to shine from nowhere in particular, and the liquid blue of the air became more transparent. The objects around him gradually took on their familiar shapes and became solid again. From the direction of the kitchen came the sounds of people beginning to work.

The attendant appeared, his rubber-soled shoes squeaking, and Father came in after him. By now it was quite light.

"She's started breathing through her throat, I see," said the attendant.

With her mouth wide open as always—or rather, with her lower jaw fairly lodged in her neck—Mother was using her whole throat to carry on her feeble breathing. "Once this starts, it's all over." The attendant looked back at Father.

Father nodded in silence. He said to Shintarō, "Shall we call the village?"

At these words, Shintarō suddenly felt the exhaustion in every part of his body. At the same time he felt irked by the two men before him, and he answered, "She's not going to die just yet, is she? Besides, even if we did call, we can't be sure my aunt will be able to come down."

The other two looked at each other. Presently Father spoke, decisively now. "We have to let them know. Even if it's just for their information. . . ."

Shintarō knew he was being unreasonable. But with Mother's death now imminent, it seemed intolerable to be preoccupied with a point of etiquette.

By the time they served the patients' breakfast it had already started getting hot. Now Shintarō began to feel terribly drowsy. . . . At night there had been only the sound of breathing in the dark; in the flooding light of day, Mother's body looked not merely weak, but stripped of any human likeness whatsoever.

Nose, cheeks, chin, all her features sagged and blurred into one another; it made him wonder if she were melting down in the heat. Only the breathing continued. Time passed terribly slowly.

Presently Shintarō's aunt showed up, dripping with perspiration and saying, "Oh good, I'm not too late." She started up a steady stream of talk once again, saying whatever came to mind—how her husband still refused to come to the hospital, how crowded the trains had been, how the rice was doing in the fields. She completely ignored the dying woman. But Shintarō felt better as he watched his aunt, who was six or seven years older than his mother, chatter away, mopping the streaming sweat from her flushed face. Everything about her radiated health, and she seemed able to brush aside in one sweep the walls, the floor, the sunlight—all the intense, oppressive things in the room.

"Oh yes. I thought you'd be getting thirsty so I picked this up on the way," she said, and produced a large, green watermelon.

This, too, helped to dispel the melancholy atmosphere in the room. When the attendant was offered the first slice, his face lit up. "I'll eat half of it and give the rest to my wife," he said.

The others hadn't realized he was married; he told them his wife also worked in the hospital. For some reason it struck Shintarō as amusing to imagine this young fellow in his scraggly mustache sharing watermelon with his wife, and he couldn't help but burst out laughing. He was sorry for his spiteful behavior toward his father and the attendant a little while ago.

With time, though, the face of their hearty visitor gradually clouded over too. They had been talking animatedly and had just started to eat the melon when the birdlike voice next door started up.

"Attendant, attendant! Watermelon, watermelon, I'm waiting! I need watermelon! Give me some too! I need some, I need some!"

Shintarō's aunt continued to eat the piece she held in one hand, but she pointed at the attendant with her other hand, dripping watermelon juice, and told him to give some to the neighbor. The attendant answered,

"No, she's got diarrhea. She never uses her chamber pot, and she made such a disgusting mess of the floor and the walls I had to punish her for it again just the other day."

Shintarō had caught sight of her through the window once, crawling around the floor on all fours, stark naked. She was a girl of about twenty with a completely innocent childlike face.

"Watermelon, watermelon, I need some, I need some, watermelon, I need some . . ."

The strange cadence of the hoarse voice continued. The cries grew louder and louder and the words came more quickly, tumbling over one another. Shintarō thought that he must not let the voice unnerve him. He had to go on eating the watermelon. . . . But as the calls grew louder, new lines appeared on his mother's swollen, distended brow, where he had thought no further expression of pain was possible, and that did it for him. His aunt and the attendant ended up hastily gathering the uneaten melon and the rinds and taking them down to the kitchen to throw away.

Even then the temperature of the room continued to rise. Though Shintarō's aunt and father took turns moistening his mother's lips with damp cotton, the water evaporated almost as fast as they could apply it. Yet if the trickle inside her mouth increased just a little, Mother moved her throat in agony. The attendant entered the room while this was going on.

"My wife made up some juice here," he said. He was carrying a feeding cup with some yellow liquid in it. "A patient's got to eat. You have to get something in their stomach, or they can't hang on."

Really though, was it possible to get anything down a patient in this condition? . . .

"Well, let's try, let's just try." The attendant seemed intent on getting the juice into the sick woman's mouth one way or the other. No one could offer any reason why he absolutely must not, and no one had the authority to stop him.

The attendant lay down on the floor and drew close to Mother's face, which was tilted slightly to the left. He peered carefully into her mouth. The jaw hung so low it almost looked dislocated, and Shintarō could see that her shrivelled tongue was stuck to the inside wall of her right cheek. The attendant pressed on the tongue with the spout of his cup to form an indentation. Then he let one drop of yellow liquid fall into the indentation. The liquid spread across the parched tongue slowly, evidently soaking in, and slid down the back of her throat. Mother's eyebrows jerked as if it had stung, but her breathing was steady.

"Good, said the attendant. He applied four or five more

drops to her tongue the same way. These went down more easily than the first. Next he administered two drops at once. Then it was three drops, as little by little he increased the speed along with the amount. By now there were hardly any dry spots left on the surface of her tongue. He held up the feeding cup to check the measure. About one teaspoon of liquid had gone into moistening the inside of Mother's mouth. . . . "Let's try giving her a little more," the attendant said, and this time he poured not into the indentation on her tongue but down the side. The yellow liquid passed like a thread along the groove between the tongue and her cheek, and trickled down her throat.

"Good!"

Just as the attendant spoke Mother made a face and coughed. Her tongue pushed on the feeding cup, from which juice now spilled out with a gurgle. When she coughed again the spout fell right into the back of her throat, and within a fraction of a second the back of her tongue was completely yellow with liquid.

A deep gargling sound arose from her throat, and suddenly Mother opened her eyes. With every breath the yellow liquid bubbled up over her tongue. Then she rasped like a dried-up suction pump, and started breathing ten times as fast as before.

Without a word the attendant ran out of the room. . . . When the doctor finally arrived several minutes later, there was just a weak scratchy sound, as Mother spewed out air only at long intervals. After standing for some time surveying the situation, the doctor bared Mother's chest and applied his stethoscope. He pressed the instrument lightly, three times on the right side and lastly once right in the middle. As if that one light tap had typed out the period, her breathing stopped. The blackish red color drained out of her face and fingertips as if it had been sucked away. The doctor stood up and called to the attendant, who was standing outside the room. The attendant turned his wide eyes to the doctor from behind his thick glasses. The doctor stretched out his arm and read off from his watch, "eleven-nineteen"; then, having the hour recorded on the patient's chart, he took off with his usual long strides and was gone from the room.

It all seemed to have happened in an instant.

Shintarō was sitting with his back to the wall. When the doctor left, he felt as if something heavy were leaving his body. A weight between "himself" and the wall at his back evaporated away. His body seemed to float weightlessly where it was, and for some time he couldn't move.

It seemed that a good deal of time had passed when he noticed the attendant closing Mother's mouth and eyelids. There was something a little unsettling about the black hair growing on the back of the attendant's pale fingers, but when he gazed at his mother after those hands were gone, Shintarō was moved. Now all trace of suffering was gone from the face that had recently been so changed, and it seemed to have reverted to the untroubled, peaceful look it had had ten years before. . . . It was then that Shintarō noticed for the first time a bizarre noise that had started up in the room some time ago. A human sound, it was at the same time not one he often heard. When he figured out that it was his aunt crying, Shintarō was startled again. It had taken him a surprisingly long time to remember that there was a precedent for people to cry when someone died. How could he have virtually forgotten that normal people cry too? Meanwhile he could hear the sobbing; for no identifiable reason it seemed threatening, and he felt as if it were putting pressure on him. Eventually this business of having to listen to someone else crying got to him. Why do you do it? he wanted to ask. Do you think that just by crying you can turn yourself into a compassionate, kind-hearted human being? Father, for his part, was down on one knee next to her, holding his big head in his hands. When he saw that, Shintarō felt horribly out of place. . . . Behind the old woman crying and the old man holding his head in his hands, the attendant dashed hastily out into the hall to return with a pious look on his face and a large ball of pressed rice with chopsticks standing in it. Having set this down with a bowl of water at the head of Mother's bed, he scolded the patients who were peering in through the windows across the hall, dispersed them, and dashed off again. . . . Watching this, it occurred to Shintarō that maybe the man felt guilty about what he had done before Mother's death, and was running around to avoid any uncomfortable confrontation. If that were the case, Shintarō wanted to reassure him not to worry about it; but the man never looked his way and there didn't seem to be a good chance to bring it up. ——On the other hand, if the attendant had looked pleadingly to Shintarō, Shintarō might very well have run away himself, rather than sit through a painful apology. . . .

Still tormented by the sound of the crying, Shintarō mulled over these thoughts until it occurred to him that there was no reason to sit where he was any longer. He abruptly stood up. His aunt lifted her red eyes to him questioningly as he left the room, but Shintarō walked on out.

The minute he stepped onto the ground outside the door, Shintarō felt dizzy, lightheaded. The fierce sunlight suddenly beat straight down on his head, and when he closed his eyes he felt unsteady on his feet. He was exhausted—no doubt that was it. Besides, in more than a week, in eight or nine days, except for one trip to buy a sunshade, he had not come out a single time into real daylight like this. It had always been evening or nighttime when he had gone out to the playing field. ——Nine days. What on earth had he been doing all that time? Why had he shut himself up in that smelly room? Had he conceivably intended living in the same room as his mother, if only for nine days, to be some kind of atonement? And even if it didn't cost enough to make it a true penance, what did he need to atone for in the first place, and why? The very concept of repaying one's mother was absurd—wasn't a son already making reparation enough just by being a son? A mother atoned by bearing a son; the son atoned by being his mother's child.

Whatever might come up between them was resolved between them. Surely outsiders had no say in it.

Lost in his thoughts, Shintarō wandered over the playing field, letting his feet lead him where they would. To know that everything was over made him free, free to stroll just like this, accountable to no one, right into the "scenery" he had been gazing at from back in the room through a window cut out of that thick wall—and this made him inexpressibly happy. Even the sunlight beating down on his head couldn't bother him now. He wanted the sun to purge away that gloomy smell that had permeated every layer of his clothes, every corner of his body. He wanted it to be borne away by the ocean breeze. . . . Shintarō looked up. He had been following the stone wall along the edge of the sea; the view he saw now gave him a start, and his feet came to a halt.

The little scene enclosed by the spit of land, boasting its solitary, storybook island, was familiar to him by now. But what stopped him in his tracks was that all across the unrippled surface of the bay, now calmer than a lake, there stood hundreds upon hundreds of stakes, looming blackly out of the water as far as he could see. . . . For a moment the entire landscape lay still. The sun that had just been beating down on his head now only daubed a few mottled yellow smudges here and there. The wind fell, the salt smell vanished, everything seemed to recede before this eerie view that had risen from under the sea. As he looked at the rows of stakes standing like the teeth of an upturned comb, like tombstones, it was a death he held in his own hands that he saw.

Modern Asian Literature Series

Modern Japanese Drama: An Anthology, ed. and tr. Ted T.
Takaya — 1979
*Mask and Sword: Two Plays for the Contemporary Japanese
Theater,* Yamazaki Masakazu, tr. J. Thomas Rimer — 1980
Yokomitsu Riichi, Modernist, by Dennis Keene — 1980
*Nepali Visions, Nepali Dreams: Selections from the Poetry of
Laxmiprasad Devkota,* tr. David Rubin — 1980
Literature of the Hundred Flowers, vol. 1: *Criticism and Po-
lemics,* ed. Hualing Nieh — 1981
Literature of the Hundred Flowers, vol. 2: *Poetry and Fiction,*
ed. Hualing Nieh — 1981
Modern Chinese Stories and Novellas, 1919–1949, ed. Jo-
seph S. M. Lau, C. T. Hsia, and Leo Ou-fan Lee.
Also in paperback ed. — 1981
A View by the Sea, by Yasuoka Shōtarō, tr. Kären Wigen
Lewis — 1984

Neo-Confucian Studies

*Instructions for Practical Living and Other Neo-Confucian
Writings by Wang Yang-ming,* tr. Wing-tsit Chan — 1963
*Reflections on Things at Hand: The Neo-Confucian Anthol-
ogy,* comp. Chu Hsi and Lü Tsu-ch'ien, tr. Wing-tsit
Chan — 1967
Self and Society in Ming Thought, by Wm. Theodore de Bary
and the Conference on Ming Thought. Also in pa-
perback ed. — 1970
The Unfolding of Neo-Confucianism, by Wm. Theodore de
Bary and the Conference on Seventeenth-Century
Chinese Thought. Also in paperback ed. — 1975

Principle and Practicality: Essays in Neo-Confucianism and
Practical Learning, ed. Wm. Theodore de Bary and
Irene Bloom. Also in paperback ed.   1979
The Syncretic Religion of Lin Chao-en, by Judith A. Berling   1980
The Renewal of Buddhism in China: Chu-hung and the Late
Ming Synthesis, by Chün-fang Yü   1981
Neo-Confucian Orthodoxy and the Learning of the Mind-and-
Heart, by Wm. Theodore de Bary   1981
Yüan Thought: Chinese Thought and Religion Under the
Mongols, ed. Hok-lan Chan and Wm. Theodore de
Bary   1982
The Liberal Tradition in China, by Wm. Theodore de Bary   1983
The Development and Decline of Chinese Cosmology, by John
B. Henderson   1984

Translations From the Oriental Classics

Major Plays of Chikamatsu, tr. Donald Keene   1961
Four Major Plays of Chikamatsu, tr. Donald Keene. Paper-
back text edition.   1961
Records of the Grand Historian of China, translated from the
Shih chi of Ssu-ma Ch'ien, tr. Burton Watson, 2 vols.   1961
Instructions for Practical Living and Other Neo-Confucian
Writings by Wang Yang-ming, tr. Wing-tsit Chan   1963
Chuang Tzu: Basic Writings, tr. Burton Watson, paper-
back ed. only   1964
The Mahābhārata, tr. Chakravarthi V. Narasimhan. Also
in paperback ed.   1965
The Manyōshū, Nippon Gakujutsu Shinkōkai edition   1965
Su Tung-p'o: Selections from a Sung Dynasty Poet, tr. Bur-
ton Watson. Also in paperback ed.   1965
Bhartrihari: Poems, tr. Barbara Stoler Miller. Also in pa-
perback ed.   1967

Basic Writings of Mo Tzu, Hsün Tzu, and Han Fei Tzu, tr. Burton Watson. Also in separate paperback eds. 1967

The Awakening of Faith, Attributed to Aśvaghosha, tr. Yoshito S. Hakeda. Also in paperback ed. 1967

Reflections on Things at Hand: The Neo-Confucian Anthology, comp. Chu Hsi and Lü Tsu-ch'ien, tr. Wing-tsit Chan 1967

The Platform Sutra of the Sixth Patriarch, tr. Philip B. Yampolsky. Also in paperback ed. 1967

Essays in Idleness: The Tsurezuregusa of Kenkō, tr. Donald Keene. Also in paperback ed. 1967

The Pillow Book of Sei Shōnagon, tr. Ivan Morris, 2 vols. 1967

Two Plays of Ancient India: The Little Clay Cart and the Minister's Seal, tr. J. A. B. van Buitenen 1968

The Complete Works of Chuang Tzu, tr. Burton Watson 1968

The Romance of the Western Chamber (Hsi Hsiang chi), tr. S. I. Hsiung. Also in paperback ed. 1968

The Manyōshū, Nippon Gakujutsu Shinkōkai edition. Paperback text edition. 1969

Records of the Historian: Chapters from the Shih chi of Ssuma Ch'ien. Paperback text edition, tr. Burton Watson 1969

Cold Mountain: 100 Poems by the T'ang Poet Han-shan, tr. Burton Watson. Also in paperback ed. 1970

Twenty Plays of the Nō Theatre, ed. Donald Keene. Also in paperback ed. 1970

Chūshingura: The Treasury of Loyal Retainers, tr. Donald Keene. Also in paperback ed. 1971

The Zen Master Hakuin: Selected writings, tr. Philip B. Yampolsky 1971

Chinese Rhyme-Prose: Poems in the Fu Form from the Han and Six Dynasties Periods, tr. Burton Watson. Also in paperback ed. 1971

Kūkai: Major Works, tr. Yoshito S. Hakeda 1972

The Old Man Who Does as He Pleases: Selections from the Poetry and Prose of Lu Yu, tr. Burton Watson 1973

The Lion's Roar of Queen Śrīmālā, tr. Alex and Hideko
Wayman — 1974

Courtier and Commoner in Ancient China: Selections from the
History of The Former Han by Pan Ku, tr. Burton Watson. Also in paperback ed. — 1974

Japanese Literature in Chinese. Vol. I: Poetry and Prose in
Chinese by Japanese Writers of the Early Period, tr. Burton Watson — 1975

Japanese Literature in Chinese. Vol. II: Poetry and Prose in
Chinese by Japanese Writers of the Later Period, tr. Burton Watson — 1976

Scripture of the Lotus Blossom of the Fine Dharma, tr. Leon
Hurvitz. Also in paperback ed. — 1976

Love Song of the Dark Lord: Jayadeva's Gitagovinda, tr. Barbara Stoler Miller. Also in paperback ed. Cloth ed.
includes critical text of the Sanskrit. — 1977

Ryōkan: Zen Monk-Poet of Japan, tr. Burton Watson — 1977

Calming the Mind and Discerning the Real: From the Lam rim
chen mo of Tson-kha-pa, tr. Alex Wayman — 1978

The Hermit and the Love-Thief: Sanskrit Poems of Bhartrihari
and Bilhana, tr. Barbara Stoler Miller — 1978

The Lute: Kao Ming's P'i-p'a chi, tr. Jean Mulligan. Also in
paperback ed. — 1980

A Chronicle of Gods and Sovereigns: Jinnō Shōtōki of Kitaba-
take Chikafusa, tr. H. Paul Varley — 1980

Among the Flowers: The Hua-chien chi, tr. Lois Fusek — 1982

Grass Hill: Poems and Prose by the Japanese Monk Gensei, tr.
Burton Watson — 1983

Doctors, Diviners, and Magicians of Ancient China: Biogra-
phies of Fang-shih, tr. Kenneth J. DeWoskin. Also in
paperback ed. — 1983

Theater of Memory: The Plays of Kālidāsa, ed. Barbara Stoler Miller. Also in paperback ed. — 1984

The Columbia Book of Chinese Poetry: From Early Times to
the Thirteenth Century, ed. and tr. Burton Watson — 1984

Poems of Love and War: From the Eight Anthologies and the Ten Songs of Classical Tamil, tr. A. K. Ramanujan. Also in paperback ed.   1984

Studies in Oriental Culture

1. *The Ōnin War: History of Its Origins and Background, with a Selective Translation of the Chronicle of Ōnin,* by H. Paul Varley   1967
2. *Chinese Government in Ming Times: Seven Studies,* ed. Charles O. Hucker   1969
3. *The Actors' Analects (Yakusha Rongo),* ed. and tr. by Charles J. Dunn and Bunzō Torigoe   1969
4. *Self and Society in Ming Thought,* by Wm. Theodore de Bary and the Conference on Ming Thought. Also in paperback ed.   1970
5. *A History of Islamic Philosophy,* by Majid Fakhry   1970
6. *Phantasies of a Love Thief: The Caurapañcāśikā Attributed to Bilhana,* by Barbara Stoler Miller   1971
7. *Iqbal: Poet-Philosopher of Pakistan,* ed. Hafeez Malik   1971
8. *The Golden Tradition: An Anthology of Urdu Poetry,* by Ahmed Ali. Also in paperback ed.   1973
9. *Conquerors and Confucians: Aspects of Political Change in Late Yüan China,* by John W. Dardess   1973
10. *The Unfolding of Neo-Confucianism,* by Wm. Theodore de Bary and the Conference on Seventeenth-Century Chinese Thought. Also in paperback ed.   1975
11. *To Acquire Wisdom: The Way of Wang Yang-ming,* by Julia Ching   1976
12. *Gods, Priests, and Warriors: The Bhṛgus of the Mahābhārata,* by Robert P. Goldman   1977

13. *Mei Yao-ch'en and the Development of Early Sung Poetry*, by Jonathan Chaves — 1976
14. *The Legend of Semimaru, Blind Musician of Japan*, by Susan Matisoff — 1977
15. *Sir Sayyid Ahmad Khan and Muslim Modernization in India and Pakistan*, by Hafeez Malik — 1980
16. *The Khilafat Movement: Religious Symbolism and Political Mobilization in India*, by Gail Minault — 1982
17. *The World of K'ung Shang-jen: A Man of Letters in Early Ch'ing China*, by Richard Strassberg — 1983
18. *The Lotus Boat: The Origins of Chinese Tz'u Poetry in T'ang Popular Culture*, by Marsha L. Wagner — 1984

Companions to Asian Studies

Approaches to the Oriental Classics, ed. Wm. Theodore de Bary — 1959
Early Chinese Literature, by Burton Watson. Also in paperback ed. — 1962
Approaches to Asian Civilizations, ed. Wm. Theodore de Bary and Ainslie T. Embree — 1964
The Classic Chinese Novel: A Critical Introduction, by C. T. Hsia. Also in paperback ed. — 1968
Chinese Lyricism: Shih Poetry from the Second to the Twelfth Century, tr. Burton Watson. Also in paperback ed. — 1971
A Syllabus of Indian Civilization, by Leonard A. Gordon and Barbara Stoler Miller — 1971
Twentieth-Century Chinese Stories, ed. C. T. Hsia and Joseph S. M. Lau. Also in paperback ed. — 1971
A Syllabus of Chinese Civilization, by J. Mason Gentzler, 2d ed. — 1972
A Syllabus of Japanese Civilization, by H. Paul Varley, 2d ed. — 1972

An Introduction to Chinese Civilization, ed. John Meskill,
  with the assistance of J. Mason Gentzler   1973
An Introduction to Japanese Civilization, ed. Arthur E. Tie-
  demann   1974
A Guide to Oriental Classics, ed. Wm. Theodore de Bary
  and Ainslie T. Embree, 2d ed. Also in paperback ed.   1975
Ukifune: Love in The Tale of Genji, ed. Andrew Pekarik   1982

Introduction to Oriental Civilizations

Wm. Theodore de Bary, *Editor*

Sources of Japanese Tradition 1958 Paperback ed., 2 vols. 1964
Sources of Indian Tradition   1958 Paperback ed., 2 vols. 1964
Sources of Chinese Tradition 1960 Paperback ed., 2 vols. 1964